Tenn Enchanted

a collection of romantic comedies

by

Christina Coryell

Facebook: AuthorChristinaCoryell
Twitter: @c_tinacoryell
Instagram: christina_coryell
www.christinacoryell.com

This book is a work of fiction. Names, characters, places, and incidents either are the product of the author's imagination or are used fictitiously, and any resemblance to actual persons, living or dead, business establishments, events, or locales is entirely coincidental.

No part of this publication may be reproduced, stored in a retrieval system, or transmitted in any form or by any means, electronic, mechanical, photocopying, recording, or otherwise, without express written permission of the publisher by using the contact information at www.christinacoryell.com.

Mowed Over Copyright © 2016 by Christina Coryell
Merried Off Copyright © 2017 by Christina Coryell
Crossed Out Copyright © 2018 by Christina Coryell
Individual Interior Cover designs by Christina Coryell, photos from Deposit Photos
Front Cover Artwork Copyright © 2016 by Michael Coryell
Cover Design by Roseanna White Designs
Background Image from Shutterstock

For Mike,

You gave me a dubious look when I asked you to draw a faceless person, but you still sat down and created the artwork.

Thank you.

♥

USA Today Bestselling Author
Christina Coryell

MOWED OVER

A Beards and Belles Novella

Mowed Over

a romantic comedy

by

Christina Coryell

Chapter One

It is a truth universally acknowledged that a beautiful fairy in possession of a large mushroom hut must be in want of companionship. #willowfairies

With the magnifying glass dangling from the contraption atop her head, Willow Sharpe barely touched the tip of her toothpick into the black ink and made one more slight adjustment to the book that measured only an inch in height. It might be miniscule, but the camera's close-up lens wasn't forgiving. What could be more perfect than Arabelle wistfully reading *Pride and Prejudice* while Lady, her pet ladybug, cuddled in her lap? Especially on a beautiful April day like the one she had at her disposal?

Willow carefully lifted Arabelle from her perch on the table and inspected her dainty wings, noting that one of the glitter sprinkles had shifted into the inky color that Willow had designed after staring at a monarch butterfly. With a cotton swab, she gently brushed it away while she lifted her chin to search for the tube of glue, trying to avoid looking through the magnifying glass. The slight change it always caused in her depth perception made her clumsy, and she didn't relish the idea of cleaning up anything she knocked over.

"What will your prince look like?" Willow asked Arabelle as she located the glue and readjusted her gaze to peer through the glass. "Dark and handsome, perhaps? Or with light blond, flowing hair? Perhaps he'll ride in on a . . . lawnmower!"

The low buzzing noise of the engine was unmistakable, and the sound sent Willow to her feet, attempting to dart toward the window and instead finding herself tangled in the extension cord for her glue gun. A jerk of her foot sent her sprawling over the armrest of the couch, where she glanced back and attempted another release movement. When her shoe didn't give, she wiggled out of it and nearly flung herself at the window, pushing up the blinds until they made a loud snap at the way she dented them.

The green behemoth passed through her line of vision, which was still obstructed by the magnifying glass. Refusing to release the blinds, she used her elbow to shove the magnifying glass up and to the left. It was her lawn that mower was traversing, and if she didn't resolve the problem soon it would—

"Stop!" She crossed the five feet to her door in seconds that seemed like hours, and flung it open with such force that the locking mechanism on the back of the knob smacked into the wall. Three steps led from her front door to the yard, but she leapt over them in one bound, her knees buckling under her when she hit the ground below. Pushing up to a stand, she ignored the moisture seeping through the bottom of her wooly sock and sprinted in the direction of the large oak just in front of her.

"Stop!" she yelled, attempting to be heard over the roar of the engine. Whether he didn't hear her or pretended not to, she wasn't certain. His mirrored orange sunglasses completely shielded his eyes, and underneath his blue baseball cap she could see that the cord from his earbuds stretched to what was presumably a phone in his back pocket.

Waving frantically, she screamed at him one more time, but he didn't stop. Just kept driving forward in the direction of that little divot in the grass—that bare spot that looked like a nuisance to anyone but her—not paying her any heed.

"Dear God, no," she whispered, diving forward and wrapping her arms over her head.

Hands pressed against his knees, Clint Kirkland drew in a gulp of air, trying to force some semblance of normalcy into his breathing pattern. It was no use. The air pocket expanded in his lungs, making him feel like his heart could explode at any second.

How? How had he not seen the body in the yard when he unloaded the mower? One minute he was glancing through the woods at the thick swath of trees, and the next he was nearly running over a strung out, half-undressed . . .

Anxiety gripped his chest again, and he coughed into his fist as he tried to knock the feeling loose. He had never been big on being startled, which was a fact his brother tried to use to his advantage when they were kids, always hiding behind furniture and doorways. But nothing his brother had done could compare to the sudden, unexpected sight of a dangerously thin woman lying prostrate just feet from his mower, wearing striped boxer shorts, one shoe, and a ratty brown sweater with a hole just above the pocket.

"Squirrel brains on a spitfire," he muttered as he swiped his ball cap from his head. Sweat prickled along his hairline, and he knew it was from the undue stress and not the temperature. With one quick brush of his arm against his forehead, he placed the cap back in place and scratched his cheek through his beard as he turned back to the victim.

She shoved up to her elbows, head swinging until her gaze was fixed on him. "Are you deaf? How did you not hear me screaming?"

The shock of seeing her moving glued him in spot momentarily. Her eyes were nearly too big for her face, like those posters of movies featuring waifish children. The effect could have been aided by that magnifying glass contraption she had fixed around her head like that guy who once shrunk his kids. The mere suggestion of that possibility to his brain had him glancing down at the grass near his feet, even though he knew that was ridiculous.

"You know, mowers have a tendency to be a little noisy," he sputtered out. "That and I wasn't really expecting any oddball activity."

She raised onto her knees while he reached out a hand to help her up, but she refused and placed her hand on the ground instead. Feeling the slight, he pushed his hat up further on his forehead, so the bill was facing the sky instead of the horizon. She brushed her palms against her legs, and he squinted his eyes as he watched her. The woman had so much hair that it made her look top heavy, billows of blonde fluff that looked like cotton candy with ribbons of blue, pink, and purple.

"I guess you're blind too?" She raised herself to her full height, which couldn't have been much more than five-foot-nothing. Her arms began flailing about, coming dangerously close to his face. "Didn't see that? 'Cause it seems like that would be really conspicuous."

Sweat started to form at the back of his neck, an irritating reminder that he didn't like confrontation. Ignoring it, he placed his hands on his hips and watched as she did the same, lifting her chin before she spoke again.

"I don't know who gave you permission to trot your mower across the grass, but you're not welcome."

The skin between his shoulder blades began to prickle. "What are you, some crazy tree-hugging grass whisperer? Save the nut show for somebody else, lady. I have work to do."

"You will remove your lawnmower from my property at once."

Sassy little weirdo. He pulled his sunglasses off his face so he could look her in the eye. "Jimmy O'Neil hired me to do his landscaping, and when I spoke to him yesterday, I'm pretty sure this was still his property. So if you don't mind, I'm gonna get back to it now."

Her arms clamped over her chest as her eyes shot fire in his direction. "Over my dead body."

So basically the same way the whole situation started. With a quick shrug, he returned to his lawnmower and settled into the seat. Instead of admitting defeat or continuing her argument, she sat cross-legged in front of him, or as his niece liked to call it, "criss cross applesauce." The woman's arms still remained across her chest in that defensive posture, her backbone straight as a board. Narrowing his eyes, he started the mower. When she didn't move, he reversed the machine and rolled backwards, swinging to the right and mowing around her in a large circle. To his surprise, she didn't jump up and refuse to let him continue. She sat in that one spot, unmoving, while he mowed the rest of the yard.

Thirty minutes later, he loaded his mower onto the trailer, taking a quick look back at his work. Not great, but the best he could do under the circumstances. It was only after he started his pickup and began to pull down the gravel driveway that he saw her stand up in the middle of that swath of taller grass, content that she had succeeded in whatever loopy mission she was spearheading.

Chapter Two

The more Arabelle saw of the world outside her fairy village, the greater accustomed she became to disappointment. #willowfairies

  Her knees were stiff and threatened to upend her as she stood from her perch on the grass, but Willow wasn't about to show weakness. She stood like a sentinel, guarding her territory, until the black pickup with the rusted fender began to pull away from the cabin. The instant he was out of sight, she stumbled in the direction of the house, staring up at the door that was still ajar from her hasty exit earlier.
  Talk about a close call. Her fingers shook as she took the doorknob in hand, quietly shutting the door. Lifting her foot behind her, she peeked over her shoulder to inspect the bottom of her sock. As she suspected, it was soggy and dirty. Groaning aloud, she pushed the bulky wool away from her ankle and off her toes completely before leaning down to remove her other shoe as well.
  That guy called her an oddball. A nut.
  She tossed the second sock into the middle of the room and suppressed the urge to huff. Creative people were often maligned for their idiosyncrasies, she reminded herself. The ones with the lasting genius were usually not understood.
  But she wasn't a nut.
  Turning to her left, she strode down the hall until she reached the bathroom. Twisting the knob on the faucet, she

waited for the water to warm and then splashed her face, glancing up at the mirror as the water dripped from her chin. Her hair had slipped from the improvised bun she'd formed when she woke up, and now it frizzed out on the left side of her head, except for the area where it was smashed down by the headband for the magnifying glass. Knowledge of her appearance caused her blood to heat inside her veins, and she allowed her gaze to drift down her body past the tank top to the boxer shorts, all covered gracefully by the threadbare sweater.

Okay, so she looked a little like a hobo in need of a straightjacket. But not a nut. An artist.

Not that she'd always been treated as an artist. Her hobby had been a source of contention early on in her life as she bounced back and forth between the homes of her mother and father. Mom would complain that she was ignoring her studies to doodle in class, and Dad would say that she was wasting her time on foolishness. Then both would blame the other for her lack of focus. Neither one of them realized that she actually had laser-focus, it was simply on something they didn't understand.

If she was being honest with herself, nobody understood her in those formative years. Like a lot of artists and flat-out creative geniuses, if she dared to label herself such, she had harnessed all that childhood and teenage angst into a successful venture. Not at first, and there were quite a few lean years. But once Disney decided to tap into their fairy series, the interest in the topic led people to her drawings. The drawings led people to her stories, and the stories had turned into a complete fairy universe.

A universe which, only about thirty minutes before, was dangerously close to being down two mushroom huts, a miniature rosebush, one highly detailed mailbox, and a ladybug doghouse.

Returning to her original task from which she had been so rudely interrupted, she settled onto the chair and tapped the screen of her phone until it was ringing on speaker. With her hands free, she picked Arabelle up once more and began inspecting her wing.

An unintelligible grunt emerged from the other end of the phone, and Willow didn't waste any time before launching into her story. "This renegade horticulturist appeared out of nowhere and attempted to decimate Willowdale."

A louder groan came through the speaker while Willow brushed at the glitter fleck on Arabelle's wing.

"You do realize it's six-thirty in the morning?" Sammie's voice was gravelly and sounded rather irritated, which made Willow glance at the clock on the microwave and grimace.

"Sorry. I forget that there's so much space between us." Actually, she hadn't forgotten about the *space* between Gatlinburg and Los Angeles. The *time*, perhaps.

"So this is the new storyline you've got going?" Sammie asked with an exaggerated, prolonged, and very noisy yawn. "Abandoned the whole love story angle already?"

Willow shook her head at Arabelle, as though the inanimate fairy perched in her hand could hear the conversation. "No, the *Pride and Prejudice* theme is still going strong. I'm determined to help Arabelle find her Mr. Darcy, although at the moment I can't even begin to picture him in my mind."

Sammie placed her phone on speaker too, which Willow might not have known if she hadn't heard the noisy padding of footsteps through the phone. "So who's destroying Willowdale?"

A sigh broke loose as Willow reached for the glue one more time, lowering her head to peer through the magnifying glass. "I scoped out the perfect place to set up the huts, and while I was inside preparing my subject, this mouthy hillbilly showed up with a lawnmower intent on causing maximum destruction."

"So a guy tried to mow your lawn."

"Your ability to make things sound unimportant is legendary." Using tweezers, Willow set the glitter flake in its proper place. "My props were in the direct path of his machine of death. I had to throw myself on the ground in front of him to get him to stop."

The shuffling came to a halt. "Please tell me you're being dramatic."

"No! And then he hopped off his lawnmower, acting like I gave him a heart attack, bending at the waist like he needed to put one of those paper bags up to his face to breathe in and out. When he was done . . ." She felt her neck heating again just thinking about the confrontation. "When he was done freaking out, he called me a nut."

"Probably justified."

"Traitor."

"And while we're on the subject, if you're going to brand people mouthy hillbillies, you might as well point the finger at yourself, sweetie."

That little jab meant it was Willow's turn to groan. Sammie liked to remind her that she hailed from the great state of Mississippi. To be more specific, the rural parts of Mississippi. They met several years before when they were almost literally starving artists in New York City, and it was only recently that the two had decided to part ways. Sammie landed in Los Angeles where she could create soundtracks for movies, and Willow was in Gatlinburg, Tennessee. Could she have photographed her fairies in L.A.? Probably so, but there was something enticing about the scenery she found in the Smoky Mountains. The way the fog lifted over the trees, the moss covered the rocks, and the forest acted like a thick barrier. It was practically a fairy heaven, if ever one existed.

"The guy should not have been on my property without my permission."

Sammie let out another groan, which probably meant she plopped back down on her bed. "But do you have lawn mowing in your renter's agreement or something? Maybe your landlord sent the guy."

That statement hit a little too close to home.

"The point is, it was annoying the way he kept mowing around me in a giant circle while I sat there protecting my belongings."

Laughter. Not the encouragement she was looking for.

"No wonder he called you a nut. Why is this bothering you so much? It's almost like. . .oh."

Willow twisted the magnifying glass so it stuck out to the left and was no longer in front of her face. "Oh? What is the 'oh' for?"

"You're attracted to him."

Willow's chair tilted and she found herself hanging onto the side of the table as she righted herself. "Far from it."

"What did he look like?"

"You know, country-ish." She reached up and scratched the part of her hair directly under the headband, where her head was starting to feel a little numb. "He had a beard, Sammie. A beard."

"The horror."

"Not like one of the sleek beards you see walking around L.A. or New York. I'm talking about a full-out, Hatfield and McCoy, we-should-be-duck-hunting pelt of some kind of fur on his chin. Like a lumberjack."

"Hmm." Sammie released a quick chuckle, followed by a sigh. "And here I thought you might have met someone worthwhile."

Willow leaned back in her chair as she inspected her lonely, very single fairy one more time. "Keep dreaming," she muttered, but even as the words crossed her lips she couldn't force a certain pair of striking blue eyes, or a deep voice with a hint of a southern lilt, out of her mind.

The familiar squeaking of the brakes made Clint stop what he was doing and stare out the kitchen window. The bus sat directly in front of his house, and with the window open to just the screen he could hear the laughter and loud conversation taking place inside the vehicle. Emily appeared at the front of the bus after a few seconds, skipping as she swung her lunchbox back and forth by her side.

"Bye Em!" a high-pitched little voice yelled through an open bus window. Emily waited until she was safely in the grass, then turned and gave a big wave.

Clint grabbed a nearby dish towel and wiped the engine grease off his hands, then strolled to the front door and opened it while he waited for his niece to make it to the porch. She offered a big smile as she stepped inside the house, and he couldn't help but notice the pink ring around her lips. Leftover from the fruit punch she had for lunch, he imagined.

"How was school?" he asked casually as she slid her backpack to the ground and went in the direction of the kitchen.

"Fine," she muttered. The standard after-school kid answer that he'd come to expect by now. "Can I have a snack?"

"Sure." The phone started to ring, and he moved to the coffee table and picked it up, spying O'Neil's name. Finally. "Listen, Em, not a big snack because I don't want you to ruin your dinner." He hit the button to accept the call. "Hey, thanks for calling me back. I just wanted to let you know that I had to skip mowing a section of the grass at cabin nine because that woman you have staying there went a little crazy on me."

There was an uncomfortable silence, only interrupted by the sound of a chip bag crumpling in the kitchen.

"Crazy how exactly?"

"Now, that's hard to explain." Clint grabbed the bottom of his beard and held it in his fist, watching Emily drop a chip on the floor. With a quick shrug, she picked it up and popped it into her mouth anyway. "It was kind of like one of those sit-ins you see on TV. Like she was protecting the grass from murder or something."

O'Neil muttered a string of profanity that made Clint glance at Emily to make sure she didn't hear, even though he was the only one close enough to the phone. "You just can't tell what you're getting with those city slickers. I tell ya, I had my reservations about her, but she paid for the whole month up-front. Plus, she had good character references."

The front door opened, and Clint nodded at Ruth as she stepped into the living room, hair still up in a rather droopy light brown ponytail at the back of her head. She brightened a bit when she met his gaze, and he took a second to take in her appearance. Her tan uniform had a spot at the waist where it looked like she'd tried to clean something off and made it worse, and her name tag was crooked near the top of her shoulder. She'd probably had a long day.

"Well, I have no idea about her character one way or the other," Clint continued, "but I know she just about gave me the fright of my life. I'm minding my own business, listening to the radio and mowing, and all of a sudden there she is, on the ground in front of my mower."

O'Neil let loose a few unintelligible sounds before his words began to make sense. ". . . could have been killed. Insurance . . . sky high."

"Relax, nobody's getting killed." Clint glanced at Ruth, whose eyes widened as she stood by the doorway. "I just wanted you to know, and to ask what you wanted me to do about it next time."

"Do you think it's drugs?"

Clint twisted his mouth to the side and gave that some thought, but eventually shook his head. "Naw, I don't."

"Okay." The sound of a truck door slamming punctuated O'Neill's words. "Just do whatever you need to do next time you're out there, and I'll see what I can manage from this end."

"Ten four." Clint hit the end button on the phone and placed it on the arm of the couch, turning his attention to Ruth. "Em's in the kitchen eating chips. Hope you don't mind."

She gave him a weak smile, looking far more worn than a woman should at nearly twenty-five. "It's fine. Anyway, it's not like I would complain when I don't know what we'd do without you."

"Anything for my favorite niece."

He averted his eyes from Ruth, because every time he saw her looking worn out, he wished things were different for her. She had been one of the prettiest girls in his brother's class, which was probably why Doug took up with her in the first place. By the time Em was born, though, he had already moved on to another girlfriend.

Clint had been stationed in Southeast Asia at the time, so he hadn't seen it all playing out in real time. He returned home in time to see Emily celebrate her first birthday, his brother decide to go work on an oil rig in the gulf, and his parents move to Florida so they could stay with his grandmother. He alone had been left to carry on in the house his grandfather had built decades before, old-fashioned and always in need of repairs. But it fit him. He fit the house, more accurately.

And Ruth . . . She'd been just desperate enough in the beginning to try flirting with him, and that had been awkward for the both of them. Her nearing eighteen, fawning over him every time he looked at Emily. Him twenty-six, trying not to find himself alone with her. He might have seemed like the more responsible Kirkland brother, rightly so, but he didn't feel inclined to step into shoes Doug should have filled voluntarily. Not as a father for Emily, and not for Doug's stand-in with Ruth either.

Uncle he could manage though, and he'd focused on that, doing as much for Emily – and in turn her mother – as humanly possible. He'd become friends with Ruth, which had turned into his longest and best relationship with a woman to date. Probably because there were no expectations on either side.

"So, who jumped in front of your mower?" Emily asked, a chip crunching as she spoke the words.

It was impossible not to smile, just a little. "This lady who's staying at one of O'Neill's cabins, apparently a 'city slicker' who really likes grass. All I know is, she's really tiny, she has multi-colored hair, and I didn't run her over today."

"I think I know who you're talking about," Ruth said, leaning down to grab Emily's backpack. "Someone like that came into the restaurant a couple days ago. Real noticeable, because she looked like a rainbow threw up on her head."

"That's her," he agreed, that unexplainable tickle of sweat starting to appear at the base of his neck again.

"She was real friendly." Ruth pulled her dirt-smudged denim purse to the front of her body and began rifling through. "Gave me a book to give to Em." Her fingers dragged out a small book with a colorful design on the front, and Emily crossed the living room to take it from her mom.

"Willow Fairies!" Em yelled through a mouthful of chips. "These are the coolest."

"Don't talk with your mouth full," Clint cautioned as he reached over to tug on one of her caramel-hued braids. When he was close enough, he peeked over her shoulder to take a look at the book. Fairies, just like Emily said. Nothing to get all excited about.

Emily wiped the chip crumbs from her palm and turned the page of the book. "My friend Bella has Willow Fairies all over her room. The pillows, the blankets, the rug, the walls."

Clint raised his eyebrows as he perused the drawing of a fairy flying into a yellow-hued sunset. "Fairies all over her room, huh? Probably time to call the exterminator."

Chapter Three

Arabelle might have felt guilt for her reaction towards him, had he behaved in a more gentlemanlike manner. #willowfairies

Clint swiped left on his phone, gazing at the familiar face again. If someone hacked into his Google search, they would think he'd gone completely insane. Even he had to admit, his obsession with these fairies was getting out of control.

It had started innocently. Emily had gone on about the fairies she'd seen in her friend's bedroom for a while, and after Ruth and Emily left the house that day he decided to check them out for himself. He found the books first, six of them to be precise. That led to perusing social media accounts, which was where he found a treasure trove. Drawings, of course, but there were photos also. Photos that were all part of a long, ongoing story about an imaginary flying insect person named Arabelle.

He had a dream about her last night. Sort of. The monarch butterfly wings were there, and the flowing curly red hair, but when she turned around her face was the face that had been looking up at him a week ago with that magnifying glass on her head.

Willow Sharpe. There were a lot of pictures of her on those social media accounts too, and he had looked at them enough that he now knew every inch of her face. Definitely Google guilty.

The ongoing story she had with the main fairy, Arabelle, went back nearly two years. Each of the posts had a caption with the hashtag #willowfairies. The tiny fairy was strong, spunky, and fiercely independent. He'd been watching the accounts all week, waiting for the pictures to change. And each time they did, he studied them with fresh eyes.

He berated himself again, not that it would do any good. It had been exactly a week since he'd nearly killed her with his lawnmower. A week where he went about his routine of mowing lawns on Mondays and Wednesdays and helping a roofing crew the rest of the week.

And this one little added nuisance of stalking the fairy woman.

"It's just because I'm going to her place to mow the lawn," he muttered, clicking on the account so he could look at the latest post. The drawing from the day before held the top spot, with over six thousand likes. Those monarch wings were set against the background of a field, and she was gazing over her shoulder to the woods beyond. A simple figure stood at the edge of the trees, clad in green with wings that resembled military camouflage. Male, as evidenced by the shadow stretching across his chin.

If he didn't know better, he would say it looked a lot like himself.

With her forearm, Willow pushed a swath of hair from her brow. Using a little strip of cloth that she kept beside her canvas, she smudged the pink pencil against the sunset. After three long years, Arabelle had her love interest. Maybe. With just the glimpse of him at the edge of the trees, it was the smallest of snippets to whet her fans' appetites.

The glimpse of "fairy Darcy" was being shared like gangbusters, too. And just as she'd expected, thousands of people were breathing down her neck. *What's his name?* As though she knew that one herself.

So she focused instead on her next drawing, attempting to give him a little more detail while she pondered an appropriate moniker for the miniscule chap.

A knock on her door startled her, and she pushed away from the table, dropping her pencil beside the drawing. Who would be calling on her? The whole point of renting the woodland cabin was the privacy.

Pulling the blinds up, she stumbled back when she saw the black truck with the rusted fender. So he'd returned to the scene of the crime. At least this time she'd been prepared. The stakes with the flags on them stood in a circle around her fairy landscape, directly in the middle of her yard, forming a barrier. No doubt he wanted to complain.

Jerking the door open, she stretched to her full height, only measuring to the level of his chin, so she had no choice but to look up at him. Those blue eyes still sparkled, even when they weren't in the sun, and he had his ball cap between his hands, giving her a good glimpse of his nearly-black hair. It was cut short on the sides, unlike that beard, which was at least a couple of inches long. He did look like a lumberjack. Especially with those muscular arms on a relatively slender frame.

"May I help you?" she asked, keeping the door partly closed. He didn't need to see her messy, makeshift work area.

"Ma'am," he began, twisting the cap between his fingers. "I'm about to mow your lawn, and I just wanted you to know."

The gentlemanly demeanor was definitely unexpected. Stepping onto the porch, she pulled the door closed behind her, bare feet lighting on the wooden deck.

"Thank you for letting me know."

With a quick glance at his mower on the trailer, he returned his attention to her, scratching the side of his beard. "You don't have any objections?"

She stepped past him and down the steps, letting her toes sink into the grass. A feeling she hadn't experienced in nearly a decade. It was refreshing and made her want to relish it for a moment, just standing there with her eyes closed, listening to the breeze rustling the leaves. But she didn't, because he already thought she was a nut.

Instead, she moved to those stakes with the flags at the top, placing her hand against one. "If you could just avoid this area, that would be great."

"You've staked out your yard," he said, meeting her on the grass. His boots marked quite a contrast next to her pink-painted toes.

"Yes, I've staked out the yard."

She expected some kind of crack about her level of sanity, but he simply nodded his head and topped it with the ball cap. His eyes roved over her, crinkling at the corners as he squinted from the sun. "Oh, the name's Clint."

His hand extended in her direction, and she stared at it for a second. Long fingers, tan hands. An inexpensive, utilitarian watch on his wrist.

Shaking herself from her stupor, she reached her own hand out, folding it in his. "Willow."

"Nice to meet you," he stated, releasing her fingers and heading toward the trailer.

Clint, she thought to herself as she watched his back, shoulders wide above jeans that hung low on his hips. Her hand somehow still felt the gentle pressure of his fingers, so she stared at it, wondering at the odd sensation.

He fought the urge to shake his fingers out as he walked away. Staring at that beautiful face online had been one thing, but when she looked up into his eyes, he'd had the strangest sensation.

It was foolish to feel like he already knew the woman, unless he was somehow equating her with that red-headed fairy. All those little flying people were characters, he reminded himself, not real. As though he needed the reminder that two-inch tall women with butterfly wings were imaginary.

Besides, the fairy was beautiful in those drawings, but she couldn't hold a candle to the woman he'd just touched. Blonde hair cascading over her shoulder, streaks of color twisted into the mix. And those eyes, violet-blue and so large he'd almost imagined himself lost in them.

Almost, because he wasn't crazy.

Firing up his mower, he drove off the trailer ramp and forward to the grass, dropping the blade. She'd moved to the deck, standing there on the steps where she could see his every move, which meant he'd have to be extra careful not to face his mower in her direction. Rocks timed perfectly from a mower blade could bust through windows. No telling what they'd do if one of them hit her, and he certainly didn't need that on his conscience.

Affixing his sunglasses on his face, he tried not to look in her direction. The woman flat-out dressed like a hobo, again wearing the same ratty sweater she'd been wearing the first time he met her. The magnifying glass was thankfully not still perched on her head as she leaned herself against the railing next to the steps, staring down at her fingernails.

So she wasn't actually opposed to him cutting the grass, it seemed. But she still cared enough about it to sit there in case he made the wrong move. At least she wasn't watching him like a hawk, instead content to peer at her own hands or stare at the freshly stained boards on her deck. That fact only gave him the opportunity to look at her with more brazenness, and he found himself doing so as he rounded the corner of the yard to make another turn in her direction.

The closer he got to that section of the yard—the one littered with those reedy stakes she'd somehow gotten to stick in the ground—the more her eyes followed him. And when he made the closest pass, narrowly missing the new barrier by about six inches, she rose from her perch on the porch, giving him an intense inspection. He could feel the sweat begin to trickle down the center of his back, even though the sun wasn't particularly overbearing.

And then he swung away, following his path to the far corner of the yard, having finished the area she'd marked. By the time he turned the lawnmower around and started a return pass, she was gone.

Clint couldn't help feeling like he'd passed some kind of test. Why else would she have removed herself from her post after watching him so intently? Somehow she'd convinced herself that he wasn't going to decimate the section of the grass that she thought so valuable. He tried not to think about it as he finished up the last portion of the yard, because standing sentinel over a patch of grass was still pretty weird, no matter whether the woman intrigued him or not.

Plain, dopey, bizarrely weird, if he really wanted to spell it out.

While he drove the mower back to his trailer, he intentionally took the path closest to those stakes again. Partly to see if she'd come roaring back out the door, and partly because he wanted to understand what was so special about it. Maybe she'd planted a tree there that he hadn't seen before? Seemed like she could be the tree-hugging type. Or maybe she had some flower bulbs in the ground right there and she was afraid he'd mow them over.

As he drew close, a little flash of red caught his eye. Just enough that he nearly choked the engine as he jerked his mower to a stop. Mushroom huts. Two of them, that he could see. What else resided there he couldn't tell, because he spurred his mower on, afraid of being found gawking at her little fairy village. But as he loaded his mower back on the trailer, he allowed himself the tiniest of smiles. Protecting her artwork was a lot less strange than some of the things he'd been imagining.

And in avoiding the little village's destruction, he'd suddenly found himself a small part of the story.

Chapter Four

Only the deepest love would tempt Arabelle into matrimony. Such being the case, she was fully prepared to spend her days teaching other fairies' children to fly very ill. #willowfairies

Clint paused in front of the glass door, turning around to stare at his truck and trailer. He was a man who made up his mind. Had been right out of high school when he'd joined the military. Had been when he returned from overseas and couldn't imagine settling anywhere other than his childhood home. Had been when he decided he wanted to be a landscaper and started his own business.

So why was he waffling about mowing one little lawn?

Shaking his head in self-disgust, he turned back to the glass door and jerked it open, making just enough noise that the few heads remaining in the café at the odd hour popped up to see who was making an entrance. Keeping his own head down, he moved to a booth out of the way and seated himself, extending his legs in front of him beneath the table.

Ten o'clock. Shouldn't be many patrons at ten o'clock. The breakfast crowd would have dispersed and the lunch crowd wouldn't be making an appearance for a while yet. So he could sit at the booth and think for a bit before he made any potentially dumb decisions.

At least that was the plan, until Ruth settled into the seat across from him, placing her palm-sized notebook on the table.

"That's a face I don't see often."

Glancing up, he set his phone on the table between them as well. She looked a lot more energetic than she usually did at the end of her shift.

"Yeah, I tend not to do much besides work during the day, so I don't get in here often enough."

She tapped her fingernails against the tabletop. "I didn't mean your face inside the café. I meant that expression you're wearing. You look worried."

"Naw, I'm not worried."

"Good, because the Clint Kirkland I know doesn't worry about things. He fixes things."

He could attest to the truth of that. At least, he could have before.

"So what is it, huh?" Ruth continued, dipping her head in an attempt to get him to meet her eyes. "Business problems? You don't want Em getting off the bus at your place anymore? I could talk to Jess about my shift and see what we can—"

"Em's fine getting off the bus at the house. And I'm not worried. Just got a lot on my mind's all."

Her eyes softened, and she propped her elbows on the table between them. "Want to hash it out? I got a break coming."

Lifting his hand to his cheek, he rubbed the side of his beard as he stared out the window at his truck. "Nothing much to hash out." The thought of running that truck and trailer across town swept through his mind again. "Okay, just for grins, say you met this person. Not someone you're well acquainted with or anything, just a random stranger. And you've got nothing in common with them. Nothing. But they make up people who seem like they could be . . . What I'm trying to say is—"

"You've met a woman."

"Yes." His gaze drifted to her face, and he quickly shook his head. "No. I mean not exactly." Leaning in, he brought his voice down to a whisper. "You remember Em's fairies? The woman who draws the fairies?"

"The one you almost killed."

Glancing behind him, he pinched his eyebrows together. "I didn't almost kill anyone, now hold your voice down. The thing is, I think that she . . ." Nearly groaning at his inability to spit out the words, he grabbed his phone and pulled up the account he'd become so familiar with in the past two weeks. Clicking on the picture, he slid the phone across the table to Ruth. "This is from the first time I mowed the lawn."

A slow nod accompanied her perusal of the picture. "I see."

Grabbing the phone, he clicked again and brought up a more recent photo. "This is from last week, after I mowed the lawn."

Ruth's jaw slackened as she glanced from the phone to his face and back again. "She's drawing you."

"Look at his name," he prompted, watching as her eyes scanned the photo.

"Flint." Pressing her hand over her mouth, she giggled. "The fairy lady has a crush on you."

"No, she doesn't."

"Oh my word. Clint Kirkland, you have a crush on her!"

He peered over his shoulder again, sinking a little in his seat. "Didn't I tell you to keep your voice down?"

"You're going to ask her out, right?" Ruth waited expectantly for an answer, and when he didn't respond, she crossed her arms against her chest. "Please tell me you're going to ask her out."

"To do what? Paint our hair pink and stare at butterflies? We're not the same, Ruthie."

Pulling her pad nearer her side of the table, she scribbled on it while he sat watching. "Men are infuriating, you know that? Have you bothered to find out what she likes? Asked her what her interests are, besides her hair color and her job? Because painting is her job, you know. I'm sure she likes it or she wouldn't do it, but how would you like to be described that way? 'Oh, that landscaper guy? What would we do? Comb our facial hair and stare at grass?' Give me a break."

The little outburst startled him enough that he leaned back against the booth seat and pulled his baseball cap from his head, readjusting it a little too forcefully.

"Look at this drawing," she continued, pointing at his phone again. He grabbed it from her hand, staring at the red-headed fairy standing so close to the bearded newcomer. "Did she draw this guy with pink hair and dainty hands? No. She drew a big, strapping guy with a black beard. A big idiot, if you ask me." Ripping the top paper from her pad, she tossed it at him. "Your tip, sir."

While she rose from the seat across from him, he flipped the paper over in his hands. *Try being yourself,* it read. Not an entirely scary prospect in a normal situation, but he'd never been good with women. Couldn't force himself to say more than a few words in their presence, and what woman would want a guy who couldn't even carry on a basic conversation?

"Shove over," Ruth ordered, scooting next to him on the bench. "Really look at the picture. Maybe it'll give you some clues."

Trying to give her a little extra space, he moved to the far side of the booth as she grabbed his phone again, studying the drawing while he peeked over her shoulder. Arabelle stood at the door to her mushroom hut, saying goodbye to Flint. Her eyes almost looked alive, and as he stared at them, he imagined those huge, blue-violet eyes of Willow's staring back at him.

"He took her for a jaunt in the woods," Ruth finally stated.

"Huh?" Shaking his head, he tried to remove those eyes from his line of vision.

"The fairy boyfriend. He took her on a nature walk, basically. So you ask her to accompany you into nature."

Looking at Ruth next to him, he squinted his eyes skeptically. "So I'm supposed to ask her to go into the woods with me?"

"Seriously, how do you function on a day to day basis?" Tapping the brim of his cap, she twisted her mouth to the side. "Tell her you know the area, and you could show her some of the best natural landscapes. Ask if she'd like to go hiking. Or just hog tie her and throw her in the back of your truck, Caveman."

"Very funny." Taking his phone from her hand, he hit the home screen to remove the fairy scene. "Thanks for the tip."

Ruth slid out of the booth, offering the slightest hint of a smile, but he couldn't really take it to heart. Especially when he was no closer to committing himself on what to do than he had been when he sat down in the first place.

Willow's living room blinds made a metallic snapping noise as they bent from the force of her fingers. The sound came as a surprise, and it made her pop back from her spying position. Straightening the offending slat, she attempted to peek out the window a little more gracefully.

He was back, right on schedule. A little later in the day than he had been the other times, but exactly one week from the last time she'd seen him. And even though he hadn't knocked on the door before he started, he still avoided that little section of the yard that she'd fought so hard to guard.

The mere sight of him swinging the mower in a circle around the area made her feel like something was doing backflips in her stomach. It was irrational, having a spark of attraction for the burly southerner who did her lawn maintenance. But no matter how she tried to convince herself of that fact, that spark still managed to settle itself somewhere deep inside, enough so that she found herself drawing his face for Arabelle's mate. And naming him Flint . . . a desperate plea for help if she ever heard one.

The urge to snap a picture of him struck her, but she didn't dare move. Much better to commit his face and physique to memory than to be caught hounding him like a member of the star-struck paparazzi. Even imagining him catching her snapping photos made her blush like a teenager.

His face turned in the direction of the cabin, and she released the blinds and stumbled back, pressing her hand against her heart. *Enough*, she told herself. *No more staring at the poor guy.* Sitting down at the table, she pulled her sketch pad closer, ready to plan a new adventure for Arabelle. Her fans had already fallen in love with Flint, even though Willow wasn't sure she was willing to allow Arabelle that same luxury. Flint could turn out to be a jerk, after all. Or he could just manage to be wishy washy and spineless like most guys she'd had the pleasure of knowing.

Silence settled over the cabin, and she realized that the noise from the mower had ceased. She could go peek out the blinds again, but he'd likely be securing the mower on his trailer or climbing into the cab of his pickup. Best to stay put and focus on Arabelle.

Her pencil touched the paper right as a knock sounded on the door, sending the tip of the lead off course until it left a dark trail all the way to the corner of the sketch pad. It couldn't be someone new, because there hadn't been enough time since she sat down for another person to arrive. Which meant he was knocking again.

Why would he be knocking?

Pulling her hair over her shoulder, she twisted it around her hand as she rose from the chair, heavy wool socks shuffling against the hardwood floor. She'd spent her fair share of time sliding back and forth across it like her own personal skating rink in the short time she'd spent there, but that was out of the question at the moment. Instead, she carefully stepped to the door, twisting the doorknob as she pulled it toward her.

"Hi," she said, her gaze lifting until she'd swept it across his muscular forearms while on the path to his face. By the time she got to his eyes, she was already feeling self-conscious. The weight of the tattered sweater on her shoulders reminded her to fold her arms protectively across her chest.

"Clint."

He thought she might have forgotten his name? Her heart swelled just a bit. "Yes, I remember."

His eyes bore into hers for a minute, and then he flipped his gaze to his truck, wrapping one hand around the back of his neck. "I grew up around here."

She used his distraction as an opportunity to peruse him more closely. The little sliver of skin that separated his beard from his ear. The thin white line that scarred his cheekbone. The way his facial hair looked curlier the closer it got to his neck.

"So you grew up here, on this land?" she finally asked, leaning against the door frame.

"No, not right here, just in the general area."

The guy was awkward as all get out, which only made her like him more. "Fascinating."

"I know the land," he said, shoving his hands into his pockets. "Not specifically this land, but—"

"The general area." A huge smile made its way to her face. "Sounds like you're a good guy to be acquainted with."

His cheeks reddened above his beard, but he kept those ice blue eyes focused on her. "Thank you, ma'am."

"Willow."

"Willow." The way he said her name made her feel like she'd just been wrapped in a blanket of sunshine. "If you'd be interested in having someone show you around, I know the land." One hand slid out of his pocket and came up to pinch the bridge of his nose as he closed his eyes. "I said that already."

A laugh trickled out as she crossed one of her socked feet over the other. "Maybe so, but I liked it each time." One corner of his mouth tipped up, and that only served to embolden her. "Thank you for your offer. I accept. Should I get my shoes?"

"Oh." He brought his arm up, glancing at the watch on his wrist. "I have to be home for Emily soon."

Emily. The three syllables dragged her heart down to the pit of her stomach as he said them. Married? He didn't have a ring on his finger, but sometimes guys working manual labor didn't wear them for safety reasons. No wonder the poor guy was having a hard time spitting out his words. He was trying to be neighborly, and she was throwing herself at him.

"I understand," she managed to squeeze out.

"She usually shows up at the house around four."

The more her heart ached, the more she wanted him off her deck. "You should definitely go home then."

"But you can come with me, if you like. My niece will only be there for a few minutes, between the time she gets off the bus and when her mom's shift ends."

His niece. The man watched his niece when the bus came. Uncle Clint, superhero.

Willow's erratic heart came back to life beneath his watchful gaze, and she reached up to fiddle with a piece of her hair. So maybe her first impression was right. He was trying to flirt with her? If so, there was no hesitation whatsoever in her spirit. Grabbing the door knob, she stepped inside, holding her fingers aloft in front of her in an expressive gesture.

"Give me five minutes."

Chapter Five

Arabelle feared she had proven herself unladylike, but Flint was only thinking of the way her fine eyes were brightened by the exercise. #willowfairies

Clint glanced at Willow walking beside him as he stepped over a rock embedded in the trail. He'd tried not to stare when she emerged from her cabin earlier, hair pulled over her shoulder into a multicolored braid. Tried even harder when she was in the truck cab with him, her cargo shorts settling about halfway up her thighs. Wanted to ignore the way the tank top hugged her frame under that baggy button-up shirt, the ends of which were knotted together near her waistband. Didn't even want to think about how practical her tan hiking boots were.

Thankfully, she didn't seem to notice his silent perusal.

"This is why I didn't move to L.A. with Sammie," she said with a sigh as she glanced at the greenery surrounding the trail. "I've had enough of the concrete jungle to last me a while." Two more steps forward, she started inspecting the ground around her feet instead. "Sammie was my roommate in New York. She'll be a great Hollywood composer someday, so you'll have to remember that name. Samantha J. Moore."

He thought about agreeing with her, but before he had the chance to open his mouth she started in again.

"It really does creep into your soul, doesn't it? The land, I mean. Sometimes I feel like it could totally envelop me." She paused to glance at him, pushing a little pink strand of hair away from her eyes. "Am I talking too much? I have the tendency to do that when I'm nervous, and since I barely know you, I think this qualifies. Barely know you . . . I don't know you at all, really, besides the fact that your name is Clint and you mow lawns and you're extremely polite in your manner of speech. I'm sure you'd like to say something too, so go ahead."

He focused on the ground, avoiding another rock as his mind reeled. Whether he preferred to say something or not, doing so under pressure wasn't so easy for him. Clearing his throat, he glanced at her again.

"You like to wear baggy clothes?" His conscience cringed so hard, he could actually feel the constriction in his chest.

Willow glanced down at her outfit, shrugging her shoulders. "Not especially. The tank top will be good in case I get hot, and the shirt over it will keep the sun off my shoulders or serve as a jacket if I get cold. I tend to be susceptible to the sun, with the blonde hair and the fair skin. But I'm sure you're probably also referring to that sweater I always seem to be wearing when you see me. Just to be perfectly clear, I don't wear that in public. It's my work gear."

Letting her control the conversation was a far better option, so he feigned the appropriate level of interest and repeated her words. "Work gear?"

"There was a woman who lived two floors beneath me when I first moved to New York, Mrs. Campbell. Her family had emigrated from Scotland when she was six years old. Growing up, her mother had told her the most fascinating fairy stories. She'd tell me about them over the most horrible tea imaginable, and then I'd go upstairs and sketch them for her. She was the first person who really believed in my talent, although I'm sure I could have given her childish drawings and she would have loved them. The woman was ninety-three, so I think she was just reliving the past through me somehow. But I didn't mind, because it was nice to have someone—anyone—tell me that something I made was good." She paused and looked in his direction again. "Did I tell you that I sketch fairies? I sketch fairies."

The woman did a lot more than sketch, but he tried to hold back his smile as he shook his head.

"That was her sweater, the one I'm always wearing. She was cold there in her apartment, so she never took it off. After she passed, I stole it. No one would have missed it anyway, since the poor woman didn't have any family that anyone knew about. Someone would have cleaned out her apartment and thrown it in the garbage, but that sweater . . ." Her eyes drifted heavenward as she stared past the trees to the blue of the sky. "That sweater reminds me that, whatever my talent is, regardless of how it appears to other people, there's a Mrs. Campbell out there somewhere who needs fairies. Maybe I'm destined to be a fairy doodler and nothing more, but we changed each other's lives, Mrs. Campbell and me. That has to count for something."

She quieted for the first time since she'd stepped foot inside his truck, and it couldn't have come at a more inopportune moment. He could make small talk well enough, but how was he supposed to follow a story like that? *So, weather's nice, ain't it?*

"Clint."

The way she said his name, all breathy and captivated-sounding, made him stop in his tracks. He turned his own mesmerized gaze in her direction, but she wasn't looking at him at all. She was looking straight past him, to the area where the waterfall spilled over the rocks in front of them.

"Gorgeous," she whispered.

It was. The waterfall. It was gorgeous. But she was too, and he couldn't pull his eyes away while he watched the wonder cross her face. She took three steps in his direction, never removing her gaze from the scenery in front of her. When she slid her fingers into his hand, standing there so close, he could do nothing but watch her expression shine through those large violet eyes.

"I think God settles in these hills," she breathed, leaning even closer as her hand tightened around his, her fingers seeming small and fragile against his own. "Wouldn't you, if you were Him? The minute I got here, it felt like He was closer to me."

"Maybe you were closer to Him, in the peace and quiet."

Apparently he'd chosen his few words wisely that time, because she tilted her head up and smiled. "Maybe you're right." Her free hand closed around the back of his palm, and she lifted both of her hands to her chest, his fingers held tightly between them. "But it was so good of Him to send you to mow my lawn, so you'd bring me here. I'm indebted to you, and to Him too it would seem."

The thought of God arranging his first meeting with the beautiful artist, sprawled out in front of his mower, almost made him want to laugh. Almost, because laughing would have proven impossible with her staring at him like that. Holding his hand so firmly between her own.

Turning her gaze back to the waterfall, she kept her firm grip on his hand. "Do you hunt God here, in places like this, where it's quiet and peaceful? I think I would, every chance I got."

He looked at the waterfall too, his gaze dipping so he could see the top of her head in his line of vision. "Sometimes I find Him here. And other times He finds me."

Willow stepped onto her deck, secretly loving the sound of Clint's boots tapping against the wood behind her. She'd imagined his face in front of her many times, daydreaming some rendezvous or another for Arabelle. He was always stoically riding in to sweep the little fairy off her feet. It had been fun creating a personality for Flint, but this was different.

Clint was solid, real, and sturdy, like an immovable wall. A quiet, handsome, strapping immovable wall. Simply being in close proximity to him was making her a blubbering imbecile. She'd barely taken a breath the entire time they'd been together, but she couldn't seem to stop the words from pouring forth. A nervous habit that she thought she would have outgrown by now.

"How tall are you?" she asked as she reversed course at the door, bumping straight into his chest. The man didn't even move as she stumbled back a step.

"Six-foot-two."

Her clumsiness had placed her close enough to him that she had to tilt her head to look into his eyes. "No wonder you seem like a giant. I'm five-foot-three, probably five-foot-four with these boots on. But you're wearing boots too, so that would make you an inch taller as well, so I'm sure it evens itself out."

"Maybe so," he said simply, staring down at her. His eyes were far more fascinating than the waterfall, but she wasn't about to blurt that along with everything else she'd blurted during the course of their time together.

"Thank you for the lovely evening," she added, her fingers reaching out to touch his abdomen. Fingertips connected with navy blue T-shirt against muscle right before he flinched. Jerking her fingers away, her eyes went wide. "The lovely hike, I mean. I had a . . ." She caught herself right before she said lovely again. "I'm grateful that you showed me the waterfall. Thank you."

Why had she touched him? All night long, one thing after the other, she hadn't been able to keep her hands off the poor guy. Back at the waterfall, she'd been staring at the scenery and mumbling something about how beautiful it was when she realized she had his hand clamped against her chest. And like a trooper, he never said anything about how weird she was acting.

He continued to watch her, seemingly unaware of her inner turmoil. "It was my pleasure."

"I've dominated the conversation, and I'm sorry."

"I'm not." A smile tipped up the corners of his lips, and she let herself relax just a bit. One thing she'd been sure of as they hiked down the trail tonight: she'd never felt so safe. The simple way he watched her as they walked let her know that he'd do whatever it took to protect her.

"There's a space in my yard where I set up my fairy houses. I'm really not crazy."

"Where you had the stakes," he added.

"Yes. I mean, not crazy as in I wouldn't sacrifice myself for grass, but still the crazy person who makes fairy houses for a living."

"So a normal amount of crazy."

If he didn't say something rude, and soon, she was in danger of falling for the big lug. "I should say good night."

He nodded, taking two steps away from her. "Good night, Willow."

Sliding the keys from her purse, she unlocked the front door and pushed it open. When she stepped through the threshold, he turned to walk down the steps.

"Don't be a stranger," she called to him.

Stopping in her yard, he glanced her way and touched the brim of his cap. "Yes, ma'am."

Chapter Six

Arabelle talked as a rule while flying. Spending half an hour in Flint's company without conversing would have been entirely too overwhelming. #willowfairies

The front screen door banged closed, and Clint jerked his gaze up from his phone where it rested on the kitchen counter. Too early for Emily to be home from school, wasn't it? But the clock near his stove told him otherwise. Time had gotten away from him again.

Emily stepped into the kitchen, dropping her backpack on the ground. Her hair had some flyaway static from the backpack fabric, and she smoothed it down as she stepped to the cabinet that held his stash of snack food.

"Something small," he reminded her, just like he did every day. She grabbed a chocolate cupcake and worked the wrapper while he watched. "Last week of school?"

"Next week," she mumbled as she stuffed a bite of cake into her mouth. "But we're not doing work."

"I remember that. Goofing off the last week of school. It's a rite of passage."

"A right of what?" She licked her fingers, transferring the cupcake to her other hand.

"It's just a figure of speech." Grabbing his phone, he swiped to activate the screen and stared at the drawing again.

"Looking at fairies?" Emily asked, her "r" sounding like a "w" with her mouth full of her snack.

"Yeah." With a tug at one of the wooden chairs at the kitchen table, he lowered himself to a seated position as he continued to study the picture. Emily plopped down next to him, looking over his arm. "Why are women so complicated, huh? I feel like I spend half of my time trying to read minds and the rest trying to figure out what I screwed up."

Emily shrugged and popped the last bite of the cupcake into her mouth. "You're bad at girls."

"You too?" Giving her a fake growl, he pressed his lips together. Careful study of the outings Willow created between her fairy couple had given him ideas for every date they'd shared. If she would have even called them dates. He wouldn't really go that far himself, because he didn't have the nerve to ask her out as such. Despite the fact that Ruth insisted they could be a couple, he remained unconvinced. She was the most fascinating woman he'd ever met, but what would she want with him? He couldn't even uphold his end of the conversation most of the time.

Even so, the trip to the waterfall had been good. The picnic he took her on the next week a little awkward, but she still agreed to go hiking with him later that same week. She even faked such an interest in his landscaping that he took her to mow three lawns with him one day. That had been the longest workday of his life, trying to keep an eye on her and off her at the same time. A very delicate balance.

But still he hadn't clarified their relationship, and she hadn't clarified anything between Arabelle and Flint. Since he took their cues as his own, he was more confused now than he had been in the beginning.

"What're they doing this time?" Emily wondered, placing her chin on his upper arm.

"Fairy stuff," he muttered, shoving the phone over so it was sitting in front of his niece. She huffed and gave him a sideways glance full of seven-year-old sass before she took the phone into her hand.

"They're on a bird."

"Probably contracting all sorts of bird flu."

She shrugged as she turned the phone sideways, scrutinizing the drawing more closely. "They look like they're having fun."

That comment made Clint glance at the phone again. Arabelle did have a giant smile on her face. Flint looked kind of stoically present. Maybe a slight hint of a smile tilting up one corner of his lips. If she was having fun, that was good enough, right?

But what was he supposed to do, exactly? It wasn't like using a bird as an airplane was a picnic or a hike. Last he knew, there were no giant birds in the area capable of carrying fully grown humans. Which meant his little hints had dried up. So he'd have to resort to something cliché like dinner or a movie.

"Too easy," Emily said as she dropped the phone on the table, moving back to the snack cabinet.

"Easy? What do you mean, easy?"

Grabbing a package of crackers, she closed the cabinet door and turned back in his direction, crossing her arms over her chest. "Where can you go for rides in the sky? Duh. Dollywood."

"You're going to have to sit this one out, big guy." Willow stepped into line, turning to smile up at Clint. "It has a height restriction, and you're dangerously tall." She glanced at the sign again, noting that the maximum height was six-foot-six.

"If there's a height restriction, it would probably be that you're too short," he told her, sliding his sunglasses off his face and placing them instead on the brim of his baseball cap.

Teasing. She was finally breaking him out of his shell at last. A little bit, anyway. Their first outing together he had been largely quiet, but he said a little bit more each time she saw him. Which she would like to happen more than once a week, if she was being honest. He didn't even ask her to spend time with him as if he considered their excursions dates. Just casually mentioned places like he was already going somewhere and she could tag along.

This time, though, had been different. It hadn't been a weekday jaunt to some secluded place. A smile crept onto her face as she remembered him standing on her doorstep a few mornings back, asking if she'd ever been to Dollywood. She hadn't let him off the hook easily, either. "No, I haven't," she said simply, waiting for his next move. It had taken several painful, agonizingly long seconds before he uttered another word. Then, when she was afraid she'd have to ask him out herself, he asked, "Would you like to go with me?"

And now there he was, just inches away behind her in line, driving her slightly crazy with temptation. She'd been habitually trying to break herself from the strange desire to touch him, and she'd mostly avoided the embarrassing habit today. It was still a little early to declare her prevention a success, though.

"Have you ever flown?" she wondered aloud when the line stopped in front of her. "I mean, of course you have. Overseas, military, dumb question. Forget I asked."

He stepped right next to her, placing one of his large tennis shoes in between her two boat shoes on the asphalt. Her eyes swept up and over his shorts and snug T-shirt before realizing he'd taken her braid in between his fingers. She watched as his fingers worked over the twisted ridges she'd formed in her hair that morning, first tracing a purple line with his fingertip, and then blue.

"Sure, I've flown. Several times. You?"

She tried to ignore the fluttering feeling in her chest and the goosebumps spreading across her arms. "No. There's something that scares me about flying."

His gaze left her hair and instead traveled to her face, and she studied his pale blue eyes while he placed her braid against her shoulder, his fingers brushing against her collarbone in the process. The guy behind them in line cleared his throat, and she glanced over to see that the line had moved in front of her. Stepping away from Clint, she took a deep breath while she tried to calm her fidgety nerves.

Clint stayed behind her this time, close enough that she could feel the warmth of his body through the back of her T-shirt. "What is it that scares you about flying?"

He was propelling the conversation on his own. Normally that wouldn't be something she'd notice when speaking to someone, but Clint was usually so quiet it felt like a milestone.

"I don't know, the falling to a fiery death part?"

Willow could feel his beard tickle her neck as he leaned in behind her. "You do realize this ride simulates flying?"

Unable to keep the smile from spreading on her face, she dropped her head back until it was against his chest. "Of course, but you're with me, so I feel fearless."

That was a little too much. She knew it the moment the words left her lips, but she remained there with her head against him, enjoying the few seconds of touch. About the time she decided she should lean forward, lest he think she was being too pushy, she felt a feathery sensation against her right arm. Training her eyes near her elbow, she saw his fingers brushing against her skin the way they'd been sweeping her hair a moment ago.

The clearing throat behind them almost made her groan, and she moved forward again, breaking her contact with Clint. She wasn't willing to undo the momentous "normal-dating" progress they'd made in the past moment, though, so she turned to him the minute she reached the line again.

"Is there anything you're scared of?" she asked, standing sideways so she could glance back at him as the line moved forward.

"Tiny people."

She wrinkled her nose as she gave him a good-natured eye roll. "Tiny people, seriously? What else?"

"Things with more than one hair color."

Turning fully toward him, she crossed her arms over her chest. "What else?"

"People who talk too much."

A rumbling scream sounded behind her as the roller coaster went by, and she narrowed her eyes as she studied Clint. "If I didn't know better, I'd think you were describing me."

The slightest hint of a smile made his lip twitch as they stopped moving forward again. "You're terrifying."

Willow pressed a hand against her chest, moving her lips into a wide O shape. "Me? I can pretty much guarantee you're the only person in the entire universe who would be scared of me. But you know what? I'm proud of you."

"You're proud of me?" He crossed his arms against his T-shirt, accentuating his muscles merely by the way they pulled against his sleeves. Willow tried not to notice the lines that formed on his upper arms where the skin followed the contours of those muscles, instead staring up at those eyes that she found only slightly more interesting than biceps.

"Sure, it's normal to be proud of someone who's conquering their fears. And look at you, willingly spending time with me when I'm so personally terrifying to you."

"I deserve a medal."

She nearly giggled, but fought it back. "Certainly, and had I a medal at my disposal, I'd bestow it upon you right now. A medal of courage for Mr. Kirkland, who showed extreme bravery in the face of certain forced conversation with a petite woman."

"You forgot the rainbow hair."

"How could I have forgotten that? Petite women with multi-faceted hair colors are the absolute scariest of them all. Bravo, sir, for your extreme courage."

He unwrapped his arms and placed one hand on her shoulder, rubbing his thumb against her neck. She couldn't make her mind up regarding where to move next. Circle his body with a hug? Put her hand atop his on her shoulder? Maybe stretch to tiptoe in the hopes of landing a kiss on his cheek?

The throat clearing behind them for a third time dragged her out of her daydream. "Maybe you two could just get a room? You obviously can't pay attention to the line."

That wasn't even close to being on her list of options, so she smiled sweetly at Clint, turned to see that the line had moved about twenty feet, and told herself for the millionth time to let the poor man make the first move.

Chapter Seven

Arabelle could not fix the moment or the scene which started the story. She was already in the middle when she realized it had begun in the first place. #willowfairies

"What should we do next?"

The attendant had barely closed them into the little cart on the Ferris wheel when Willow asked the question, and Clint waited a few seconds to answer while he studied her profile. She looked around her, eyes wide, drinking in every single thing she could see. It was fascinating to him the way everything . . . well, fascinated her. She met every new thing she came across with the kind of awe that he imagined a blind person would feel on the first day of sight.

"I don't know that there'll be a next," he finally answered. "Park's getting ready to close."

"That's a shame," she said with a sigh, letting out a little squeak when the cart moved forward. "I do believe I could stay here all night and never get tired."

The sun had already set and twilight was waning too, but the bright lights of the park meant he could still see her face as well as he could all day. She hadn't been quite as touchy feely as she usually was, and her lack of contact somehow had him reaching out to touch her instead. Rubbing her multi-colored hair between his fingers. Grazing the back of his hand down her arm. Even taking her hand in his while they walked.

"Look at that view," she whispered, her eyes settling on the far end of the park. "I can't even remember when I've had more fun."

"You're exaggerating," he said, stretching his arm out behind her. "I'm sure you found plenty of fun in the city."

The view disappeared as their cart dipped down toward the ground. "Of course I found ways to enjoy myself, but this is different. Here in your mountains, my heart's happy."

He chuckled as he avoided the gazes of the attendants while the cart passed. "I don't own the mountains."

A smile brightened her face as she focused on the scenery once more. "I'm not so sure about that. I think the mountains belong to you, just as much as you belong to them. You're imprinted on their face, and they're stamped on your soul."

That.

That was the kind of thing that made him half crazy. The way she spouted her poetic little phrases kind of offhanded like she didn't even have to think about them. But if he had been thinking about what to say all day, to explain why he couldn't settle anywhere else, he would have said something simple like *it's just home.* Which it was, but so much more than that. She saw things deeper than most people, his little fairy painter.

The realization that he was starting to think of her as his wasn't as surprising as it should have been, either. He'd been doing that for quite a while, although he was hesitant to admit that fact.

She continued to study the landscape, and he studied the side of her face. Everything about her seemed dainty, from the slope of her nose to the curve of her cheek to the way her chin almost came to a point. Even her ear seemed delicately perfect, the way it framed her face with no hints of any marks there. Not even the telltale little spot where earrings usually were, or had been. Flawless ear lobe. Had he ever really looked at a woman's ear before? Probably not, he decided.

Willow mentioned something about the lights, and he watched her lips move as she spoke. The top one lifted to an exaggerated peak in the middle, while the bottom one was fuller. It wasn't good to be so distracted, he knew that. Any second now she'd ask him about something she said and he'd be clueless, but she was so stunning. He imagined himself showing her picture to his buddies in the service, like they'd shown him their girls back home. They would have said she was too good for him, and he would have agreed, because sitting right next to him like she was, he thought she was the most beautiful woman in the world.

The cart jerked to a stop, leaving the two of them at the top of the wheel, gently swaying in the evening sky. Her violet eyes turned to look at him, too quickly for him to avoid her notice. Caught staring. He probably should have looked away, but he didn't. And when he didn't, she brought her gaze up to meet his, focusing directly on his eyes. He felt the tips of her fingers against either side of his face, her hands settling against his beard.

She drew her bottom lip between her teeth, then glanced at his mouth. "Would it be okay if I kissed you?"

He swallowed hard as his eyes widened. "I think I'm supposed to ask that kind of stuff."

Shrugging her shoulders, she gave an awkward little sideways smile as her fingertips swept down his cheeks. "You're right. I keep telling myself that, but you're moving too slow."

"Moving too—"

His words were cut short by her fingertips settling on his mouth. She let them linger there for a few agonizing seconds while she stared up at him, and then dragged them away only to move her lips to his instead. He drew his breath in as she kissed him, but she leaned back immediately like she'd only wanted a taste, pressing her lips together while her eyes scanned his face.

For someone who thought he was moving too slow, that was barely movement at all.

Besides, it was time he took control of the situation. She seemed to like him, if her actions were any judge. The fairies she drew had been nice for giving him hints, but he knew her well enough now that he could come up with his own ideas. And he'd start with . . .

Wrapping his hand around the back of her slender neck, he drew her closer as her eyes drifted closed. That was all the hint he needed before pulling her into another kiss. It probably wouldn't have been his first choice, kissing her atop a Ferris wheel, but the goal had been to take her flying, and he felt like he was doing just that. Flying when he usually had his feet firmly on the ground.

He deepened the kiss as the ride started again, unable to tell if it was the motion that had him off balance or the woman beside him. Perhaps a combination of both, since Willow seemed to keep him off balance all the time. Had since the instant he saw her, really, spread out on the ground in front of his mower. She'd been sending his heart into palpitations at every subsequent meeting.

The sensation of dipping and rising back into the air let him know that they'd passed the bottom of the ride and were heading back up to the top. He leaned back and their lips parted, her mouth open as though in surprise. While he wondered if he should kiss her again, her fingertips trembled a bit at the neck of his T-shirt, connecting with his skin just above the fabric. She had such a dainty, delicate touch, like a butterfly softly landing against him.

"Well done," she whispered, all wide-eyed innocence again.

It was impossible to contain his smile as she nestled into his shoulder, staring out at the scenery once more. He wrapped his arm around her a little tighter, making sure she was firmly against his side. No woman had ever praised him for his kissing ability before, especially not in the moment. Had any of them done that, he would have thought it strange. Not with Willow, though. Somehow everything she did managed to seem uniquely suited to her.

And the fact that she enjoyed the kiss made him feel like he was on top of the world, even more so than the Ferris wheel could.

Willow stepped down from the truck, accepting Clint's offered hand. Hers was a hopeless case. She'd tried to be poised and suave and ladylike, but still couldn't help throwing herself at him in the end. Not that she regretted it now. That kiss on top of the Ferris wheel had pretty effectively blown her mind.

Now she was the one who was struggling to find words, and he was carrying the conversation. Quite a difference from their norm.

"Thank you for going with me today," he said as he walked her across the yard to her cabin. "It's been ages since I've been to Dollywood."

"Well, if you really wouldn't have gone if you hadn't asked me, then you're welcome."

They reached the steps, and instead of walking up them, she sat on the top one and waited. He ran the palms of his hands against his shorts as he lowered himself next to her. It seemed easier to relate to him when they were sitting down. Maybe because he wasn't towering over her and they were almost eye to eye.

"So . . ." he muttered, looking out at the woods beyond the yard.

"So," she repeated, focusing on his truck in her driveway. "I have a thing for you." An awkward silence stretched between them, and she tried to ignore the lack of response as she tried not to look in his direction. He inspected the side of her face, brow wrinkling in concentration.

"You have something for me."

"No, not something. A thing. I have *a thing* for you." Leaning her head back to stare up at the sky, she placed her right palm against her forehead. "There should be a law against me doing this. I'm dreadfully bad at it."

Clint didn't seem to notice her consternation, continuing to thoughtfully watch her as she dared to peek at him through her fingers.

"Bad at what, exactly?"

Life, she wanted to say. Instead, she let out a huge sigh. "It's just that I haven't had many dates, per se. I suppose it's easier to just keep myself away from the opposite sex than to be reminded over and over again that guys aren't interested."

"Why wouldn't guys be interested in you?"

He was either sweet as syrup on a candy cane or a little delusional. She didn't want to take a guess at which was accurate.

"There really isn't a great demand for women who spend most of their time thinking about fairies. Especially not women who lack the necessary curves to attract men in the first place." She wrinkled her nose and fully turned in his direction. "Sorry. Talk about being bad company, right?"

He didn't smile or shake his head or offer any answer to her question. Instead, he watched her carefully. "I don't date much. Most women want me to . . . you know . . . talk."

"And here I thought you were just so awestruck by my charm that I shocked you into silence."

A deep laugh broke into the muted sound of insects chirping and buzzing in the background. Clint's smile was so genuine that it created little crinkles around his eyes. "Sassy little weirdo."

She let her mouth drop open at those words, finally giving him a mock glare even though she couldn't keep the corner of her lips from rising into a grin. "Tell me what you really think of me," she demanded, her heart pounding as he took her hand in his.

"Willow Sharpe, fairy painter, feistiest woman I've ever met." He sobered a little as his bright eyes lingered in that sweet spot where they focused on her own. "I confess, I have *a thing* for you."

Her face broke into a smile while her heart fluttered inside her chest. Trying to keep from launching herself at him, she traced the lines on his palm with her finger. "What are we going to do about this, then?"

Clint swallowed as he watched her finger move against his hand. "Does something have to be done about it?"

"I think so. I don't spend nearly enough time with you for my liking. It's growing very difficult for me not to touch you, as you can see at present. And I wouldn't be opposed to having you kiss me . . . thoroughly and often."

He nodded his head as he appeared to thoughtfully process her statements. "Seems reasonable. Is now a good time for you?"

Willow closed her eyes with a smile as she leaned into Clint's hand against her cheek. "Now is actually perfect."

Chapter Eight

Finally, at long last, Arabelle felt that it might be possible to find love after all. #willowfairies

The cabin was going to cost her a fortune if she continued to rent it through the summer months, but Willow couldn't make herself care. She'd paid her fee for the month of July to Mr. O'Neill that morning, even though it was only halfway through June. She'd rent the place for five years if she had to, if it meant continuing to live the near-perfect existence she was living.

Arabelle had found her niche here in Tennessee. Her social media followers were loving her relationship with Flint, most everyone declaring him dreamy or rugged or a real man's man (for a fairy, of course). And Willow was happy in her own skin for the first time in . . .

Well, ever.

It was liberating to have someone like her for who she was. Her parents had tried to make her into something she wasn't. The company who published her books tried to get her to follow certain storylines. Even Sammie occasionally told Willow how to act when they went to parties together.

But Clint was unique. On paper, the two of them were as far apart as night and day, but he embraced their differences and liked her anyway. She'd never felt more free to create, or even to breathe in the space she was occupying. And in the month following their date to Dollywood, she'd never felt more loved.

The mere thought made her smile all over again as she adjusted the magnifying glass and studied the miniscule mug Arabelle would be drinking from. It needed just a hint of gold paint on the upper rim. Moving the magnifying glass to her left, she grabbed her finest brush and reached for the paint at the same time her phone began trilling with the sounds of a harp being strummed. Replacing the brush, she grabbed the phone instead, hitting the speaker button before glancing through the glass on her forehead once more.

"Hi Sammie."

"Willow. You haven't returned my calls, what could you possibly be doing out there in the middle of nowhere?"

"Living," she breathed almost dreamily with a smile as she picked up the paint brush once more.

"Living. Becoming a hermit is more like it. Things are going really well here, and I've met so many people. People who want to meet you, fairy girl. I've been spreading the word about you like crazy."

Peering through the glass at the enlarged details of the mug, Willow spread a hint of gold near the handle. "That's sweet of you. Thanks."

"When are you coming to see me?" Sammie asked. "I can't wait to show you around."

Barely touching the tip of the brush in the gold paint again, Willow used her other hand to scratch her cheek. "Why don't you come and see me? I'd love to show you some of the sites, and take you to Dollywood."

Sammie laughed on the other end of the line. "Oh Willow, I'm glad to see you haven't lost your sense of humor. There's a house I have my eye on, and it will be just perfect for us. Let me know what day works for you and I'll schedule a tour so we can look at it together. Now that you've got this earthy, woodsy phase out of your system, we can do L.A. like we were meant to."

The tiny splash of gold gleamed at the edge of the mug like perfection. Willow tilted it back and forth to make sure nothing needed adjusting before setting the paint brush down. "Sammie, you were the best roommate. The best. But I don't want to move to L.A. I like it here. In fact, I—"

"Please don't tell me this has something to do with your lawn man."

Taking a deep breath, Willow pushed away from the table. "Clint isn't just some random person. He's . . . my person."

"I'm your person. He can't be your person."

"I know. I know. But something's happening here, Sammie. It's like heaven leaned down and kissed the earth, like God filters through everywhere and into everything. And I think maybe I belong here just like Clint. He's part of this place, and I love it."

"You love it, or you love him?"

Willow leaned against the wall, peeking through the curtains to that one slightly taller section of grass. Every week she watched as he mowed around it so carefully, growing ever more grateful for the simple pleasure of knowing him.

"I'm in love with him. I admit it."

Sammie sighed on her end of the phone, like the words were disappointing somehow. "Honey, I'm sure you're lonely there and the guy is paying attention to you so it makes you feel good. But please don't buy into that, okay? A little stop over, that's all your getaway was supposed to amount to."

"Paying attention to me," Willow repeated, crossing her arms over her chest as she stared at her makeshift workspace, filled with paint, fairy paraphernalia, and paper. "It's not like that, honestly. Clint looks at me like I'm the most amazing person he's ever met. He treats me like I'm the most fascinating creature on the planet."

"He mows lawns. He can't have that many prospects, Willow."

"When did you become such a cynic? I didn't hold much stock in romance when I came here, you know. I wanted to give Arabelle a love interest, and it was almost impossible because I didn't believe it existed. But I've seen it with my own eyes. I've felt sheer joy from simply being in another person's presence. That's not something that we can produce in one another simply by pretending to like each other's company. Clint has made me a better version of myself, and I can't go back to living at half-brightness. Not when I've seen the light up close."

"You sound just like the dreadful romantic comedy I'm working on right now."

"I'm not trying to be funny."

"I know. You're *in love* and it makes you do nutty things. I get it. Why couldn't you fall in love with someone here? We have lawn maintenance people. The one at my place doesn't speak English, but he seems nice enough."

"Sammie—"

"I'm kidding, mostly. And trying to be happy for you." She sighed, and Willow picked the little Arabelle figure up from her place on the table while she waited for her friend to continue. "Let me know if you change your mind."

"I will, and best of luck on your romantic comedy."

Sammie said her goodbyes, and Willow whistled while she gathered her supplies and prepared to take them outside. She didn't take pictures of the fairies often—only on special occasions. But lately life felt like a special occasion. And today was Clint's birthday. She'd snap her pictures of the fairies, pick up the cake, and then they'd have a wonderful evening.

Carefully setting Arabelle next to the mushroom hut, she placed the mug next to her on the ground. The little redheaded beauty with the butterfly wings would be telling Flint she loved him soon. It was time. Past time, really. Flint had shown himself to be more than worthy.

Pulling her phone out, Willow checked the time. Eleven-thirty. She told Ruth she'd pick up the cake at eleven. Time had gotten away from her again. With a long look at the mushroom huts, she pondered her options. It was unusual that Clint wasn't around yet to mow the lawn. She could pop over to the café before taking the photos, though. He knew the drill with the grass and the fairies.

Practically skipping to the house, she grabbed her keys and checked her appearance in the mirror. The magnifying glass contraption had left some red marks around the side of her forehead, but otherwise she looked fairly normal. She smiled at her reflection, blowing herself a kiss. Stupid, she knew, but she felt giddily ridiculous. It was going to be an unforgettable day.

Willow arrived at the café right before noon, and Ruth ushered her to a table at the corner. She wanted to talk about Clint's birthday, she said, as soon as she got a break. So Willow ordered a sandwich. And a milkshake. And a piece of lemon pie. And it wasn't until she was so full she felt like she wouldn't be able to walk that Ruth was finally able to slide onto the chair across from her.

Of course she wanted to chat about the surprise pop-up birthday party they were having for Clint. Willow knew without a doubt that Clint would be mortified, but she couldn't seem to talk the younger woman out of doing something for her daughter's favorite uncle. And if she knew Clint, which she thought she did by now, he'd be kind of calmly present, smiling every once in a while, but secretly wishing he could be anywhere else. In the most gracious of ways, naturally, because he was a gentleman. Without a doubt, though, he'd be pining for an escape.

Willow hoped to be the escape by showing him the perfect place she'd found while hiking the woods around her cabin. The place where she'd set up the chairs so they could just sit in silence and watch the stars that evening. She was suffering intense anticipation herself, although she tried to hide it.

Ruth didn't seem to notice, going on and on about anything and everything. Had Willow talked to Clint yet that day, she wanted to know. Which of course she hadn't. Hadn't called him the day before either, because he was busy re-roofing someone's house. So it had been nearly forty-eight hours since she'd seen him, heightening the anticipation that much more.

By the time Willow finally headed back to the cabin, cake in hand, it was nearing two in the afternoon. The sun would be directly overhead, which might make her picture more difficult to take, but she'd manage. Clint would likely have come to mow her lawn and gone already, but she tried not to be disappointed. After all, it wasn't like she wouldn't see him soon.

As she pulled down the final stretch of the road leading to her cabin, a shiny white truck brushed past her. Odd, since hers was the last cabin on the road, but maybe it was some tourist checking the place out. Pulling up in front of her temporary home, she carefully extracted the cake from the passenger seat and turned to glance at the place. It looked nice and clean, like always. Freshly mown.

So he'd been here, then. The little twinge of disappointment snaked up her spine, even though she knew it was silly. She could go a few hours without seeing the man, couldn't she?

But something looked different. A little too perfect, really. Like a picture on a postcard instead of the yard she'd been staring at every day through the window, keeping an eye on her . . .

The cake box slid from her fingers, landing on its side by her feet, as she placed both her hands over her mouth.

"No, no, no."

Her first step was impeded by the cake box, causing her to trip enough to place one hand on the grass in front of her, but it didn't slow her momentum. Reeling forward, she fell all the way into the grass, taking big, gulping breaths as she crawled on her hands and knees toward that familiar spot where she spent so much time. Not surrounded by taller grass. Cut short, just like everything else.

She stopped at the edge of the little bare spot, knees aching from her fall and fresh grass stains on her palms. But it didn't matter. Arabelle lay on her side about a foot away, one of her wings wrenched from her body. The mug she'd spent her time on that morning was pressed into the dirt, the fresh paint marred and scratched. And the little mushroom huts that had taken her weeks to perfect, both decimated.

Cradling Arabelle in her hand, she dropped her head to her knees and let the tears come freely.

Chapter Nine

Arabelle wished no present contact with her neighbors. Assistance would prove impossible, and their sympathy unbearable. #willowfairies

"Clint?"

His head pounded, but he tried to clear the fog enough to see where that voice was coming from. With a blink, he squinted his eyes against the light overhead. He hadn't turned a light on. He'd probably remember that.

"Uncle Clint? Mom, he's in bed."

"Clint? For heaven's sake, what's going on? I've tried and tried to call you, and you wouldn't answer. Em, step back honey. Uncle Clint looks like he's going to be sick."

"I'm fine." He waved them away with one very heavy, nearly impossible to lift hand. "Just need to get up and moving."

Cool flesh pressed against his temple. "He's burning up. Have you taken your temperature, Clint? Taken anything for your fever?"

"Wha— No, I don't get sick. Just a headache." He attempted to sit up, but couldn't seem to make himself move.

"I've no doubt you have a headache, but you're feverish too. See what he has in the bathroom, Em."

The blankets were strangling him. Who tucked them in? He never tucked them in. Jerking against them once more, he gave up and plopped back against the pillow.

"You hot under those blankets?" Ruth lifted the blankets away from him as though they were nothing.

"Mom, Uncle Clint doesn't have anything in his bathroom except beard stuff and armpit perfume."

That hand touched his forehead again, and the cool feel of it against his hot skin actually felt good. Maybe he *was* sick.

"Okay, don't move. Em and I will go straight to the drug store and pick something up for you, so you just relax. Or sleep, or whatever makes you comfortable. We'll just be a few minutes."

He didn't even answer. It would have taken too much effort. Instead, he squeezed his eyes closed and tried to forget everything.

With a start, Clint sat up in bed, sweat prickling against his forehead. The sun was already streaming in past the curtains, and he had a lot of work to do. The mere thought instantly irritated him. He wasn't prone to oversleeping.

Throwing back the covers from his bed, he spun his legs around and attempted to stand, having to prop his hand against the wall for balance. Man, he was weak. Sleeping through breakfast wasn't a great idea either, apparently.

His gaze drifted across the glass of water and the bottle of pills on the nightstand. Ruth. She'd been in his bedroom, and Emily too. Forced him to take pills when she said he had a fever. Flickers of memory started filling in all the blank spots. Nearly falling off the roof when he got dizzy. Jenkins telling him to get home before he passed out. Actually passing out. Thank God it only lasted one night.

So it was Wednesday. His birthday. He grabbed the phone on his way to the bathroom, checking the time. Ten-thirty. Not as bad as he thought it might be. So he'd be running late, but wouldn't actually miss any jobs.

He'd feel better once he had a shower, he told himself. Heated it so hot that it nearly scalded him, then turned it to ice cold to force life into his bones. Brushed his teeth while he stared into his lifeless eyes in the mirror. His body needed fuel. Fluids. Wrapping the towel around his waist, he crossed into the kitchen, pouring himself a cold glass of water.

Sinking onto the couch, he breathed a sigh of frustration as he searched his phone for O'Neill's number. He couldn't remember the last time he'd been sick. Couldn't stand being weak and not being able to do what needed to be done. Closing his eyes, he leaned his head against the couch and rubbed one hand through his wet hair as he waited for O'Neill to pick up.

"Yeah," came the abrupt greeting.

"Hey, I'm running a little late today. Must have come down with some kind of bug, but I'm up and around. Just wanted to tell you in case anyone asked why I hadn't come by yet. I'm on my way out."

"Oh, Clint. Hang on." He yelled some orders to someone in the background before continuing. "Listen, you should just take it easy. Jenkins called and told me you were sick, that you'd gone home. I had Atkins fill in for you on the lawns."

"Well, just call him and tell him I'm on it."

"I'm sure he got through them all yesterday. Just take it easy today, buddy. No worries."

O'Neill dropped his end of the call, and Clint furrowed his brow as he glanced past the window again, studying a sun-splashed spot on the wall. Why would he do them yesterday, unless . . .

He pulled his phone back into his line of vision, pressing the button to activate the screen. Thursday. No, it couldn't be Thursday. Thursday meant he slept through an entire day. It meant he missed the surprise birthday thing

Ruth and Emily were plotting. It meant he'd missed his date with Willow.

Willow. Why hadn't she called or come by or texted or . . . anything? No missed messages from her on the phone at all.

This time, the sick feeling churning in his gut had nothing to do with a virus.

As soon as he got some food in his stomach and felt human again, Clint drove to Willow's cabin. Her car was in the driveway, which only gave him a fleeting sense of relief. Closing his truck's door, he shoved the keys in his pocket, scanning the area for anything out of place. The only thing he noticed was the dented white box plopped haphazardly in the yard.

His steps seemed like they were happening in slow motion as he moved in the direction of the box. It looked like an ordinary bakery box, if it weren't for the ants crawling out of the side and over the white cardboard. Flipping it open with the toe of his boot, he studied the cake inside, which was broken down the center and smashed against the side of the box. The ants were making quick work of their task, swarming the sticky sweet icing. It was easy to see them disappearing into the short grass.

Short grass. His eyes lifted to scan the yard, and immediately he settled on the section that he knew to avoid. The section where Willow painstakingly set up the little fairy huts. Every ounce of his breath left his body as he took the few steps to the designated spot in the yard, dropping to his knees. Carnage. Fairy carnage. The huts were missing their tops, shattered into dozens of pieces scattered across the dirt. The mailbox had been crushed, probably beneath a lawnmower tire. No signs of anything else she might have used to decorate the space.

Closing his eyes, he let what must have been her acute disappointment wash over him. The pain she must have felt at having her work destroyed like that. But she didn't even call to let him comfort her. He should have been there for her, and he would have been. Had she stopped by the house and thought he was ignoring her?

God, help me, he breathed as he rose to his feet. His steps were still a little shaky, but he tried to remain steady as he crossed to the front door, climbing the stairs. She was notorious for peeking out the blinds, which usually put a smile across his face when he was mowing the lawn, but there were no signs of life. Knocking on the door, he waited with his fist resting against the door frame. She didn't immediately answer, so he banged on the door again.

Surely she wouldn't have left. Especially not if her car was still sitting there in the driveway. Rubbing a hand against his forehead, he pulled his phone out of his pocket and dialed the number of the café. Lunch rush. Definitely not the best time to call.

"Um, yeah, can I speak to Ruth please? It's an emergency."

"She's got a slew of tables. Who's calling?"

"It's Clint. Please, it'll just take a second."

The woman who answered the phone yelled Ruth's name, and Clint tried to slow his breathing as he paced across the porch.

"Clint, everything okay? Do you need me to take you to the hospital?"

"What? No, I'm feeling much better." He lifted a hand to try to peek into the cabin, but couldn't see anything past the blinds. "Have you talked to Willow at all today?"

"No. I tried to call her last night, but she didn't answer. I figured maybe she'd been by to check on you or something."

He covered his mouth with his fist, staring out at the cake box in the yard again. "If you hear from her, let me know. I'm sure everything's fine. Sorry to bother you."

With one deft move, he canceled the call and placed the phone in his pocket. His breath hitched in his chest, the same way it had the day he saw her on the ground in front of his mower. Willow felt things with all her heart. The slightest little thoughtful gesture could make her day. How low would something like this take her?

Turning back to the door, he turned the knob, but it didn't budge. Bracing himself, he rammed his side into the door. A little splinter started near the doorknob, and he shoved his body against it again, hearing the cracking sound as it gave beneath his weight. He shoved his fingers into the gap and worked at the latch, fumbling to get it open. As soon as he released it and pushed the door open, he felt a wave of embarrassment. Two months he'd spent trying not to act like a hillbilly brute in her presence, and the instant the opportunity arose he did just that.

Shaking his head, he looked around the living room. A little figure of Arabelle rested on the table near the door, one of her wings missing and her leg broken off. The area around her was a mess of paint and fabrics and sketches, the odd magnifying glass Willow used sitting awkwardly atop them.

"Willow," he said, voice relatively quiet in comparison to the way he busted into the place. When she didn't reply, he stepped further into the house, glancing around as he did so. Her phone sat on the kitchen counter, blinking enough to inform him that she had messages. He pushed the button and saw that it was only at around ten percent and hanging on by a thread.

"Willow," he repeated, stepping tentatively into the hallway. Fear gripped his chest as he wondered what he would find, then told himself to stop worrying. *God,* he thought again, unable to even finish a prayer. *Please.*

He'd never been inside her bedroom before, and as he stepped into the space, he couldn't help but notice that the bed was made. The space was tidy, no clothes littering the floor. Nothing out of place. It made him feel better and worse at the same time.

The slightest groan sent the hair on the back of his neck straight on edge. Turning, he let his gaze drift to the bathroom door. It was barely open, just enough to see that the light was on.

"Willow? Willow, I'm coming in."

She didn't answer, so he pushed the door open, nearly gasping at the sight of her form on the bathroom floor. Her face was pressed against her arm, which was propped under her head, the rest of her body curled up in a fetal position.

"Hey," he whispered, brushing her hair away from her face. "I'm here." She didn't move, but the feel of her hot skin on his fingers motivated him enough to act. Sliding one arm beneath her neck and the other under her knees, he lifted her from the floor, leaning back just enough that her head rolled against his chest. He could feel the warmth emanating from her even through his T-shirt.

She couldn't have weighed much more than a hundred pounds, but as he placed her head against her pillow atop her comforter, he braced himself against the side of the bed. His strength obviously still hadn't fully returned. He'd managed pretty well, though, since he was able to break into the place. He started to sit next to her on the bed, but the action shifted her body in his direction, so instead he knelt on the floor.

"Willow, can you wake up?" He pressed the back of his hand against her cheek, feeling utterly incompetent. "Hey, I just need to know you're okay."

Her eyelashes fluttered, and the brief glimpse of her eyes told him they were glassy. "I'm dreaming," she whispered, barely audible even though he was right by her side.

"No, you're sick, but I'm glad to hear your voice. It's Clint. What can I do for you?"

She rolled her head from one side to the other but didn't open her eyes. "Clint can't be here. I want to look nice."

"You're always beautiful to me." He pushed all the hair away from her forehead, grimacing a little at how warm she felt to the touch.

A slight smile pulled up one corner of her pale lips. "That sounds like something Clint would say. Isn't he wonderful?"

He couldn't decide whether to be concerned at how delirious she seemed or smile at the compliment. "How are you feeling? I want to help you."

A tremor shook her entire body. "Cold."

Lifting her slightly, he pulled back the comforter. She was wearing those barely too-short running pants that people wore - what did they call those again? Not that it mattered. He wasn't about to change her clothes, but he could find those giant wooly socks she was always wearing. Pulling out the top dresser drawer, he closed it almost immediately when he realized it contained her undergarments. Instead he went for the second drawer, finding almost a whole compartment full of those giant socks. Jerking out a pair, he unfolded them and knelt beside her once more, taking her icy little foot in his hand.

"I'm going to try to get you warmed up," he explained as he gently slid the sock over her foot and up her calf muscle. "If you have what I had, hopefully it won't last much longer." The second sock was on her foot, but he let his hand linger on her shin. Would the same virus hit her harder, since she was so much smaller than him? That probably wasn't how such things worked, but he really didn't have experience with caring for sick patients.

He grabbed the comforter and pulled it over her legs, dragging it all the way up to her chin. Once he got it there, he rubbed his hands against her shoulders, trying to be a little gentler when a tiny groan escaped her lips once more. Leaning down, he kissed her forehead, once again being reminded of the fever raging in her body.

"Got to get the fever down," he whispered, rising to his feet and heading back to the bathroom. The rug next to the tub was wrinkled and shifted to the side where she'd been centered on it, and he moved it out of the way, straightening it before he glanced through the bathroom drawers, trying not to be nosy. She had a thermometer right on the top, one of those old-fashioned numbers that had the mercury in the middle. Trying to think fast, he grabbed it and then looked for something to treat the fever. He found a couple boxes of pills that might be helpful, so he studied the ingredient lists and their suggested use before he decided on a winner.

Before going back to her side, he located a plastic bag in the kitchen and filled it with ice, wrapping the makeshift ice pack with a dish towel. By the time he had a glass of water, his hands were more than full. Jostling everything, he stepped back into her room, where he watched the rise and fall of her chest. He placed all of his supplies on the table beside the bed and laid one hand on her cheek.

"Willow, can I take your temperature?" Her lips were slightly parted, but he didn't want to try to do anything without her consent. "Willow, hey, can you hear me? I'd like to take your temperature."

She roused herself just enough to flutter those eyelashes again and drop her mouth open a little more. It made his heart ache the way she instantly did what he asked, but he ignored the feelings rising inside as he placed the thermometer beneath her tongue and tipped her chin up to get her to close her mouth. He vaguely remembered his mom taking his temperature when he was a kid, so he held the thermometer in place while he moved the ice pack against her head. She shoved the thermometer aside with her tongue, but he pushed it right back and tapped her on the nose.

"Hold still now, or it won't be accurate."

It seemed like an eternity while he waited for her temperature to register, but he finally pulled the thermometer back and held it aloft as he tried to read it. And tried, and tried, and tried, rolling it around in his fingers. One tiny glimpse of the red line indicated that her temperature was close to one-hundred-and-four. If he read it correctly, of which he wasn't convinced.

Sliding his hand behind her neck, he tipped her head up, keeping his arm behind her head for insurance purposes. "Come on now, you need to drink some water. Do you think you can swallow a pill?"

Those wide violet eyes slowly opened, gazing directly at his own only inches away. "Are you really here?"

"Of course I am. Did you think I wouldn't come?"

"I dropped your cake."

"You think I care about that?" he whispered, keeping his eyes focused on hers. "I care about you, which means I want you to take these pills. Will you do that for me?"

"For you I'd do anything."

God, I love this woman, he thought as he tried not to smile. *More than I thought possible.*

Setting the ice pack aside so he could grab the pills instead, he gently placed one against her lips. "Let's start with the pills and then talk about that," he teased quietly. She took a drink from the glass, so he gave her the second pill. When she was done, he asked her to drink more of the water, which she took while she looked up at him with that same awestruck expression that usually filtered onto her face at some point during any conversation.

"Get some rest," he whispered, placing the glass on the table. He moved the ice pack back to her forehead, and she rewarded him with the makings of a smile, allowing her eyes to drift closed.

Chapter Ten

Arabelle must know, of course, that everything Flint did . . . It was for her alone. #willowfairies

Clint checked the latch on the door, making sure it was secure. He didn't feel guilty for barging through it to help Willow, but he'd wanted to fix it as soon as he knew she was okay. Helping her feel better was one thing, but keeping her safe inside her cabin was just as important. At least he could rest a little easier knowing that the door was off his to-do list.

Wiping his hands against his jeans, he went to the back of the cabin, poking his head into her bedroom. Eight hours he'd been inside the space with her, beside the little stint of time picking up the new door. She'd been sleeping most of that time, only waking up when he asked her to take more medicine. It made him feel helpless, the waiting.

He touched her forehead with the back of his hand. Still too warm, although the medicine was doing its job. Leaving the premises definitely wasn't an option. She didn't stir, so he went back out to the living room, looking around to try to decide how to fill his time.

The house was clean, other than her work space, which he wasn't about to tidy up without her permission. Even looking at the broken fairy figure made him uncomfortable. Would she be able to replace the wing easily? And the leg? Or would she have to switch to sketches and paintings instead?

Letting out a sigh, he ran his hand against the back of his neck, trying to work out the tension that had gathered there. If her little huts had been full-size dwellings for human beings, he could have done something to help her. But fairy-sized mushrooms weren't really his specialty.

He slowly released his neck, opening the front door and staring at the bare spot in the yard. It wouldn't hurt to check everything out once more. See if it was salvageable. His boots seemed loud against the porch, set against the backdrop of only insect noises. Swinging his hand, he waved a mosquito away as he sank to his knees once more in the grass. The colorfully-painted tops of the mushroom huts were definitely not going to be reparable. The bottoms were mostly intact, though. And the mailbox, although the metal was smashed, wasn't torn or damaged otherwise.

Leaning down, he took one of the mushrooms between his fingers, lifting it enough to place it on his palm. The structure was probably about the size of Willow's hand, although smaller than his. The woman was so creative, it made his mind spin. The way she dreamt something up from nothing. He certainly didn't have that ability. The closest he could come was fixing something that needed repairs, like shingles on a roof.

"Shingles on a roof," he whispered, staring down at Arabelle's damaged home. The circular frame that gave it that signature look. The little wooden door at the front, its rounded top featuring a tiny window. The little curtains hanging at the larger side window, navy blue with pink polka dots.

It didn't need to be created all over again. It needed repairs.

Repairs were totally up his alley.

Willow groaned as she shifted her body to the left, tugging the comforter away. The thermostat must have malfunctioned and turned on the heat instead of the air conditioner. Flinging the back of her hand up to her forehead, she cringed when she realized she was perspiring. But she didn't feel half-dead like she had before. And the sweating meant the fever broke, right?

Sitting up in bed, she swayed as she attempted to adjust her eyes to the light in the room. Natural light from the window, letting her know it was daylight. Blinking a couple times to try to clear the fog from her eyes, she pushed her hand up into her hair and glanced at the doorway, considering whether she should get up and head to the bathroom.

Her gaze instead landed on the man in the corner, his legs stretched long against the floor, back against the wall, head tilted slightly up like he was trying to sleep.

"Clint?"

His eyes popped open, and he awkwardly attempted to rise from the floor. It was obvious to her that his stint sitting there had been uncomfortable, simply by the fact that his movement was impaired.

"Hey," he said gently, sitting himself at the foot of the bed. "Feeling better?"

"I think so, yes." She drew the comforter back up to her chin, holding it between her fists. "You stayed with me?"

Without bothering to answer that question, he rose and stood by the door, glancing into the hallway. "There's fruit in the kitchen, and some canned soup. Oh, and bread for toast. Do you want me to fix you anything?"

She couldn't help but smile, because she knew she didn't have any canned soup. He must have gone shopping. "I'm sure I can manage. How did you get in here? Did I leave the door unlocked?"

"Hmm. . .yeah. Definitely make sure you lock the door." His hand went to the back of his neck, that telltale sign that he was nervous. "You sure you don't need anything? If not, I should probably—"

"Thank you. I don't even know what to say."

He pressed his lips together, taking a step back into the hall. "I'll call you later, okay?"

She nodded, and he gave a quick wave as he disappeared from her line of vision. The sound of his boots on the hardwood floor gave way to the door clicking closed, and she knew he was gone. Allowing a huge grin to spread across her face, she dropped her chin to her fists, still holding her comforter in place. Sweaty and clammy and pale as she was, she'd never felt more desired in her life. A good man . . . No, a *very* good man, cared about her enough to completely disrupt his life and sleep on her floor, waiting for her to feel better. She could almost sob at the sheer joy of it, except she felt a little too dehydrated for tears.

Rising from the bed, she carefully made her way to the bathroom, where she tried not to glance in the mirror. One glimpse of her face and all her carefully crafted euphoria would no doubt be thrown to the wind. Instead, she turned on the shower and prepared to wash all traces of her illness away, if possible.

Willow emerged from her bedroom, dragging a comb through her wet hair. She felt better already, clean and with her teeth brushed, wearing clothes that smelled like fabric softener. The kitchen came into her line of vision, bananas and a can of soup sitting on the counter. He'd even set out the little soup pot she had in the cabinet. Thoughtful. Yet another thing she liked about Clint.

Grabbing a banana, she pulled back the peel and hesitantly took a bite before letting the events of the past few days return to her mind. Clint's cake that she dropped in the yard. Completely missing his birthday. And yet there he was, taking care of her. The tears sprang to her eyes, and she brushed one away with the back of her hand while she pulled the can opener from the drawer. She wasn't even sure she was hungry, but if he could bring her soup, she could make herself give it a try.

Snapping the can opener onto the top of the can, she took a good look at the ingredient list. He hadn't purchased one of the cheap cans of soup. This one claimed to be all-natural, filled with only high-quality, good-for-her foods. She nearly giggled, imagining him standing in the grocery store staring at the rows of soup and trying to pick the right one.

She heated up a bowl of the soup in the microwave, then raised her spoon and blew on it for a few seconds before lifting it to her lips. It did taste good, surprisingly. Normally when she'd been sick it took her a few days before her appetite revved up again, but springing back would be a good thing. Especially since she had so much work to do.

Closing her eyes, she allowed the mess she'd found in her yard to play like a newsreel in her brain. She'd taken a picture of the mushroom huts and put something cryptic about a disaster on her social media sites. So stupid and impulsive. Being sick meant she hadn't been checking on the posts, either, so there was no telling what kind of chaos she'd created by that split-second decision.

At least she hadn't taken a picture of poor Arabelle. She could envision a bunch of little girls Emily's age logging onto their mom or dad's phones, pulling up the account and finding a damaged fairy. The destroyed houses were bad enough.

Quickly pulling her hair over her shoulder, she absently braided it as she stepped across to the living room. She could begin damage control, at the very least. Her phone was plugged in at the side of the table, which had to have been Clint's handiwork. She didn't remember charging it and it probably would have died while she was sick. Picking it up, she looked at the scary number of notifications that had amassed in her absence.

"We have a lot of work to do, Arabelle," she whispered, her eyes shifting over to glance at the fairy where she rested on the table. Remaking her wing would take a little time, as would trying to recreate her leg. Letting out a sigh, she scanned the supplies scattered over her table until she spotted the little mailbox on the corner, a little worse for wear but no longer smashed as it had been. The metal looked a little crinkled, but functional. And the little slip of paper folded inside almost called her name.

"Arabelle, what have you been doing while I was asleep?" she asked, smiling at the little fairy while she pulled the paper out of the mailbox with her thumb and forefinger. The fairy remained impassive, guarding her secrets. Willow unfolded the slip of paper, holding the tiny little parchment in the palm of her hand.

Arabelle,

I'm not sure how to fix legs or wings, but I repaired your roof. I hope it makes you feel better.

Flint

Willow's eyes shot wide open as her fingers trembled. She raised her head until she was looking at the ceiling, which hadn't changed in appearance. The cabin didn't need any roof repairs, as far as she knew. Which could only mean . . .

Pulling the door open, she gazed out at the grass, almost afraid to move. Those huts were beyond repair. She saw them with her own eyes, before she took pathetic photos of them and cried in her bathroom until she made herself sick. Or maybe cried until she actually was sick, since the fever wasn't imaginary. Either way, they had been destroyed. Absolutely destroyed.

She stepped onto the porch, then glanced down at her feet in the wool socks. Plopping herself on the steps, she pulled off the socks one at a time, stretching her toes before she placed them in the warm grass. She'd grown accustomed to the sensation since that first day she'd gone shoeless, often walking around her yard with her feet bare. As she walked in the direction of that sparse place in the grass, she felt each step as though it was heavy with purpose.

The grass cleared and her little fairy dwelling came into view, now amounting to an ordinary dirty spot in the midst of green. But she saw them. The two tiny mushroom huts, their structure still intact, with new roofs. Not the traditional mushroom roofs that she had used before, but sloped roofs covered in shingles. Tiny, scalloped shingles made from tree bark, placed one atop the other, like a perfectly formed little cottage in the woods.

Willow tried to imagine Clint's large hands affixing each of those tiny shingles, and the thought made her press both her hands to her chest as she choked on a sob. The repairs were perfection. Absolute perfection. She couldn't even dream up anything Flint would manage that would be so . . . Flint-like. Lowering herself to sit beside them, she reached out a hand and ran the tips of her fingers over the bark, admiring the craftsmanship. The shingles perfectly represented everything she had found while living in the cabin. Natural beauty that spoke of God's handiwork, made even easier to appreciate because of Clint.

She would take pictures of this, of course. Rewrite the note from Flint on a tinier parchment. Let all the people who followed her fairies know what simple, sweet, and pure love looked like in action. And then she'd find Clint, throw her arms around him, and never let go.

Chapter Eleven

She had grown to realize that he was exactly the one who would most suit her. Though they were clearly unalike, he perfectly met all of her wishes. #willowfairies

A Few Months Later…

The front door opened before Clint heard the sound of the bus outside the house, so he jerked his gaze up to see that it was Ruth, not Emily, who stood in his living room. She dropped her purse on the coffee table and plopped down beside him on the couch, leaning against the cushions with a sigh.

"Rough day?" he asked, eyeing her with curiosity.

"Pretty dead, actually, which is why my shift ended a little earlier than normal. I can't even remember the last time I was out of the café before the bus showed up."

"Yeah."

He couldn't seem to make himself say anything else, and she sat up and studied him, letting her eyes rove from his face to his hands.

"Whatcha doing?" she wondered, mischievous smile on her face.

"Nothing."

"Liar. What's in your hand?" She grabbed his fingers, and he reluctantly loosened his fist enough that she managed to pry his hand open. Once his palm was visible, she reached inside and pulled out the ring he'd been holding.

Her eyes widened as she held it between her fingers, glancing over at him.

"I know I've only known her five months, but it's not like I need time to make up my mind. And I know that cabin has to be costing her a fortune."

Ruth smiled and held the miniscule ring up to the light. The diamond wasn't very significant, but the ring was small enough that it actually made it look a little bigger.

"Clint, if you're asking because you're afraid she'll leave, trust me – she won't go anyplace where you're not."

He shook his head as he took the ring back from her hand. "It's not that. I'm thirty-three years old, and I know what I want. Waiting doesn't make much sense."

Ruth's eyes filled with tears as she placed her hand on his arm. "I'm sure she won't be able to contain her happiness." Averting her gaze, she pressed her lips together.

"What? You want to say something."

"It's just . . . this doesn't have anything to do with that fairy, does it?"

He couldn't keep the frustrated smile from appearing on his face as he wrapped one hand around the back of his neck. "I suppose I wouldn't mind beating that little dude to the punch for a change."

Ruth rose to her feet and moved to the window, sweeping the curtains aside to watch for the bus. Clint pushed away from the couch, shoving the ring into his pocket as he stood to join her. "Listen, Ruth—"

"Don't mind me," she said, brushing a tear away from her cheek. "I'm super happy for you, really. I couldn't be happier. It's just hard not to wonder if I'm ever going to break out of the cycle, you know? Working a job that barely keeps us afloat, shuttling Emily to stay with my mom during the summer while I'm at the café. Begging you to be here for her when she gets off the bus."

"I'd do anything for Emily, you know that."

Ruth sighed as she let her hand drop from the curtain. "I know you would, but I wish . . ." She self-consciously tugged at the bottom of her uniform shirt as she attempted to straighten her clothing.

"Please, say whatever you want to say."

"I wish someone was willing to do anything for me, the way you are for Willow. It feels like I'm destined to be alone forever."

He dropped his arm around her shoulders in what he hoped was a brotherly gesture. "Good things take time, you know. And you're only twenty-four."

"I'll be twenty-five next week."

"Oh, that changes everything. You're definitely an old maid."

"Shush," she ordered him as the bus pulled up in front of the house. "Emily doesn't need to know about any of this. Except you having the ring. That's news that needs to be shared with everyone within a fifty-mile radius."

He narrowed his eyes at her as she stepped away from his arm. "Don't you go breathing a word about that until I ask her."

"Lips sealed," she assured him as Emily burst into the room, her backpack dropping immediately to the floor. His niece said nothing as she moved toward the kitchen looking for snacks, not even acknowledging her mom's presence. "Is that normal post-bus behavior?"

Shrugging, he looked into the kitchen, where Em was going straight for the chips. "Yep, pretty much."

"What did your fairies do today?" Clint asked, pulling Willow a little closer to avoid a rock in the path. Despite his best efforts to make sure the storyline Willow had going with her fairies wasn't somehow directing his own efforts, he couldn't help being a little nervous that somehow she'd figure him out. Being worried that she might ask why they were visiting the same waterfall they saw on their first date. Or that she'd wonder why he might be acting a little strange.

Wrapping her arm tighter through his, she watched the trail ahead as they walked. "Oh, nothing special. Arabelle was helping some of the other fairies with girl drama. Flint is still on his mission to locate Karin's brother."

"Good. I mean, I'm sure he'll find him. Flint seems like a good guy."

"The best." She grinned up at him, then stepped away toward the edge of the trail to bend down and inspect something. He'd grown accustomed to that over the summer. The woman never missed anything with her eagle-eye vision, seeing even the tiniest details in the scenery around her. She never touched anything, though. Sometimes she pulled out her sketch book and tried to recreate what she saw, and other times she snapped a photo to look at when she got home.

"What did you see?" he asked, waiting for her to rejoin him on the trail.

"Some kind of hard-shelled little roly-poly bug."

He watched for another minute while she remained in that position, her hair loose and hanging down her back. Even Emily wouldn't get excited about a bug, unless maybe it was in her hair. In her hair . . .

She rose next to him, and he widened his eyes as though she might be able to read his mind. Instead, she gave him a goofy grin and continued walking down the trail, reaching for his hand. "Do you remember the first time we came here? I think I talked until I was blue in the face."

"Yep."

She laughed, and the sound reminded him of the water tripping over the rocks that they'd hear in just a few minutes. "Yep that you remember, or yep that I talked your ear off?"

"Both."

"That sounds about right." Her boot came untied, and she stopped at a large boulder on the side of the trail to sit and tie it again. Clint quickly settled behind her, grabbing her hair in his hands. To his surprise, she didn't ask what he was doing. Just tilted her head back with a sigh as he began sloppily braiding her hair. She seemed to like it so much, he wondered why he hadn't thought of that sooner. Somewhere about the middle, he slid the ring onto one of the three strands, then continued braiding until he reached the end.

"Hair tie," he muttered, holding his hand against her shoulder. Reaching into her pocket, she extracted one and placed it in his palm. Yet another thing he'd learned about her over the summer – she never left home without at least three hair ties in her pocket.

"I'm pretty sure that was about the sweetest thing you've ever done, braiding my hair like that. Now I feel all warm and fuzzy inside."

He smiled as he wrapped the hair tie around the end of her braid, but cleared his throat in an attempt to keep the smile from his voice. "Yeah, or I could have been ensuring all that hair would stop slapping me in the face," he mock-complained, stepping away from her.

She reached up to feel the back of her head as she started walking, and his breath hitched a little as he wondered whether she'd find the ring. The corner of her mouth tilted up, but it didn't go any farther.

"Not bad, really," she stated as she pulled her hand away from her hair, swinging it by her side instead. "I'm impressed at your braiding skill. Is it like building a rope or something?"

"Building a rope?" He scratched his cheek, making a sound like sandpaper against a two-by-four. "Can't say as I've ever made a rope with my bare hands before."

"You could though, I bet." She spun around on her heel, facing him on the trail as she walked backwards.

"What's the weirdest thing you've built with your hands? Come on, spill it."

"Probably that ladder thing you had me build out of toothpicks and hay for your fairies. Or the time we gathered those tiny pebbles to make that creek bed you—"

"Okay, I get it. Everything I do is weird. Think about how enlightened your life has become since I entered the picture." Willow's boot caught on a root, and she started to stumble backwards before Clint grabbed her elbow and steadied her. With a grin, she held onto his arm. "Guess I'm still falling for you, aren't I?"

Clint didn't let her go after the little trip, holding her steady while she made a silly joke and stood smiling up at him. She needed to get ahold of herself. Going back to the waterfall was making her feel nostalgic, like something big was about to happen.

She was going to see a waterfall. That was the extent of it. Sure, it was beautiful and breathtaking, but more than that it made her think about the slow and steady way her relationship with Clint had developed. Not like the waterfall itself, rushing over the rocks, but like the water above that point, slowly going along not realizing it would soon be racing over into the unknown.

She'd been just like that water the first time she visited. Walking along next to Clint, chattering away like it was any ordinary meeting. Attracted to him but not knowing the depth of his character, the extent of his loyalty, or the impact meeting him would have on her life. Now as she stood beside him, she didn't feel like they were so different. Oh, their personalities weren't similar, or their interests, and definitely not their manner of conversing, but it didn't matter. They fit together like wings on a fairy. Blades on a lawnmower. One didn't work right without the other.

Extracting herself from the gravitational pull he seemed to hold over her, she started walking again, moving toward the waterfall that was now in her line of sight. "This is making me think about the first time we came here," she tossed over her shoulder. "Call me sappy or sentimental or whatever, it's probably true anyway."

"Yeah," he said from his position behind her.

"Yeah, you're thinking about it too? Or yeah, I'm sappy and sentimental? You have to expound on your thoughts a little, mister, or I can't know what you're really expressing."

He chuckled as he continued to walk a step behind. "It was more of a vague agreement so I wouldn't have to say anything else."

"That figures. Do you remember the day we met? Of course you do. I'm fairly certain you almost passed out on my lawn." Willow focused on the sound of the water as she walked, then stopped to gaze at the waterfall just in time for an unruly toddler to sprint past, his mom yelling for him to slow down. The little guy raced up the trail only to have to stop behind another couple blocking the way.

"You gave me quite a start that day," Clint finally answered, placing his hand against her waist.

"Quite a start. I'd say it was a little more serious than that. Besides, I'm the one who should have been hyperventilating and having trouble breathing."

"Why is that?"

"You nearly mowed me over, didn't you? A terrifying prospect."

Shaking his head, he hooked his finger under her chin, forcing her eyes up so she looked at him next to her instead of the rushing water. "Actually, I think I'm the one who was mowed over that day. And you're right, it *was* terrifying. But now I know it's the best thing that ever happened to me."

She stepped to the edge of the trail to let another couple pass, wrapping her arms around his waist as she did so. "I do believe that might be the most beautiful thing you've ever said to me. Mostly because I know how much it cost you to verbalize it, given your fear of tiny, chatty women."

He pulled his face into a scowl and took her braid between his fingers, moving it to the front of her shoulder. "Actually, I love tiny women. One, anyway."

"And tiny women love you." She lifted to her tiptoes to kiss him quickly. "One, anyway. Will you take my picture in front of the waterfall?" Reaching into her back pocket, she extracted her phone and handed it to him, giving him her most effective pleading, wide-eyed gaze.

"Sure. But there's a line." Clint pointed in the direction of the waterfall itself, where a crowd of people had filled in, each waiting for their turn to step behind the waterfall and snap a photo.

"Oh, out here's fine. Just a picture with the waterfall behind me. I could sit on the rocks. Unless you want to be in the—"

"Nope."

"I know you so well." She carefully stepped to the boulders well in front of the waterfall, lowering herself onto one of the dry stones. "Okay, shoot." She smiled, pointing over her shoulder at the waterfall, and the corner of Clint's lip turned up as he snapped her photo. He liked to pretend he was immune to everything, kind of impassive and above the moment, but he wasn't. She'd broken past his exterior enough to know that.

Hopping down from the rock, she stepped over to him and took the phone in her hand, glancing at the photo. "Clint, that's horrible! You didn't even get the waterfall in the background. All you got was my shoulder."

Letting out a sigh, he peeked over the top of the phone, then shrugged. "Looks okay to me."

Turning, he started walking back in the direction from which they'd come, and her mouth fell open as she watched his retreating back. "What are you doing? Come on, you can't be serious. That's just about the worst picture I've ever seen." She jogged a few steps until she caught up with him. "Would you stop walking? I'll be nice. I won't make you talk and I'll even try to curtail my own words a bit, which you know is probably the most difficult thing in the world for me to do." Grabbing his arm, she held on with both hands. "Clint, just one picture."

He came to a halt, giving the briefest hint of a smile before he took her phone again. Looking at the photo, he tilted his head to the side, then twisted the phone the other way. With a quick nod, he handed it back to her.

"It looks good to me."

Placing a hand on her hip, she stared at the photo again, her eyes narrowing at the complete lack of water in the frame. Not a single drop. All he'd managed to capture was the side of her shoulder, that sort of sideways and lumpy braid he'd formed hanging there over her T-shirt, and the bottom of her chin.

"I don't—"

"You're not looking hard enough," he said, the corners of his eyes crinkling like they usually did when he laughed or smiled. "You can see a roly-poly bug sitting in the dirt. A tiny speck on an acorn yards away that looks like a fairy footprint. You notice things no one else would ever see. Trust me, you're not looking hard enough."

Without tearing her gaze away from Clint, Willow thought about those words. Did she really notice things others didn't? She seemed so much more aware here than she had before. Aware of the beauty that rested in the most ordinary things. Aware of the purpose that marked each moment of her day. Aware that all of it was orchestrated to work in perfect harmony, even when her involvement wasn't perfect or harmonious.

And aware most of all that she didn't have to change who she was to be loved.

Finally taking her eyes off Clint long enough to look down at the phone, she let her gaze swim over the surface, beginning at her chin and going across every centimeter of the image, onto the blue and pink in her hair twisted over one another, even to that little flash of light that strangely filtered into the frame. There was a little mark near the bottom of the photo, which on closer inspection looked like the pocket of her T-shirt. But . . .

Zooming in on the photo, she studied the flash of light, hoping to find its source. It seemed to be somehow drawn to her hair, maybe even emanating from her hair. That couldn't be possible. Tilting her chin down, she looked at the end of her braid resting on her shoulder, a gasp escaping her lips. Fumbling with the phone, she attempted to shove it into her pocket, then gave up and handed it to Clint. He took it wordlessly as she grabbed the bottom of her braid, sliding off the hair tie. With quick fingers, she unwrapped the design Clint had made only moments before, until finally the little jewel slid away from her hair and into her palm.

"You want to marry me," she whispered in awe as she stared at the ring resting in her hand. "That was the most romantic thing in the world. Did you learn to braid just so you could do that, or have you known how to do it all along? The thought of you practicing braiding makes my heart do funny things." Pausing to take a breath, she pushed the ring onto her finger, admiring the way the sunlight reflected off the stone. "I had a feeling something huge was going to happen today, but I told myself that was silly. Yet here we are, in the same spot where we had our first date, you asking me to be your wife."

"I didn't ask you," he muttered, causing her gaze to dart up in his direction.

"Oh. When I saw the ring, I just assumed—"

"I didn't ask because you won't be quiet long enough to let me."

"Oh." She laughed, unable to keep a grin from spreading across her face. "You've never let something like that stop you in the past. But my answer is yes, of course. I can't imagine anything more wonderful than being right here with you for the rest of my life. I love you so much." Rising to tiptoe, she threw her arms around his neck, hanging on as he wrapped his arms around her waist and lifted her off the ground. Twisting her face ever so slightly, she pressed a kiss against his cheek. "When should we get married?"

The rumble of his chuckle in his chest could be felt in her own as he held her against him, and the movement made her smile. "Sometime after I ask you, which I still haven't done yet."

"Okay, okay." She let out a sigh as he lowered her to the ground, the look in his eyes worth more than a thousand rings. "Is fall beautiful here? I bet it's gorgeous. We could get married in the fall, or close to Christmas. A Christmas wedding would be unbelievable, don't you think?" Trying not to laugh again, she pressed her fingers over her mouth in a flawed attempt to stop the flow of words. "All lovely things that we'll talk about *after* you ask me, which you will. Very soon, I hope."

Epilogue

And so the residents of Willowdale celebrated Arabelle and Flint's impending nuptials. They could not have parted with her for anyone less worthy. #willowfairies

Leaning her chin on her left hand, Willow added shading to one of the miniscule petals in Arabelle's bouquet. It was the little fairy's big day, but she wasn't going to be wearing a giant dress or a veil in her hair. A slightly fancier version of her everyday short dress, convenient for flying, and a few wildflowers in her hair were all she needed.

Clint stepped up behind Willow, placing a warm hand against her shoulder. "Staying up much longer?"

"No, I can work on it in the morning. Doesn't hurt to keep the suspense for a few days." She placed the pencil on the table, tilting her head back to look up at her husband. "You know, I think the fairies like your house even more than they liked the cabin. So many more places to get lost and find marvelous creatures."

"A fancy way for saying we're further in the woods."

Pushing away from the table, she rose to a stand, stretching her arms wide to ease the aches out of her muscles. "When will you learn that nothing is ordinary? The most mundane things are always worth a second look."

Extending his hand in her direction, he lifted his eyebrows as he gave her a crooked, half-smile. "It's slowly sinking in, but I'm working on it."

She placed her hand in his, stepping away from the work space he'd designed especially for her in their living room. Mrs. Campbell's old sweater sat on the corner of the desk, folded up just like it had been when she'd taken it out of the box during the move. After all her years of wearing it while she worked, it didn't feel necessary anymore. She didn't need a token to remind her to be who she was. The man gently holding her hand let her know it was okay to be who she was, with or without fairies involved.

A lesson she was happy to have learned, since it's a truth universally acknowledged that fairies, and humans, simply want to love and be loved in return.

And she was.

USA Today Bestselling Author
Christina Coryell

MERRIED OFF

A Beards and
Belles Novella

Merried Off

a romantic comedy
by
Christina Coryell

Chapter One

"It must be sheer ecstasy to be known not by a name first and foremost, but by a song." Celeste Jordan sighed as she sank deeper into the scratchy cushion on the old wooden chair. "It's tempting to choose such a song for myself, but I'm afraid it would be impossible to narrow it down. All of life is one lingering melody."

The harrumph from the other side of the porch didn't manage to put a damper on her spirits. "I don't reckon that bird cares what you call him one way or the other," John stated from his end of the space, clearing his throat before taking a sip of his morning coffee.

"Well, I'm in complete awe of him. He has to be the most splendid, beautiful bird in the entire state of Tennessee."

Even without turning, Celeste had the distinct impression that John was shaking his head. "An ordinary wood thrush the color of dirt." His voice lowered to a whisper. "See for yourself, kiddo. He's lighted on the railing right in front of you."

Breathing in a deep breath of the crisp misty air, she pressed her eyes closed and wrapped her arms over her chest. "No, I think I'll keep seeing him exactly the way I see him now. He's a brilliant blue with a crest of red and some purple in his tail feathers. And proud . . . I've never seen a bird puff its chest so." Tilting back her head, she caught the scent of wood smoke in the air as she crossed her boots at the ankles, her long skirt fanning out about her feet. "Yes, he's glorious.

I wish you could catch a glimpse of him. Everything is so much clearer when looking through the eyes of the heart."

Chapter Two

"I'm pretty sure Willow turned you into a fairy."

Doug Kirkland swung the axe over his shoulder, splintering the black oak in front of him but not breaking it. "Say that again?" Dropping the axe to the ground, he reached down and grabbed the wood with both hands, ripping it apart where it had remained intact before pinning his gaze on his brother a few yards away.

"She has this theory that what she creates in her fairy world happens in real life," Clint continued, tossing another chunk of wood in his direction.

"And she thinks I'm a fairy?" He narrowed his eyes while he set the new piece of wood on the flattened tree stump before him, angling it so his axe would have the most impact. With a glance at his chest, he gave his pectorals a good flex beneath his T-shirt just to accentuate his argument. "I'd be more likely to believe she wanted to turn me into a toad."

"A toad would sure fit you better, but in this case I think you're a three-inch tall dude named Cap."

"Cap?" Doug grabbed the axe again, placing it behind his shoulder and then swinging downward with enough force to send the wood flying in two different directions.

"Probably because you said you were in charge of the roughnecks on the oil rig. Like a captain."

Bringing the hem of his shirt up, Doug wiped his forehead to remove the sawdust he felt clinging to his skin. If he looked anything like Clint did at the moment, he probably had it in his beard, too. Although his beard was a lot more in control than Clint's, so it wasn't really a good comparison.

"So she's trying to put a hex on me? Some kind of voodoo stuff?"

"No." His brother grabbed the back of his neck and stared out at the tree line—a surefire sign he was embarrassed. Clint had never been one for talking things out. Usually kept himself all bottled up and stoic, preferring listening to verbalizing. The match he'd made with his new wife had seemed completely bizarre to Doug at first, until he'd spent a little time with the pint-sized, pastel-haired painter. Clint barely had to worry about getting a word in edgewise with that one.

"She makes stories with the fairies," Clint finally continued.

"Yeah, I've seen the tiny houses, the paint, the glue—"

"She uses it to make characters. She did one about me when we met, and then added in Ruth and Emily later."

Doug's gut clenched, making him cringe even as he took in Clint's cheeks tinting a darker shade. "Well, you can tell her I appreciate the effort and all, but there's nothing there with Ruth and there never will be."

"It's not about you and Ruth, it's just about you." Clint shoved his hands into his jeans pockets. "She started this storyline where fairy Emily was looking for something, and then you showed up in real life."

"Because I decided it was time, that's all. Wasting years on that rig wasn't appealing anymore." *Neither was the life I was living,* he added to himself. "I'm only back because of Emily and to see Tennessee soil again. Just coincidence with your wife's art."

Clint nodded, the beginning of a smile barely discernable under his facial hair. "Just wanted to give you a heads up. I remember the way I felt the first time I saw Willow's drawing looked like me."

With a sigh, Doug sat on the tree stump, both hands on his knees. No way would Willow draw something that looked like him. Clint was being ridiculous.

Running a hand over his hair, Doug left the wet ends disheveled and pointing straight out away from his ears. Clint had insisted earlier in the afternoon that the feeling would be uncomfortable, but he had been wrong. Seeing an almost precise image of himself on Willow's drawing was eerie, but the feeling settling on him wasn't discomfort. Something closer to foreboding.

He'd always controlled his own destiny. Decided when to come and go. Moved here and there based on his own desires and wishes. The thought that something uncontrollable out there in the universe could be directing his steps, brought on by Willow or not, wasn't very appealing.

It was also fantasy, he reminded himself as he unwrapped the towel from around his waist.

Probably a general uneasiness brought on by trying to assimilate himself with this way of life again. Seeing Clint living in the house his parents had owned. Clint with a wife, no less. Reacquainting himself with Emily and Ruth—and knowing the latter would probably rather run a spear through him than willingly be in his company. Not that he could blame her for that. He felt like a different person now, though. The Doug they remembered ages ago was still stuck back there somehow, a part of history.

He barely remembered the person he'd been in Tennessee. For the last several years, he'd been known as Deke—the guys on the oil rig calling him by a shortened version of the initials D.K. The nickname hadn't just made him one of the guys—it had given him a sense of anonymity. Deke was whoever he wanted to be. He wasn't Clint's smaller kid brother. He wasn't the guy who ran off and left his ex and kid so he could earn a better life. He definitely wasn't the guy struggling to fit into a world one size too small.

No, he'd simply been part of the crew on the rig earning money, living life, and having fun while he was young. The job wasn't for everyone, but it had served him well. He had a state of the art pickup, a pile of money in the bank, and . . .

And direction to find, he supposed. Three weeks back in Gatlinburg and he still couldn't figure out what to do with himself.

"You'd better shape up," he muttered to the phone in his hand, staring at the painted guy staring out into the woods. It was a pretty solid likeness, all the way down to his muscular forearms and the color of his beard. The wings were weird, tinted the pigments of tree bark and almost blending into the background. If he didn't like Willow and think she had a good heart, he'd call and tell her to knock off the stalking.

Shaking his head, he exited the screen, instead opting to go to the contacts on his phone. He needed a distraction, but he had turned over a new leaf when he moved back to Tennessee. That included swearing off casual dating, so the bar scene was out of the question. He'd been gone long enough he didn't know who was single or taken around his old hangouts anyway.

No, being romantically involved with anyone was off limits until he got his head on straight. What he needed was good solid work to keep his mind occupied. He had spoken to a woman the day before who needed a tree removed from her yard . . . what had her name been? The one with the high-pitched laugh who kept touching his arm while they talked. He'd added her number to his contacts.

"Laugh," he whispered, bending over to grab his jeans before stepping into them. Tugging up on his belt loop, he paused before buttoning his jeans to type in the search bar. L-A-U-G-H. A string of several contacts popped up. Ashley Laugh. Dana Laugh. Kristin Laugh.

Ashley, he decided as he pressed his finger against the name, the sordid remains of his dating past taunting him from that contact list. Last names had rarely come into play, and descriptions had been easier to remember. Funny laugh, snake tattoo, tongue ring. The list of names stared back at him now like a nightmare laundry list, but he hadn't convinced himself to erase them yet. Maybe when he was one-hundred percent certain he'd actually moved out of the past, he would do something about deleting it.

The phone started its trilling so he placed it on the bedside table as he grabbed his T-shirt to pull it over his head. He should find an apartment and move out of the hotel, but he hadn't quite convinced himself that staying was the best bet. Being in Emily's life didn't necessarily mean being within a few miles. It could be thirty or even fifty.

"Hello?"

The breathiness of that voice sounded almost nothing like the woman he'd met yesterday, a round tone instead of the thin voice he remembered when discussing tree branches. Plucking the phone from the table, he held it closer to his lips. "Ashley, it's Deke. We met yesterday."

A heavy pause preceded her answer. "No, you're mistaken."

His eyebrows tilted together as he lowered himself to the bed, tipping his head to the side. "Yeah, I distinctly remember. You were wearing a shirt with the word PINK on it."

A breezy laugh whispered through the phone, but instead of being high-pitched, this was rich and almost lilting. "I'm sorry, what did you say your name was?"

"Deke."

"Deke? That's a very unusual name. What does it mean?"

The line of questioning settled confusion squarely on his shoulders. Reaching up to smooth down his wet hair, he gave the phone a scowl. "It's a nickname from my buddies on the oil rig."

"An oil rig? That sounds fascinating." She paused as hints of bluegrass music filled the background. "I hate to tell you this, Deke, but you must have written your pink friend's number down wrong."

A wrong number felt more like a metaphor for his life than a mistake. "Then who is this?"

"You've called Roy Coble's phone."

"Are you Roy?"

The laugh seemed to flow right through the phone and skim over the hair on his arms. "Goodness, no. Roy's a sixty-year-old man who likes to whittle, and I'm pretty sure he's never worn a shirt with the word PINK on it."

Something about her tone made him feel a new shade of ridiculous. Add the fact that he couldn't seem to hang up even though he had the wrong number, and he was about to question his own sanity. "Why are you answering Roy's phone? Are you his daughter?"

"Work colleague."

He glanced at the clock by the bed to see that it was just after five o'clock. "What kind of work colleague?"

"Mostly I play the fiddle and Roy tries to marry me off."

Rising to his feet, Doug crossed the room to push back the drapes, staring at his shiny black truck in front of the building while he pondered ways to keep the melodic voice talking. "Why would he do that?"

"It's our gig. I'm his moony-eyed daughter who does nothing but play music, and he's trying to get rid of me."

Doug lifted a hand to scratch his beard, unable to keep his forehead from wrinkling. "I thought you said you worked together."

"Yes. I really must let you go because I have to grab my fiddle. I thought you might be Elizabeth or I wouldn't have answered the phone."

The distinct tinny sound of banjo music drifted in from the background, and with it came an irrational sense of panic. "Wait, what's your name?"

Nothing but a dial tone met him as a response.

"There's lots of people who can't take a hint. Take my daughter," Roy said. "No, seriously. I'll pay you to take her."

"Pa, don't be silly. If I was gone who'd play the fiddle for you?"

"Exactly."

The tittering of laughter Celeste heard in front of her was enough to bring a smile to her lips, but she forced a bit of a pout instead. Routine like every other day, but the thought of performing for new people still made it feel fresh. Bringing the instrument up to her chin, she placed the bow against the strings and loosed a torrent of notes that caused her toe to start tapping beneath her long skirt. The crowd was hushed, with the exception of the one gentleman in the front who was prone to chuckling and the mother on the edge shushing her child. They would clap when she finished. The older crowds usually did, and she had the distinct feeling this crowd was significantly above an average age of fifty, with the exception of the youngster on the end.

The last note sang off the end of her string, and the smattering of applause broke out just as she'd expected.

"Now that's what I call some fine fiddlin'," Roy stated. "I'll let you take her off my hands for the low sum of two dollars, on account of the fact that she can't cook."

"Aw, Pa, don't be teasing the fine folks when they've been so kind standing here and listening to me play. Thank you!" She waved with her right hand while hugging the fiddle against her chest with the left.

The crowd began to disperse, and she nearly turned to go inside the cabin before the shuffling to her right caught her ear. Remaining where she was, Celeste gave a bright smile.

"Go on and ask," the mom whispered to the child.

"Hi," Celeste said, kneeling down on the weathered boards of the porch. "What's your name?"

"Alice."

Shifting her gaze to the left and back again, Celeste caught the flash of a blond pigtail. "I'm glad you stopped to see us today, Alice. What can I do for you?"

The young girl didn't readily answer, so Celeste kept the smile on her face while she glanced in Roy's direction. Within seconds, his hand was firmly cupped over her shoulder. "Young'un is pointing at your necklace," he said, giving her shoulder a final squeeze before stepping back.

"Oh!" Celeste wrapped the fingers of her right hand around the little wooden bird. "Pa made this one special for me, but if you go two little shops down around the bend there, you'll find a sweet lady named Millie. She has bunches of things just like this. Tell her Celeste sent you, and ask to see the angel. It's my personal favorite."

"Thank you," the child's mom said as Celeste rose to her feet.

"You're welcome. Enjoy the rest of your day." Sighing, she released the wooden bird from her fingers and leaned back against the porch post, keeping the fiddle snug against her chest. "People have seemed to be in a jovial mood this afternoon, not that I can blame them. There's a crispness in the air today that makes me think of snow."

"Won't be any snow here in mid-October," Roy stated, dragging his rocking chair away from the edge of the porch. "Anyhow, it's over fifty degrees."

Pressing her eyes closed, Celeste held out her hand and imagined the snow drifting down and lighting on her fingertips. She could almost feel the icy pinprick of the flakes on the breeze. "Made me think of snow, that's all I said. If I want to see the whole world around me covered in the powdery whiteness, it wouldn't impact you a bit."

"Suppose not." Roy chuckled as the chair scraped the wood when he shoved it into place. "Long as you don't go wandering around with your hands in the air so I have to explain it to people."

She couldn't keep the grin from tipping up one corner of her lips. "I told you I would try very hard not to do that again. Oh, and someone called your phone right before I came out here. I answered thinking it might be Elizabeth, but it was a man named Deke."

"Doesn't ring any bells."

"No?" She lowered her hand back to her side, rubbing her palm against the cotton fabric of her dress. "It seemed like he had the wrong number, which was a shame. I'd have enjoyed talking to him longer. There was this quality to his voice—a richness, like the melted dark chocolate center of the candies they make across the park. Made me wish I knew him."

Roy stopped shuffling behind her and stood perfectly still. "Talking to strange men probably isn't a wise decision."

Her mind echoed his sentiment, but her heart couldn't keep the smile from lighting her face. "You're right, but don't worry. I doubt I'll ever talk to him again."

Chapter Three

"Uncle Clint looks like he's about to bust that swing."

Doug drew his eyes up from the buckle he'd fastened near his waist and focused on Clint about ten feet in front of him. "Yeah, it seems like there should be a Jolly Green Giant rule on that sign back there. *Guests must not live on a cloud above a beanstalk.*"

Clint turned his head like he wanted to make a remark, but the swing's restraints held him fast, ensuring he couldn't actually twist in his seat.

"I wish Willow could ride with us," Emily added, wistfully turning her gaze toward his sister-in-law standing past the barrier, a gray stocking cap covering her pink braid. "She screams the best."

Widening his eyes, Doug tugged on the latch once more to make sure it was secure. "I'm sure she'd like to ride too, but you spun her out of commission and she feels a little sick. Besides, I kind of hope she screams for your benefit and that's not real. Otherwise she's the most easily terrified person I've ever met."

Emily seemed to sink a little into her seat as she wrapped her gloved fingers over the bar in front of them, growing pensive like she usually was around him. This was the hurdle he was afraid he'd always have to cross, and knowing he deserved it didn't make him feel any better. He'd barely seen her over the years, and he doubted the fact that he was trying to get his head screwed on straight would impress the little girl next to him.

Both Ruth and Emily had been wary when he'd suggested the trip to the amusement park—right up until he made mention of the fact that he'd invited Willow and Clint. Ruth had visibly relaxed, clearly trusting his brother more than him, and Emily's face lit up like she'd been given the golden ticket to Wonka's factory. His daughter had made her preference even clearer when they arrived at the park, sticking to Willow closer than a shadow. Except for the few well-timed instances where Willow began feeling motion sick. He supposed it could have been true on Willow's part, but it seemed more likely that Willow was removing herself from the situation purposefully.

Doug looked down at Emily, studying the way her lips puckered almost like she was trying to blow a kiss. She had a tendency to wear that expression when she was thinking, and Willow's glittery lip gloss only accentuated her pout. He'd already discovered so many things about her in a short period of time. She was part tomboy, part princess, her usual outfits consisting of some type of frilly lacy skirt with motorcycle boots and knee-high socks. Obviously didn't like to brush her hair, because the only time it looked tame was when her mom braided it. Couldn't pass a dog without stopping to learn its name. And her profile reminded him a little of his mom's, which brought a sad smile to his lips.

Pulling himself out of his thoughts, he draped his arm over the back of her seat as the ride operator had instructed. "You warm enough? We could go inside after this, or maybe I could buy you hot cocoa."

She forced a tight-lipped smile and nodded her head. "I'd like cocoa. And maybe we can go look at the old houses after this."

"Sure, kiddo."

The ride began lifting the two of them into the air, and Emily withdrew her attention to stare down at Willow, waving one gloved hand. Willow waved back, her smile wide across her face. Within only a few seconds, they were sailing through the air, the force of the motion pressing Emily into his side.

Neither one of them screamed.

The scent of warm apple cider permeated the air, and Celeste leaned against the hand-hewn logs while she imagined the apple aroma clinging to her like a sweet perfume. A woman to her left wistfully told Roy about a sweet potato dish her grandmother used to cook in a replica of one of the pots hanging in the old cabin, and she couldn't help but listen intently to the conversation. It was strange and fascinating what items people linked with emotion. Some remarked about her fiddle, others the antiques inside the cabin, and even a few the old farm implements scattered around the place and leading down to the barn. Without fail, every time she would play an old hymn on her fiddle, someone would tell her it reminded them of a simpler time.

It was easy to believe in a simpler time here, where people were generally kind to each other and happy with the simplicity of her corner of the park. That was probably why she never desired to be anywhere else, content to let the place encompass her world.

"Celeste," one of those kind voices said from her right.

She pulled her gaze down but turned in that direction with a smile. "Hi, Miriam. Beautiful day, don't you think?"

"A little bit colder than yesterday, but I suppose I'll take it. Got something for you."

Extending her right hand, Celeste waited for the wrapped candy to fall into her palm. "What kind today?"

"Cherry."

With a slight nod, Celeste closed her hand around the taffy and dropped it into her skirt pocket. "Thank you. Tell your grandson that I can't wait to hear the song he wrote."

"He's been practicing every night. Maybe I'll have my daughter bring him up here next weekend."

"That would be lovely. Tell her I said hello, too."

"I will honey. Just mind that you keep your fingers warm."

Celeste nodded before Miriam walked away. She didn't really mind the cold, and she had gloves to keep her hands warm if it became too oppressive. Days like today were near perfection in her estimation, even if everyone else thought the air a little chilly for their tastes. The world might long for sunbeams that settled on its shoulders and spread a warm swath down its back, but she was most content with the cool breezes that caused the end of her nose to tingle.

She sniffed for good measure, if for no other reason than to punctuate her mental words.

"You there, sir!" Roy called to someone passing by. "Do you take a particular liking to the fiddle? My daughter has one here and I'm wondering if you'd like to take her off my hands?"

Stretching out her fingers, Celeste took the cue and held the fiddle tightly to her chest. "Pa, surely you aren't trying to sell my fiddle?"

"Not outright, but if the feller that wants you has a mind to buy the fiddle too, I reckon I'd let him pay me for it."

Her feigned astonishment seemed to play well with the batch of onlookers who had meandered their way, so she lowered her head in her most forlorn expression as she began a mournful piece on her instrument. In character she could perform in ways she would never dare when exposed privately, so she tended to exaggerate her actions. For this particular song, she chose to end the last note with her face tilted toward the sky.

"Aye, she plays a mighty pretty tune," Roy stated. "Smart as a whip, too. Say, Celeste, do you have any words of wisdom for these young ladies who are passing by our humble abode?"

"Oh, of course," she said, snapping to attention and standing up straight. "If you can't decide if it's a snake or a stick, best not pick it up."

"Snake," Roy repeated. "Now there might be plenty of snakes around our cabin, but these here's city folks. Maybe give them something a little more useful."

Squeezing her eyes closed, Celeste nodded. "When traveling with a feller, best keep your skirts away from the wheels less'n you give him too much information unintended like."

Some giggling from a few girls in the front increased when Celeste lifted her skirt to her knee and shook her boot in the air.

"My word, Celeste. These here are genteel ladies who aren't apt to be traveling alone with wild gentlemen. Except that one there—she looks like a bit of trouble."

Celeste widened her eyes, but internally her heart broke into a smile. Roy only offered those words when there was a particularly shy little girl standing in front of him. If they weren't in the middle of an impromptu performance at that very moment, she'd lower herself to the steps and try to engage the girl in conversation. But the job came first, and then the mingling.

"I don't know as I have much to offer genteel ladies, but . . . How about this? When you fry up eggs, try to get the pieces of shell out before you start cooking. It's way harder to pick them out after."

The words rolled through the air exactly like she'd heard them countless times. Roy would tell her that she was supposed to break the shell before putting the egg in the pan. She would do some good-natured shrugging and grinning. He would offer her to a random man in the audience for a paltry bride price and spit out a few one-liners designed for laughs.

As though the whole thing could happen without her giving it a second thought, she began playing the fiddle softly in the background like she did every day. The beginning strains of "Aura Lea" drifted from the instrument, and she couldn't help but feel a sense of contentment as she played the old Civil War tune. It was traditional and fit the time period, but people would recognize it either way since Elvis Presley used the tune with new lyrics about a century later.

It was almost tempting to lose herself in the notes, with Roy's voice droning on in the background, "Now that's what I call some fine fiddlin'. I'll let you take her off my hands for the low sum of two dollars, on account of the fact that she can't cook."

She held the last note as long as she could, finally lowering her fiddle to her side as she prepared to tell Roy to stop teasing the crowd. As she opened her mouth to speak, a strangely familiar voice altogether unlike her own permeated the air instead.

"I have two dollars."

Chapter Four

Emily led the way to the taffy shop, barely slowing her pace as she sidestepped a double-wide baby stroller in the path. When sugar was involved, the girl was almost impossible to deter. Or puppies, for that matter.

With a quick glance back, Doug made sure Willow and Clint were still following them. Although they were several feet behind, a subtle nod from Clint let him know they wouldn't be separated. Although if Em didn't let up her quick pace, he might soon find himself jogging to catch her.

He'd almost decided to kick it into second gear when she made an abrupt stop, turning to her right and nudging in toward a crowd of people. His heart threatened to go into a panic when he saw the throng, but when he realized it was some kind of street performance, he breathed a sigh of relief. Nothing he'd have to distract Emily from, at least.

Stepping to her side, he placed a protective hand on her shoulder and looked at the facade of the cabin with the little lean-to porch, its rough-hewn logs obviously original from the time period or at least made to look that way. A portly man with a white goatee sat in a rocking chair with a corn cob pipe in his right hand, the left looped casually into the bib of his overalls. Beside him a copper-haired woman offered some advice about keeping skirts out of wheels and then gave a little shake of her ankle, causing Emily to giggle.

Something inside made him pause and study her a little more closely. She lifted her head and drew her gaze across the crowd, not looking at any one person. Her clothing was designed to make her appear to be from the 1800's, but the state of her hair almost gave the impression that she'd walked in from the woods like one of Willow's fairies. A few flyaway pieces about her face drifted with the breeze, the rest caught up in a messy braid over her shoulder. Forget fairies—the woman could pass for Willow's old-timey, freckled long-lost cousin.

She said something else about cooking eggs, and he tilted his head to the side as familiarity seemed to shake him. He'd met her before somewhere, maybe? Gone to school with her, although he felt certain he would remember that face. She picked up her instrument and began playing a string of notes that sounded a lot like an Elvis song, ignoring the guy playing her dad who was trying to marry her off to the highest bidder.

A rich voice filtered through his mind. *Mostly I play the fiddle and Roy tries to marry me off.*

"Dad," Emily hissed beside him, tugging on the edge of his jacket.

Dragging his eyes away from the redhead, he looked down at his daughter. Her large brown eyes held such a pleading force, he felt himself turning in her direction. "What is it, kiddo?" he whispered, leaning closer to her ear.

"Don't you have two dollars?"

The skin between his eyebrows puckered. "For the taffy? Let's see how much it is before I—"

"No, for her. That man is trying to get rid of her. You have to help."

A chuckle slipped out before he had a chance to steel himself against her accusing glare. "It's just an act, he's not going to—"

"Hurry!"

The intensity of her features had him patting his pockets with his palms looking for his wallet, even though he knew her request was ridiculous. Then again, this was the same kid who started sobbing every time one of those Humane Society commercials popped onto the television. If ever there was a bleeding heart, his daughter might be the Guinness World Record holder. It was a little funny that she was equating the amusement park actress with a lost puppy, but not so funny when he found himself pulling a wad of one dollar bills from his front pocket. Greenbacks in hand, he peered up at the cabin again.

Screwing up her nose with a huff, Emily's boot came down hard on his toe.

"Ow," he muttered, shooting a scolding glance at his daughter. She tilted her head in the direction of the man in overalls. "Fine." Shifting his attention to the man as well, he cleared his throat before raising his voice. "I have two dollars."

Both the performers on the porch stopped what they were doing and listened, the woman keeping her eyes glued to the floor while the man searched the crowd until his gaze landed on Doug and Emily. More precisely, they skimmed over Doug and settled firmly on Emily alone, who anxiously bounced on the balls of her feet.

"Well," the man said, his eyes sparking with a hint of mischief, "thank you kind folks for your attention, but it appears I have some business with the gentleman in the back."

Doug caught a brief glimpse of a hesitant smile on the young woman's face before she broke into a full grin, eagerly waving at the crowd. "Enjoy your day at the park, folks! Don't forget to stop in and see Miriam to get some mouth-watering taffy!"

His heart beat a little harder as Emily put her gloved hand in his, tugging him forward toward the porch. That voice, the fiddling, the guy trying to marry her off—she had to be the woman from the phone last night. The recognition made him instantly curious about her, but also gave him pause. Hopefully she wouldn't remember the conversation. The way he'd grilled someone he didn't know over their relation to whoever owned the phone. Or the fact that he'd tried to get her to keep talking after he knew he had the wrong number.

"What is your name, young lady?" the man in overalls asked, looking down the end of his nose to Emily. His posture said he was trying to appear intimidating, but the rosy tint to his cheeks made him look more like Santa Claus than a grumpy old-timer.

"Emily Kirkland."

"And who is this guy with you? Your stable hand?" He paused and brought a hand up to the whiskers on his chin. "No, you seem like a genteel girl. Your butler, perhaps?"

A scowl crossed Emily's features as she glanced at the woman to the left of them. "He's my dad."

"I see. And I suppose you want to conduct some business with me, is that it?"

Emily straightened herself as tall as her nine-year-old stature would allow. "We've got two dollars. I want to buy your lady."

Doug cringed as he brought his left hand up to his temple, peering around him at the dispersing crowd. He was barely into the phase of their father-daughter bonding where they could comfortably spend the day together. Having a discussion about the improprieties of offering to buy a person wasn't high on his list of acceptable topics.

"And now, what do you plan on doing with her?" the man questioned Emily, his features softening.

"I'm gonna let her go."

Doug glanced back to search for Willow and Clint, but they seemed deep in conversation several yards away. It was too bad they hadn't seen the little show Emily was putting on. Willow might have been able to use it for her fairy pictures. As uncomfortable as the whole thing was making him, he couldn't deny that he felt a little surge of pride at Emily's good intentions.

"Hi, Emily," the young woman said, lowering herself to a seat on the highest step leading up to the cabin porch. "Thank you so much for that sweet offer. Is it okay with your dad if I give you something?"

Doug started to nod, but the woman kept her eyes glued to Emily, so he verbalized a *yes* instead.

Rifling around in her pocket, she pulled out a wrapped piece of taffy. "Miriam brought me cherry today. I think you'll like it. Do you come here often?"

"Once before with my mom, and today with Uncle Clint and Aunt Willow."

"I see. Well, I love it here. In fact, I'm here every single day with Roy over there. He pretends to be my dad and I play the fiddle, but he's not really trying to get rid of me."

Emily glanced up at Roy to gauge his reaction. "He's not?"

The woman wrinkled her nose just a smidge, leading Doug to focus on the scattered freckles across her cheeks. The most sizable freckle was right in the middle of her nose, almost like it was painted there on purpose. "No, it's just a little skit we do every day to entertain people. At the end of the day Roy will go to his house and I'll go to my house, and then tomorrow we'll start our act all over again. Do you ever pretend things?"

Emily nodded and closed her hand over the piece of taffy. "Yeah, sometimes I pretend I have a dog."

"Ooh, I love dogs. Which kind is your favorite?"

"Um . . . cocker spaniel."

"Excellent choice." She continued talking, focusing her gaze on Emily's gloves instead of her face. "When I was about your age, I was friends with a wonderful sheep dog named Hoss. He had the most triumphantly deep bark, and I liked to imagine we had a secret language. People said he didn't understand me, but I still like to believe he did. Sometimes we have a sixth sense about these things." She pointed to her temple and offered a smile. "My name's Celeste. It's awfully nice to meet you, Emily."

Celeste extended her hand, and Emily placed her glove inside and gave it a shake without saying a word.

When the greeting ended, Celeste shifted in Doug's general direction, offering him a handshake as well. Her hand was pointed more in the vicinity of his knee than his chest, but he tilted himself lower so he could take her hand in his.

"Celeste," she said, the faintest hint of a smile turning up her lips as her eyes focused on his shoulder. "You have a very smart daughter, Mr.—"

"Kirkland." He cleared his throat again to remove whatever was threatening to clog his airway. "Doug Kirkland."

The grin on her face seemed a little uncertain as her focus once again drifted in Emily's direction.

"Dad, can Aunt Willow take me to the bathroom?"

He dragged his eyes away from Celeste long enough to nod at his daughter. "Sure. I'll wait here for you."

Emily skipped away while Roy vacated his spot on the porch, sauntering into the cabin. The two actions left him completely alone in front of Celeste, and he fought to keep his eyes from roving over her face lest she catch him staring.

"You said it was Doug, right?"

The shifty way she refused to look at him made him uneasy enough that he found himself stuffing his hands in his pockets. She wasn't supermodel beautiful. Didn't even look like most women he'd met, really, with no makeup and her hair swept into tamed chaos. Something about her had him fidgety, though, and he didn't like it.

"Yes, Doug."

"It's nice to meet you, although I believe we've already spoken before. It was you on the phone last night, was it not? I recognize your voice if not the name."

She turned to look at him, prompting him to flash the smile that he usually used to charm people. "Yeah, Deke but my name is actually Doug. I must have written the number down wrong when I called last night. Sorry for the interruption of your work, but I can't say it wasn't a pleasure talking to you." Her cheeks flushed pink, but she continued to stare at his jawline instead of meeting his gaze. Tilting his head down, he tried to force her to look at him. "Have you worked here long?"

"Close to five years now. Roy and I get along well over here in our neck of the woods."

"You have the perfect looks for the part," he said, rethinking his words when she still refused to meet his eyes. "I mean, the way you have your hair and clothes and everything, you look like you could have stepped out of a different time."

"That's good," she muttered, tilting her chin down until she seemed focused on the ground near his feet. "Good that I look the part, of course. It's appropriate that I'm an accurate representation."

"Sure." His eyes swept toward her hands, one still gripping the fiddle by its neck. "How long have you played the fiddle?"

She pulled it closer, tucking it against her chest. "Almost as long as I've been walking. It's my ticket to another universe."

He wasn't sure what to say to that, but the sight of Emily moving in his direction hand in hand with Willow meant he didn't have long to chat anyway. "Would you be interested in talking to me again? If you give me your number, I'd be happy to call you on purpose next time."

She kept her chin tucked down like she was inspecting her boots. "I don't have a number except for John and Ava's, and I doubt they would like me giving that to strangers. Anyway, I'm not sure it's a good idea."

He'd experienced the odd handful of rejections at bars over the years, but none of them felt this personal. Furrowing his brow, he studied her posture, the way she almost shrank away from him. She was at work, first of all. Probably not smart to approach her at work. And she seemed . . . different somehow. Almost like she really had stepped out of the 1800's and he'd have to tread softly if he wanted to talk to her.

Besides, the last time he'd checked, swearing off dating didn't include getting a woman's number.

So why was he racking his brain trying to think of an excuse to see her another time?

"Okay," he relented. "I hope our paths cross again someday."

With a deep breath, he resigned himself to the simple action of holding out his hand for another handshake. Nothing at all suggestive in that. An innocent friendly gesture. After a second passed with him staring at his fingers, he lifted his eyes to her face. She offered a tight smile and nodded, completely ignoring his offered hand as she turned to walk inside the cabin.

Dumbfounded, he closed his fingers into a fist, watching as she disappeared through the doorway. For a split second he fought the urge to grow angry at her dismissal, but then the scene began replaying in front of him. Her reluctance to look at him, the offered handshake directed toward his knee, the way she didn't return his smile . . .

Almost like she couldn't see him at all.

Chapter Five

Ava Huckabee settled next to Celeste on the worn couch cushion. The end of the afghan wrapped around the older woman's shoulders brushed against Celeste's hand. Without giving it a second thought, Celeste reached out to touch it, holding the wool between her fingers. She'd been scolded for that action many times when she was younger, the way she couldn't seem to keep her hands off things. Ava never minded, though.

"There's Roy pulling up with the truck," Ava stated, the couch cushion shifting a bit under Celeste as Ava lifted to peek out the window. "I'd imagine John will deter him for a minute asking if he knows where we can get some more firewood. I swear the man's stubborn as an ox. All I'd have to do is ask one of the young men at church and I'm sure we could get some assistance."

Celeste couldn't help but grin as she imagined John's response to that statement. Probably something about caring for the place like a man should, and how he wasn't a spring chicken but didn't have one foot in the grave yet. Ava and John might have teased each other ceaselessly, but the respect they had for one another laced every word. Besides, Celeste knew John would never let there be an issue with firewood. Ava was perpetually cold, as evidenced by her wearing an afghan every day as a shawl, and John always took care of his wife.

And Celeste as well, in the bargain.

The sound of boots scuffling across the porch preceded the squeak of the screen door, and Celeste rose to her feet as the front door opened.

"Ava, I don't suppose you have a little extra coffee this morning? Elizabeth ran out last night and hasn't been to the store yet." Roy's voice held a hint of humor, giving Celeste the distinct impression that he and John had been joking around outside. "Celeste, you might as well seat yourself back down. I can't go anywhere until I get some coffee in this thermos."

His footsteps took him into the kitchen where he helped himself to the caffeine he craved, so Celeste lowered herself back to the couch. "It's going to be a beautiful day," she stated, releasing the afghan from her fingers and spreading her hand against her lap instead. "Maybe a chance of a shower later, according to what John told me."

"No ma'am, not what John told you," John stated as he noisily lowered himself into a recliner across the room. "I was merely relating what the weatherman said. If that forecast is wrong, you blame it on him and not me."

"You mean you can't sense a storm coming in your bones?" Roy asked as coffee splashed into his metal thermos. "Elizabeth will be right sorry about that. She was planning on using you for a cheap weather forecasting tool if ever the cable goes out."

"That nonsense dish we have on the house goes out every time it rains anyway," John complained. "Works all the time 'cept when you need it. But if you want to know the weather, go over there and take Ava's hand. Whatever level of ice it's turned into will tell you the temperature."

"Always cold," Celeste added with a smile.

"Always cold," Ava repeated. "It's a might nicer outside today than it was yesterday, which is a blessing. I'd imagine that's better for the two of you standing on that porch all day long."

"Naw, we go inside if we need to warm up," Roy said, the swishing sound of his lid being twisted onto the thermos accompanying his words. "Wonder if we'll have an eventful day like we did yesterday, kiddo."

"Eventful day?" Ava's slightly chilled hand settled on Celeste's arm. "You didn't tell us something happened."

Celeste felt her cheeks heating at Ava's concern. "A very little something. More akin to nothing, really."

"Man in the crowd offered to buy her," Roy stated, ending with a chuckle. "His little girl 'bout had him by the ear dragging him up to the front, and then he waved the two dollars at me like I was actually going to sell her to the highest bidder."

"Goodness Roy, don't make it sound quite so dramatic. It was nothing but a silly misunderstanding."

"Might have been were it not that same man who talked to you on the phone the day before."

"What man talked to you on the phone?" John asked. "Nobody's called here that I know of. Ava?"

Celeste shook her head before Ava had a chance to reply. "Roy had a wrong number on his phone the other night. Happened to be the same man at the park. An odd coincidence, that's all."

"Did seem like a coincidence, but the man was dead gone on our little songbird, staring after her when she walked away," Roy said, moving into the living room until he was standing in front of the couch. "Might have to perfect my fatherly act a little more in protecting you from potential suitors."

Celeste's heart seemed to take flight inside her chest, pattering against her ribs. "Roy's only seeking to tease me. I don't even know that man."

Doug, her mind chimed as if it wanted to taunt her, too.

"And that, my friends, is a pity."

The room quieted, and Celeste wondered if Roy was winking or nodding at the others in her presence. Rising to her feet, she refused to give it another thought.

"Shall we go? Don't want to be late," she suggested, moving toward the front door.

"Thanks for the coffee," Roy said behind her as she stepped onto the porch, her hand connecting with the step rail. Her unoccupied hand instinctively gripped her dress and pulled it into her fist, keeping it free of her boots. Her soles touched the grass below the steps about the same time Roy began whistling. In an instant, the cheery tone put her at ease. Made her feel comfortable. Brought back the familiar.

He pulled open the passenger door of the truck and took her hand, waiting until she stepped up before he released her. With a deep breath, she smoothed the fabric of her dress against her knees.

"What did she look like?" she asked, the words tumbling from her lips even though she'd been nearly determined to keep them locked inside her head.

Roy paused at the open door of the truck. "Who, kiddo?"

"The girl yesterday who tried to set me free. Emily."

"Oh. I suppose she . . ." The sandpaper-scratching noise could only come from him rubbing the side of his beard. "She looked like a little girl. Brown hair in a braid. Kind of a rough and tumble sort."

Rough and tumble. Something about that description made her heart happy. "Yes, I can almost see her in my mind. Thank you."

"You're not curious about the fella? Did you get a good look at him?"

Heat stole over Celeste's cheeks. "You know I didn't, other than he seemed very dark."

"Huh. I'd imagine that's on account of his beard."

"He had a beard?"

"Yes'm. Real dark, bordering on black, but his skin's almost as pale as yours. Handsome fella, probably close to six foot tall. Looked strong but kind of wiry. Kept smiling at you, so I know he has straight teeth."

She tilted her chin toward the interior of the truck. "Honestly, Roy. Straight teeth. I didn't ask you about the man, you know."

"No, you sure didn't."

The truck door closed on her right, and she schooled her features to remain impassive while he crossed to his side of the truck. The way people looked mattered next to nothing in her world. She could catch the odd glimpse of someone if she really tried hard enough, but she preferred to let her imagination paint the picture. Fashioning a beard onto her mental image of Doug Kirkland caused the beginning of a guilty smile, so she quickly pressed her lips together in the hopes of keeping her delight to herself.

Roy asked for two dollars like he had countless times every day that month, and while she feigned surprise with the fiddle clutched to her chest, her mind mentally reran yesterday's events in their entirety. The surprise when someone spoke up. Her shock at recognizing the voice. Her conversation with Emily, and Doug asking if he could talk to her again. It all felt otherworldly, like it had happened in a dream and she couldn't quite piece it together correctly.

She grinned and waved at the assembled crowd, then leaned her back against the porch post. John and the weatherman had been correct about the beautiful day. Seventy degrees with a light breeze, perfect for lounging outdoors.

Instead of moving into the interior of the cabin as he usually did, Roy stepped over to her end of the porch, calmly wrapping his fingers around her elbow as he leaned closer. "Your friend is back."

"Pardon me?"

"The bearded man. He watched that last portion and now he's waiting just beyond the way there. I think he's hoping to talk to you when I step out. Shall I stay?"

Her heart longed to seek him out, to stare in the direction where she thought he was waiting, but she resisted the urge. Trying to actually see him would make her look frantic or strange to any bystanders, and she didn't want to create the wrong impression.

"Should I be afraid of him, do you think?" she whispered, keeping her face tilted toward Roy.

"He looks harmless. But if you need me, yell."

Celeste nodded, resting her hand against the post as she lowered herself to a seated position on the top step, pulse hammering as she waited. Instead of staring off into the distance, she kept her gaze focused downward while she arranged her skirt against her boots. Any second he would be in front of her, that strange deep voice sending shivers up her spine.

No one appeared, so she forced calm into her nerves. Perhaps Roy had been wrong and he wasn't there at all. Or maybe he had seen her and changed his mind.

"Hi, Celeste. You probably don't remember me, I'm—"

"Doug." She grinned at the way her voice cut him off. "Did you fall asleep in the bushes and stay through the night?"

She felt the step settle a little as he sat beside her. "No. Emily and I were leaving the park last night and I was kicking myself that I hadn't found a way to talk to you again. Then there was this sign telling me to exchange my ticket for a season pass. So I did. And here I am."

"Hmm. No one's ever purchased a pass to see me before." Warmth began at the crown of her head and flooded down until it reached the pit of her stomach, making her look away from him lest he see evidence of it on her face. "A roller coaster maybe, but not a silly skit. What we do isn't even very original. Same thing every day, you know."

"Yeah, I caught the act a minute ago. I enjoyed it every bit as much as yesterday, except today nobody stomped on my foot ordering me to pay your bride price." He cleared his throat, and she pulled her gaze back to the front. "Emily likes to try to set things right with the world. It's a good trait."

"A wonderful trait." Celeste forced a deep breath, pressing the fabric of her dress between her fingers. "How old is your daughter?"

"Nine."

"And where is her mother?"

The pause that proceeded his words spoke louder than anything he could have said. "She lives local, but we're not together."

One tiny phrase that left so much up to interpretation, she dared not touch it. Instead, she focused on the banjo music coming from the speakers at the leather shop nearby where someone must have opened the front door.

"Have you always had this job?" Doug asked, bringing her attention back to the cabin porch. "I mean, doing the skit at the cabin?"

"No. When I started I was in the band for the Carlisle Sisters. They stopped playing here, so I moved to the cabin with Roy." Rising to her feet, she stretched her fingers out to her side. "I could do with a bit of exercise. Would you care to walk around the bend with me? As long as we're back in a few minutes Roy won't even notice I'm gone."

"Of course." His fingers touched hers only long enough to bring her hand up, tucking it in the crook of his arm. With her fingertips resting against his warm skin, she took in the gentle flex of his muscle as he helped her step down onto the asphalt. All it took was one step to confirm that she felt small and fragile hanging onto his arm. She wasn't entirely certain whether that was a good thing or a bad thing.

But she knew without a doubt it had nothing to do with whether he was handsome or not.

Chapter Six

"How are things with your fiddle player?"

Doug looked up from the spaghetti twisted around his fork to narrow his eyes at Willow. She sat across from him at the table twirling noodles around her own fork in wide-eyed innocence.

"I haven't seen my *friend* Celeste this week. They closed the park to get ready for Christmas."

Willow released a long sigh, the end of her blond-pink braid barely missing her plate. "Christmas there is probably magical. We should go, Clint."

Doug looked to the head of the table where his brother sat trying to eat the pasta without getting it in his beard. Definitely a losing battle.

"If you want to go you should ask mister season pass over here," Clint stated, inclining his head toward Doug. "Maybe he can get you a discount."

"I probably could get you a discount, but I'm not sure how I feel about Christmas this early in November. By the time the actual holiday rolls around it's all going to seem like overkill."

"Never." Willow pulled her hands together in front of her plate, settling her chin on them like she'd completely forgotten about her dinner and was about to tell a fairytale. "Imagine the wonder of the scene. The scents of peppermint and roasted chestnuts lingering in the air. Folksy Christmas hymns ringing out from violins and acoustic guitars. Lights skirting every building and tree in sight. Carolers with their period garb singing by flickering candlelight."

Doug cleared his throat as he plunged his fork into his spaghetti once more. "It's a theme park, not a Dickens novel."

"An immersive Dickens novel," Willow repeated, her eyes going all dreamy-like.

"Thanks for starting that," Clint muttered as he grabbed his garlic toast.

Willow turned her attention to her husband, but only held a smile for him despite his teasing words. "The first time Clint ever kissed me was on the Ferris wheel at the theme park. Of course I'm sure you've already told your brother all about that, so I don't know why I bother."

Doug stared at Clint just long enough to see the apples of his cheeks tint red before he returned his attention to Willow, who had transferred that unsettling smile to him.

"Have you asked her for a date yet? Your *friend* Celeste?"

Placing the fork on the table, Doug leaned back in his chair to illustrate the fact that Willow was interrupting his dinner. Not that she would care. "I'm not sure how I'm supposed to do that."

Willow's nose scrunched up as she stared at him. "How about . . . Hey, Celeste. What are you doing Saturday night? I'm attracted to you and I would like to get to know you better."

Doug faked a shiver before picking up his fork again. "Who would say something corny like that? Wait, don't tell me. That sounds like Clint."

"Don't be silly. Your brother wouldn't string that many words together." Willow tossed a wink in Clint's direction. "Why won't you ask her, though? It's obvious you like her, so don't give me a nutty excuse."

Releasing a sigh, Doug lifted his left hand to rub a palm over his eyebrows. "I've kind of sworn off dating, if you really want to know. And she's not like anyone I've ever dated before."

"Because she's blind?"

"It sounds horrible when you say it like that, but yes. Because she's blind. Do I offer to take her to a movie she can't see? Go to a restaurant where she can't read the menu?"

Willow's countenance changed to one of deep thought as she ignored her food. "I can see why that's a problem. Someone as unimaginative as yourself would have great difficulty thinking of something that didn't involve teenage dating rituals."

"I think she's insulting me," Doug muttered, glancing at Clint.

His brother gave a short laugh before looking at his plate. "Yeah, but I'm kind of enjoying it."

"Clint didn't ask me to go to a restaurant on our first date," Willow stated. "We went on a hike to a waterfall."

Doug's throat made a garbled noise that almost sounded like a grunt as he grabbed the bread from his plate. "If you're trying to hold out Clint as some kind of ideal date planner, you're wasting your breath."

"All I'm saying is to use your imagination." A mischievous grin tilted up Willow's lips. "You do have one of those, don't you?"

The knock on Doug's hotel room door in the middle of channel surfing paused the screen's scrolling on a Spanish language telenovela. The voices came through the speakers louder than he expected, bringing the lover's spat directly into his room. Widening his eyes, he pressed the power button. If Emily had her say, it would probably be flashing the bright colors of cartoons in a few minutes anyway.

Dragging in a deep breath, he crossed the few feet to the door and tugged it open, his eyes immediately locking with Ruth's. Hers narrowed in response.

Despite the sour expression, she looked pretty in her mauve T-shirt dress and sandals, although he knew better than to make a comment. She'd always been naturally attractive without bothering to try very hard—so different from the women he'd met at bars over the years. It was probably what had drawn him to her in the first place when they were both teenagers, although he'd been idiot enough at the time to use her and toss her off. Not that they were compatible enough to stay together—that was as clear now as it had been then—but he'd forced her to change her life and disappeared. And each day that went by he felt a little guiltier about it.

"Hi," he said as he pressed the door open a little wider. Emily slipped under his arm, her blue flannel pajamas dotted with a tiny dog bone pattern. A picture of a golden lab sat front and center on her chest, tongue out and the whole nine yards.

"Nice PJ's," he tossed over his shoulder to his daughter. She gave a cursory nod before settling on the bed, plopping her tablet on her lap.

His expression must have conveyed words he didn't say, because Ruth spoke up from the other side of the doorway.

"Gift from Willow and Clint on her birthday. I don't let her use it very often but she thought she'd be bored to death."

The little dig might have been meant to sting him, but it only made him chuckle. "It's a good possibility. Spending time with me is dreadful."

Ruth could have easily knocked that softball over his head, but instead she gave a sideways quirk of her mouth. The kind that said she was disappointed in him but not enough to actually argue it aloud.

"So. . ." His eyes swept across her gently waved hair before taking in the slight hint of blush on her cheeks. "Hot date tonight?"

If the quirk had demonstrated disappointment, the pursing of her lips was more indicative of a desire to strangle him. "My mom is taking me to some motivational talk about finding your purpose. Otherwise I would have had her watch Emily. And Willow and Clint had some prior engagement they couldn't get out of."

"Got it. I'm your last choice."

She didn't argue with his statement, instead fidgeting with the keys in her hand. "I'll be back to get her around ten."

"Sounds good."

With that Ruth turned and walked back to her car. Closing the door behind him, he shoved both hands in his pockets as he stared at the reason for his return to Gatlinburg. The fact that he'd been absent most of her life was never far from his mind, although it hadn't bothered him enough until he returned for Clint's wedding. Something about seeing his daughter so comfortable with his brother when he was a practical stranger had made him snap. Caused him to leave his career, his friends, a steady stream of money.

But he was here now. That might not ever be enough to make up for lost time, but it was a start.

"You hungry?" he asked, watching the way her tongue poked out the side of her lips as she stared at her tablet.

"We had dinner, but I could eat some chips."

"Chips," he repeated, glancing about the bare room.

"Or candy. Cake. I'm not picky."

Since his selection of junk food was nonexistent, he sat next to her on the bed. "What's keeping your attention on that tablet?"

"Willow Fairies." Dropping back, she flattened herself on the bed and held the tablet above her face. "Aunt

Willow paints them. She said she'd fill my whole bedroom with them, but Mom said we can't 'cause of the apartment rules."

Leaning against the headboard, he noticed the way her pale cheeks reflected the pink glow from the screen. "Yeah, apartments always have rules. Hotels, too." He hated to ask, but the memory of that little tree bark fairy forced his hand. "What are the fairies doing today?"

"Today?" She pressed her finger to the device to scroll back up. "Cap's staring at the forest."

"Staring at the forest?"

Without a word, she passed it to him. One exchanged glance was enough to convince him that she didn't realize he was Cap.

He knew eventually he would tire of playing the tune on his own, but Cap couldn't decide how to coax the songbird forward.

So that's how it was to be then. He supposed he should be grateful that Willow hadn't created a *Little House on the Prairie* fairy for Cap to chase. In the bizarre little planet she was creating, that would have been a thousand times worse.

"So . . . you want to play a game or something?" Doug asked, handing the device back to Emily. She calmly shook her head, diverting her attention from him. Puffing air into his cheeks, he searched his brain for possibilities. "Go somewhere? Watch TV?"

"No." The short word was followed by a stifling silence, probably designed to shut him out. At least, it appeared that way. Reading Emily was still new enough that he hadn't quite figured out her quirks.

With a shrug, he picked up his phone and stared at the search bar, giving Emily the space she wanted as his redheaded friend filled his thoughts instead. Despite what Willow had said, he had an imagination. Right now it was designing all sorts of ways that Celeste could refuse him. Laugh at him. Tell him he was a stalker.

A little guidance would be nice. Maybe from someone who had walked in his shoes, or even someone on the other end of the equation who could give him some pointers.

"Dating a blind person?" Emily's voice sliced straight through his thoughts until it seemed to hit him square between the eyes, which were guiltily staring at those words he'd typed into his search bar.

With a flick of his wrist, he powered off his phone screen. "What are you doing, spying on me?"

"Looking to see if your Wi-Fi was working," she answered, crossing her arms over her chest. "Sometimes the girls on my bus look up dumb dating tips too."

The sassy tilt of her posture after that statement did something funny inside his gut. "How old are these girls?"

Her eyes widened a bit as she obviously realized the reason for his question. "Not my age. A grade or two ahead of me."

"Dear God, help us all," he muttered, dropping the phone on the bedspread. Leaning back against the pillows, he copied her posture by folding his arms over his chest. "You're not allowed to date until you're nineteen."

One corner of her lips crept up as she fought to keep them pressed together. "You're easier than Mom. She says thirty-five."

"Thirty-five then, I'm siding with your mother."

Her eyes narrowed just a smidge. "You're not thirty-five."

He couldn't help but laugh at that. "Well played, Em. Twenty-five then. I'll give a little."

She kicked back to a flat position, staring at the ceiling. His eyes naturally followed to that same spot, studying the speckled texture of the off-white tiles.

"Is this about the lady whose dad was trying to sell her?"

"Celeste." Saying her name aloud only brought Ruth's fidgeting at the door back to his mind. "Forget you saw that and let's change the subject. This thing your mom's going to tonight, was she excited about it?"

The slight wrinkling of her nose was enough of an answer. "I don't think so. Just trying to make grandma get off her case." She lifted her hand to her mouth, sliding the fingernail of her index finger between her teeth. "She gets sad sometimes, but she doesn't think I notice."

The level of guilt he felt at those words was unexpected. "Me being back here is the right thing, but I'm sure it's not easy for your mom."

"Oh, she don't care about you."

Her blunt words caused a laugh to slip from his lips. "That's nice to know."

"I just mean that I know the whole deal. Mom told me the only good thing that could come out of her and you together was me, and since that's done it's best to leave it alone."

A little smile formed at the corners of his mouth. "If that's her explanation, I won't argue with it. And you're a pretty awesome kid, if I do say so myself." Her words also made him respect Ruth even more. Had he been in her situation, he probably would have filled Emily with poison toward the vacant party in the relationship. The fact that she hadn't done so meant she was a way bigger person than he had been. Hopefully he could live up to her example from here on out.

"She seems nice," Emily said.

"Your mom?"

"No, Celeste. She dresses weird, but that's probably her job. And it's not her fault that she's blind."

That statement didn't seem to request a response, so he pressed his lips together and stared at the picture on the wall across from him. Cheap representation of the Smoky Mountains.

"Last year in Sunday school we had this craft we were making for Father's Day. Mrs. Rayford made a big deal about letting me do another craft since you weren't around. It was embarrassing."

His heart pinched right along with the corners of his eyes. "I'm sorry about that, Em. I really am."

She turned her head against the bedspread, causing her braid to stick out to the side. "The year before that, Miss Dana was our teacher and she didn't say nothing about it. Just gave me the craft like the other kids."

"Yeah? What did you do?"

"Colored it and gave it to Grandpa. Sometimes it's annoying having people remind you about what's different. It's nice when they forget and treat you just like everyone else."

A genuine smile spread across his cheeks. He doubted he could have received a better sermon had he been sitting in a church pew.

"You're a pretty smart cookie, you know that?" Reaching out, he poked her in the side.

She wiggled away, sticking out her tongue. "Yep. I got that from Mom's side."

Chapter Seven

"You look different today. I was beginning to think you only had one outfit."

The little tingle of delight Celeste felt at hearing Doug's voice was familiar, but the sense of relief was new. She hadn't been near him in over a week, and part of her had been worried he might forget she existed.

"One isn't allowed to wear ordinary clothes at Christmas," she said, hugging the fiddle against her chest. The dress she wore wasn't so unusual compared to her normal uniform, other than the fact that it was hemmed with a strip of velvet and she wore a cape trimmed with white fur.

A lull fell over their conversation, and she dropped her chin to avoid his inspection, if indeed he was studying her. "You're unusually quiet," she finally said.

"I was just wondering why no one had bothered telling me about the Christmas clothes rule before."

"Perhaps they were afraid of being honest with you." She couldn't resist the urge to smile, tipping her chin up in the process.

"You think so? Am I so frightening?"

"You did tell me you weren't sure how you felt about Christmas."

"Early Christmas," he corrected. "It's still the beginning of November."

She brought the fiddle up to her shoulder, then lifted her bow to play a line of "You're a Mean One, Mr. Grinch." After her bow stilled, she allowed her eyebrows to inch up while he laughed.

"Careful, Celeste. You might slip out of character."

"Heaven forbid." She tucked the fiddle under her arm, like her ever-present shield. "Have you sampled the wassail or tried some roasted chestnuts?"

"I parked my truck and walked straight up to your front porch."

A flush stole over her cheeks at the blunt statement. "Whatever for?"

"Because I enjoy your company and I'd like to ask you to go to dinner with me."

"At the park?"

"The park?" The sound of his boot connecting with the first porch step announced the fact that he had moved closer. "No, I'd like to pick you up at your house and take you to a restaurant."

The muted sound of "It Came Upon a Midnight Clear" sang over the speaker nearby on acoustic guitar, the sole thing she could hear over the sound of her own heartbeat hammering against her ribs. She'd been to a restaurant only a handful of times, usually on someone's birthday. Most recently it had been Ava's, and she'd taken off work special so they could go early. No one outside of her adopted family had ever taken her to dine in public.

"If your answer is no, I understand," Doug added.

She lifted her gaze to him, the suddenness of her movement bringing a brief glimpse of dark hair. "My answer is yes. Thank you for asking." She swallowed, lifting her free hand to the ties of the cape around her neck. "When should I expect you?"

"Any day or time you like."

Pressing her lips together, she offered a nod. "I should be home around six-thirty tomorrow night."

He paused for only a second. "Tomorrow then. I'll pick you up at seven."

The driveway came into view, two grooves of dirt through the weeds that had grown up on either side. A lower string of weeds littered the center, probably beaten down by continually greeting the bottom of a car. Turning his truck onto the driveway brought the house into sight—dark brown siding that made it seem to melt into the night sky. The only things saving it from completely fading were the pole light several feet away and the porch light above the door, shining like a beacon. A trail of smoke rose above the chimney where it seemed to disappear into the air. The house was small, though certainly bigger than the hotel room he currently occupied.

Stepping out onto the grass, he let his gaze drift over the two vehicles in front of the house. One low-sitting car as he'd imagined, probably fifteen years old, and a pickup with an even older model year than the car. A marked contrast to his big shiny truck, the latest variety with all the gadgets and gizmos inside to make him comfortable. He'd never stopped to think about her circumstance before, somehow always tripping over the mental image he had of her inside that century-old cabin. Of course that wasn't her real existence, but she'd fit there. Strangely, this vibe fit her, too.

The sneaking suspicion that his fancy truck wouldn't fit followed him up the porch steps. Sucking in a deep breath, he knocked on the metal frame of the screen door and then took a step back. A few seconds passed before the doorknob creaked, the white-painted wooden door swinging inward. The man on the other side looked far too old to be Celeste's father, the grooves in his forehead unmoving as he lifted a pair of bushy eyebrows.

"Hello," Doug said when the man didn't make a move to push open the screen door. "I was looking for Celeste. Do I have the wrong house?"

"No, you have the right place." Clicking the lock on the screen door, the man gave it a push. "Come on in."

Pressing the metal frame back so he could step over the threshold, Doug extended his hand. "I'm Doug Kirkland. Celeste and I met at the park."

"John Huckabee," the older man said before gesturing to the slight woman sitting on the couch. "My wife, Ava."

Doug stepped forward to offer his hand to her as well, and she unwrapped the afghan from her shoulders to accept the handshake.

"Nice to meet you," she stated, removing her chilled fingers from his. "I'm sure Celeste will only be a minute."

"Thank you." He stood in the middle of the room, drumming his fingers against his jeans. "I almost missed the driveway, the way you're tucked away in the trees. It's quiet here."

"Yes, thank goodness." John dropped his gnarled hands to the arms of the recliner before he sat. "There's something to be said for quiet amongst all today's noise."

Nodding his understanding, Doug glanced at Ava again, who offered a timid smile. "Celeste said you have a daughter?"

"Yes ma'am, Emily's nine."

John gave a soft grunt. "She's a very special young woman, Celeste. I trust you have good intentions."

"John!" Ava's voice was quiet but firm, silencing her husband as Doug widened his eyes, ready to give an affirmative response. Instead, he was cut short by Celeste's sudden appearance at the entrance to the hallway between the living room and kitchen.

"You found us," she said, gliding toward him like she was skimming water instead of walking across the carpet.

Her white dress was flowy and reached halfway down her calves, topped off with a dark pink cardigan. "I was worried you might not."

"No need to worry. You gave excellent directions."

Ava hid a smile, almost like she knew he was telling a fib. Celeste's directions had been pretty horrendous, but the map on his phone had filled in the blanks when he typed the address.

"Good night," Celeste said to the room without turning her face toward anyone in particular. "Should I lock the door when I come back, or will you wait up for me?"

John cleared his throat before answering. "I suppose you can lock up, but remember that you have to work tomorrow."

"Oh, John. She hasn't abandoned her scruples." Ava tilted her head as she gazed at Celeste. "Have a nice time."

"I'll have her back early," Doug felt the need to add as he pushed open the screen door. Celeste stepped out onto the porch in front of him, waiting while he pulled the door closed. He paused as he let his eyes graze over the sweater showcasing her thin arms, the large loops of her braid resting on her shoulder.

"I hope what I'm wearing is okay," she said, standing at the front of the porch near the steps. "Ava helped me pick out my clothes but she wasn't sure what would be appropriate."

"You look . . ." A thousand words seemed to lodge in the back of his throat. "Nice." Squeezing his eyes closed, he shook his head. Nice?

"That's a relief." She extended her left hand, letting it rest in the air between them. "Shall we go?"

With a step forward, he tucked her hand into the crook of his arm.

The hostess settled them into an oversized booth in the dimly lit room, several tables away from the nearest couple in the quiet restaurant. Sitting across from her, he waited as the menus were placed on the table and they were asked what they'd like to drink. He answered quickly, content to study her instead of the menu. She looked like she'd been pulled straight out of that Disney movie Emily had been watching the other night. The name escaped him, but the cartoon woman had popped through a manhole into the real world, all wide-eyed and dressed like she belonged in another dimension. If Celeste weren't wearing that sweater over her dress and had a couple of wildflowers tucked into her braid, she'd fit right into such a storyline. A chipmunk could wander up any second and start prattling away in her ear.

"You seem very far away," she stated, dragging him out of his mental picture.

"Sorry. Lost in my thoughts."

A little smile marked her lips. "No, I meant you seem to be a great distance from me. How big is this table?"

He glanced at the tabletop, his eyebrows inching together. "Maybe three feet, a little over. I could join you on that side if you like."

"Would you mind terribly?"

Would he mind terribly? He couldn't help but smile even as the gut-check hit his conscience. She seemed so innocent. Almost too innocent to be out in public with a man like him.

"No, I don't mind," he said, rising and moving to the spot next to her. Instead of looking at her profile, he picked up the menu and popped it open. "There's a menu on the table. Do you want me to—"

"Choose for me. I enjoy trying new things."

"Really? Is there any food you don't like?" He willed himself not to peek at her while he tried not to notice the light vanilla scent drifting from her side of the bench.

"Not especially." She paused, but then her fingers grazed his elbow. "Oh, except cow tongue. I don't like that at all."

"No?"

"No, although I suspect it's less from the taste and more from the idea. Ava insists that I wouldn't have even known had she not told me, which is probably true. I might have eaten tongue hundreds of times over and been none the wiser, but I don't like to think of it."

A chuckle slipped out and he glanced at her beside him, the dimness of the room somehow highlighting the faded freckles on the bridge of her nose. "I doubt they serve that here. Do you like pizza?"

"That sounds lovely. I haven't had it in ages."

He nodded before letting out a sigh. Of course she wouldn't see his reaction, so he'd have to say something instead. That thought brought a wry grin to his lips. Thank goodness she had the correct Kirkland brother by her side. If Clint had been the one with Celeste, she'd never have any idea what was going on.

Nervous energy had made her warm enough that she took off her sweater moments before, but she could still feel the heat emanating from Doug's arm next to her. He seemed bigger sitting beside her than he usually did standing with her, so she tried to sit as straight as possible so she wouldn't disappear into the vinyl seat.

"So . . ." He drew in a noisy breath beside her, causing her attention to perk up. "I'm curious to know about your . . . history."

"History?"

"Yeah, where you grew up, what you were like as a kid, things that might have happened to you."

"You're curious about my eyesight."

The lengthy pause told her she'd hit the nail on the head. "That too, I suppose."

She ran a finger along the edge of the cloth napkin in her lap. "I have a genetic condition that gives me a very limited field of vision. It's something like looking through a fogged-up window, according to what I've been told. On good days there's a little spot of clarity, but I have to move my eyes around to try to get the big picture. It's hard to do without looking a little frantic."

"So you can see?"

"Very fuzzy, but yes. Bright colors are better. If there's too much going on, trying to focus gives me a headache."

He cleared his throat, tapping a finger against the table. Rather than wait for him to say something, she turned her chin slightly in his direction.

"Please don't worry about the menu. I wouldn't have been able to see it with the dim light anyway. Things are very hazy to me in here."

"And your eyesight has always been this way?"

"Not always, but as long as I can remember." That familiar chill crawled over her arms, the one she got every time she started to fret about the fact that she was different. Instead of continuing the line of conversation, she reached out until her fingers came in light contact with her glass of water. "You've never told me about your relationship with Emily's mom."

The seat moved beneath her, a physical sign of his shifting beside her if she hadn't heard the movement.

"There's not a lot to tell. She was my girlfriend in high school, and I was a Class A jerk. I'm sorry to say I've only recently been part of Emily's life. More than a child support check, anyway."

"Oh. Because you were working on the oil rig?"

"Because I chose to work on the oil rig, yes."

She tapped the tip of her fingernail against the water glass. "I'm very sorry, Doug."

He cleared his throat before answering. "Sorry?"

"Yes. Emily seems like a wonderful girl. You've missed so much of her life. Cheated yourself out of her early memories."

"You've cut right to the heart of it, haven't you? I don't feel I should be pitied. Scorned maybe." He let out another noisy breath in a huff, instantly making her wonder if most people were so dramatic and she simply never got close enough to notice. "Enough about me. How are you related to John and Ava?"

"John is Pete's brother." Wrinkling her nose, she tilted her chin down. "It's a long story."

"I have all the time in the world."

She turned her head so she could look up at his face, a blur of cream and shadow sitting this close. "When I was seven, I was placed with Pete and Mary Huckabee. That was the best thing that ever happened to me—I couldn't have asked for kinder foster parents. When they passed away, Ava and John took me in."

Celeste knew the pizza was arriving before she heard the waiter's voice or the clank of the tray rattling against the table. A handful of scents seemed to war for her attention: tomato, garlic, basil, yeasty bread . . .

"Here you go, folks. Hot out of the oven so be careful."

Doug thanked the waiter, his rich voice a beautiful sound from her close vantage point. She let her eyes linger on him, hoping for a moment of clarity that continued to be elusive.

"He wasn't kidding about it being hot," Doug mumbled, pushing his plate back just a smidge. "Think I'm going to let mine rest a minute. I want to hear more about you anyway. What was life like with Pete and Mary?"

She rolled the idea around in her head for a few seconds. "A relief, I suppose. I'd bounced around so much, it felt like heaven to be in one place for so long. I didn't have to struggle in school, because Mary taught me at home. She was a retired schoolteacher, and I didn't mind being her special pet project."

"What did Pete do for a living?"

"Operated a tree farm north of here. He sold to greenhouses and landscaping businesses, but around Christmas we'd set up the little shack on the corner of the property with hot cocoa and Mary would sell her hand-crocheted ornaments when people picked out Christmas trees. Those were my favorite times."

"And who taught you to play the fiddle?"

"I taught myself. Music was my great equalizer back then. I didn't need to see the instrument to make it sing. Only had to feel it." A heavy silence descended over the table, bereft of any sighing or shifting. "Did I say something that bothered you?"

"Of course not. That was beautiful. I was just playing your words back in my head."

She couldn't hold back the smile that broke across her face. "Do you do that often? Play back words in your head?"

"No," he said, so quietly that she felt herself leaning a little closer. "Not often enough."

Chapter Eight

Bells jingled overhead—just the ordinary kind and not anything Christmas related—but they annoyed the dickens out of him just the same. Ignoring the sound, Doug pulled his stocking cap from his head and slid into the booth by the window. The glass had been painted with fake snow around the corners, although it didn't boast any Christmas messages yet. Probably because it was still a week until Thanksgiving, so blatantly switching to Christmas decorations was a faux pas.

At least, it should have been.

The scent of coffee permeated the air, with a faint hint of pumpkin spice. He distinctly remembered his time growing up in Gatlinburg as typical small-town happenings, games with his brother, home cooked meals with his parents. But his return had been like stepping into a fully-formed storybook universe. Willow's fairy occupation. Celeste's nonstop Christmas celebration. The café near his childhood home should have been safe and familiar, but even it seemed destined to jump into the fray, judging by the aura of fall floating in the air.

The distinct sound of tapping drew his attention up and to his right, where Jess stood rapping the end of her pen on her notepad. Her lips were scrunched up into what he could only imagine was a disgusted pout, causing the tiny wrinkles around her lips to fan out in a circle. "You here to cause trouble or you want something to drink?"

"Coffee," he said, tightening his fist around the stocking cap. "Why would I come in here to make trouble?"

"Exactly what I was asking myself," she stated as she stepped away.

He deserved that type of treatment. Absolutely deserved it, which made it a lot easier to take than the kind of trusting relationship he had with Celeste.

The coffee mug hit the table so hard, a little of the dark liquid sloshed over the side. He didn't have to look up, because Ruth slid into the other side of the booth, dropping her crossword puzzle to the table underneath her note pad. Before she said a word, she grabbed a napkin and wiped up the spilled coffee. He had to smile at that one. She'd never been able to abide a mess long, even if she were the one to make it.

"Is something the matter?" she asked, her light eyes flashing even though her face remained impassive.

"Other than the fact that you threw coffee at me?" He lifted an eyebrow in her direction, but her expression didn't change. "No, nothing's the matter. A friend of mine has invited me to Thanksgiving dinner, and I'd like to take Emily. If it's okay with you."

"The woman you're dating from the theme park?"

Setting the cap beside him on the seat, he wrapped both his hands around the coffee cup. "Her name is Celeste, and we're not dating. We're friends."

Ruth stared down at the newspaper with the crossword puzzle partway finished. "You can be honest with me, Doug. I know about you Googling dating a blind person. Emily's not exactly a great secret keeper."

That tidbit of information about Emily might have been useful a couple of weeks ago. "I thought about dating her, but I'm pretty sure I would corrupt everything good about her. So we're friends. How's that for honest?"

"It could be the most honest thing I've ever heard you say."

Trying to roll the tension from his shoulders, he picked up the coffee and took a sip, staring through the sprayed fog on the window. With a jolt, it made him think of

Celeste and how she'd explained her eyesight a couple of weeks before. Seeing through a fogged-up window.

"My mom has Thanksgiving at noon, so if it's that evening, I don't see why Emily couldn't go." Ruth settled both of her wrists on the tabletop. "Have you thought any more about getting an apartment? It's odd you being at the hotel so long. And it doesn't help if you're trying to convince Em that you're here for the long haul."

"I've given it some thought, but haven't decided yet. Not about leaving, just about where to live."

"And what about a job?"

He resettled the mug on the table. "Right now I'm still cutting wood. Reimagining my entire life has proven a challenge."

"Yes, well try doing that at seventeen."

Doug allowed himself a good long look at Ruth, taking in the high tilt of her cheekbones and her pale blue eyes. He remembered the way the guys used to talk about her back in high school, like she was the end all. Sixteen-year-old Ruth wouldn't have imagined her life like this. He couldn't even remember what she had been passionate about back then. Showing off in English class when she knew all the big words, maybe. Parading around in her cheerleader uniform.

"I've done a lot of things I'm not proud of, and I want you to know I'm sorry."

The corner of her mouth tilted up as she stared down at her hands. "We both made mistakes back then. Yours might have been a bit more egregious, granted, but we have Emily. I wouldn't take back any mistake in the world if it meant not having Em."

Words evaded him, so he nodded instead. He wouldn't trade Emily either, now that he was part of her life. And regret over missing so much time with her would eat him alive if he let it.

"You've changed," Ruth whispered, barely audible above the din of customers talking in the background.

A sigh escaped as he nodded, glancing across the room at the bar stools facing the kitchen. "Not enough, but I'm trying to."

No noise filled the cab of the truck, except the sound of the tires vibrating on the asphalt beneath them. Emily had switched the radio to a station that played nothing but Christmas music. He'd turned it off on the way to the Huckabee place, unable to take another second of "Rockin' Around the Christmas Tree." Now he wished there was something other than the silence, but he was hesitant to turn the radio back on, lest he find a song even more obnoxious than the ones he'd heard before.

"The pie was really good," he said before pressing his lips together, keeping his focus out the dark windshield on the white and yellow lines directing his path.

"I don't like sweet potatoes." Emily drew her feet up to plant them on the seat, hugging her knees to her chest. "I liked the hot rolls though. Ava makes them just like the lunch ladies at school."

He couldn't help but raise his eyebrows at that statement. Usually school lunch and praise didn't tend to go hand in hand. "They seem nice, the Huckabees. And the Cobles. From what Celeste said, they always invite Roy and Elizabeth because they don't have any family around here."

"Yeah, I guess. It was weird to have him being so nice to Celeste after I saw him try to sell her." Emily gave Doug a pointed stare. "Don't tell me it was just play acting, 'cause I know that. It's still weird."

With a smile, he turned the radio on so it was barely registering a notch above the road noise.

"Celeste's grandma kept telling me how nice you were to give them wood to burn," Emily continued. "She acted like that's all you did all week was stack wood around their house."

"Ava's not her grandma, and I had some extra wood, that's all. I brought it over in my spare time, so there was no need to make a big deal about it."

"You should have told her not to be making a big deal then. She acts all excited about you like you're Justin Bieber."

Narrowing his eyes, he turned the radio up a little louder. "I'm definitely not Justin Bieber, and I'd appreciate it if you'd never say that again."

"No. You're older."

The mischievous grin she shot his way told him she was trying to goad him. "Watch it, little miss."

"And you can't sing. I've heard you."

He chuckled as he looked in her direction. "Now you're hitting a sore spot. Got anything else before I drown you out with 'Blue Christmas'?" He placed his hand on the radio knob, poised to crank the music up.

"Yep. You're way beardier."

Chapter Nine

The first thing Celeste did after she stepped over the threshold was take a huge breath, closing her eyes as she inhaled the scents in the air.

"Pine and neglect," she decided. "A little musty. Wouldn't hurt to air the place out."

"I need to prop the windows open one of these days." The sound of Doug's footsteps came closer until he stopped behind her. "It's not very big, but it will work for now. At least Emily can come over and play in the yard without me worrying about her being in a parking lot or wandering into the street. And I'm sure it will make Ruth feel better about leaving her with me."

With her eyes still closed, Celeste wrapped her arms across her chest, hugging her sweater closer to her sides. "You need a Christmas tree, that will make it homey. Maybe Emily could pick it out."

He groaned, the closeness of the sound letting her know he stood right behind her. "Can't we have one conversation without being bombarded by Christmas? It's barely December."

It made her feel slightly off balance, the way the timbre of his voice filled her with delight. She'd never been this close to someone of the opposite sex, so emotionally open with anyone who didn't live in her home. But he wasn't interested in her the way a man was interested in a woman, and she forced her mind to come to grips with that fact once again even though her heart went skating off in its own direction.

"I'll try to rein myself in," she said, opening her eyes to reveal a bright shaft of light coming in through a window to her left. "You have a lot of natural light in here. Are you sure you'll be comfortable with that?"

"What? Why wouldn't I want light to come in?"

"Those restaurants we go to are always so dark, that's all. I thought maybe you liked that."

He stepped past her, the whoosh of sound to her right letting her know that he'd shoved the window up. The cool breeze that followed would have confirmed it even without the sound. "Most quiet restaurants aren't lit up like the sun. Maybe fast food or kid-friendly places. If that suits you better, all you have to do is say so."

"I wouldn't say I'm in a position to say what suits me, really. Everything suits me, you know." She pulled her gaze to the window to her right, where she could see the light outside the space but it wasn't cascading into the room like from the other side of the house. "I don't mind light one way or the other, except on the days when it gives me a headache. Today I feel lovely."

"Hmm. Well, I'm glad about that."

The shirt he was wearing seemed gray—definitely not yellow like the one he'd been wearing yesterday. She trained her eyes somewhere in the area of his abdomen, a splotch of silver leading up to a darker shade. Her gaze darted up, a momentary flicker of clarity between her eyes and her brain. A shock of dark hair, not combed over neatly but sort of messy in the front. Slender face leading down to a short, trimmed beard.

She heard the hitch in her breath before she felt it, bringing her fist up to stifle a cough. Within seconds he was at her side, his fingers brushing her elbow.

"Everything okay?"

No, everything was not okay. Every time he was near her something inside woke up, and it was beginning to feel like torture. Being next to him but not being able to touch him. Always waiting for his move but not feeling like she could reach out first. It was like being the faithful sidekick in those Hallmark movies Ava was always watching. She was in the friend zone. The friend never got the guy. She was the one in the background making him comfortable and giving him the courage to go find the woman he wanted.

She didn't want to make Doug comfortable.

Right?

"Um, yes. Everything's okay."

"Good. You scared me for a second." He stepped away, his boots tapping out a rhythm on the hardwood floor. "The landlord said the oven is on the fritz, but I'm not much of an oven user anyway, so I told her it was no big deal. As long as the microwave works, I'm good to go. Hot shower, warm bed, can't really ask for more than that. Are you sure you're okay? You're making a face."

"Am I? I hadn't noticed."

"You are. A scrunched-up face like you smell something bad. Does the house stink?"

"No."

The volume of his voice dropped. "Is it me?"

She fought the urge to smile at the defeated sound of his tone. "I'm not sure I would tell you if it was."

"You're kidding, right? I think you owe me that much as a friend, to tell me if I stink."

She let that statement run through her brain a few times. He *was* her friend, no matter what she wanted or didn't want from the relationship. "You're right. As your friend, I would tell you. But you don't stink."

"You're sure?"

"Very sure." She took a step across the empty room in the direction of the window, feeling the instant warmth across her arm when the sun's rays touched her. "You know, there aren't many things that can physically touch you without actually doing so. The sun. The wind. I feel the heat off the sun just as easily as if it were reaching out and sweeping its fingers down my arm."

Doug cleared his throat as he stepped up behind her again. "First of all, if the sun were close enough to touch it would probably burn you alive. Second, I doubt it has fingers." He traced his fingertips down the back of her head, brushing aside her hair. Despite the sun's warmth, it caused a shiver.

"I was being philosophical," she said, stepping away from him. "Your Christmas tree could go right over here in this corner."

He let out an exasperated laugh, just as she expected. "Fine, Lady Christmas. I actually do have a holiday-related question for you, but don't get too excited."

She smiled as she placed her palm against the wood-paneled wall. "I'm all ears."

"I'm having a hard time figuring out what to get Emily for Christmas."

Reaching her hand out until she felt the sun's rays on her skin again, she tilted her head to the side. "What have you thought of so far?"

"Getting her a dog, although that would irritate Ruth, and I don't know whether they can have dogs in their apartment." He crossed the room and pushed the open window back down. "But what do you think about getting a dog that would stay over here?"

She pulled her hand back, placing it against her heart. "I have no doubt Emily would love a dog, but what if it causes problems? If Ruth can't have a dog, Emily might fight with her mom about coming over here because of the dog. You don't want that, do you?"

"I hadn't thought of that."

"And if you get a dog, you should only do that if you're ready to take care of it yourself. Dogs are a lot of work."

"Ugh, you're such a buzzkill. Here I thought I had a great idea."

She grinned as she focused on him once more, only a haze of gray. "No one's ever called me a buzzkill before. Keep thinking. I'm sure you'll come up with a perfect gift."

"I will, because you're going to help me."

"Me?" His fingers caught hers, gently pulling her back into the sunshine. "I don't know how much help I'll be in finding gifts."

"We should discuss it tonight in the truck."

"In the truck?" she asked, scared to move lest he release her hand. "Are we going somewhere?"

He paused for a moment, in one of those instances where she desperately wished she could see his facial expression. "Would you like to go to the movies with me?"

The excitement built inside her so quickly that she giggled before she could tamp it down. "The movies? Would I ever."

He was definitely losing his mind. First he'd dressed in a button-up shirt, all tucked into his jeans. Then he'd practically bathed himself in cologne, regretting it so much that he spent at least five minutes trying to rub it from his skin with a hand towel. To top it off, he'd listened to Emily's Christmas station the entire way to Celeste's place, not even realizing what was happening. It wasn't until Celeste was firmly in position on the passenger side humming along with "God Rest Ye Merry Gentlemen" that he realized the error of his ways.

Heaven help him, he couldn't keep this up much longer. Hanging out with her, talking about how they were friends. Eating next to her while that vanilla scent she always carried clouded his brain. Seeing her sitting daintily on the other side of the truck like she belonged there. Witnessing her sheer joy at the thought of going to the movies.

"I haven't been to the movies in ages," she said, clutching her hands together in her lap. "Thank you for asking me."

He let his eyes linger on her appearance for a minute—her black jeans and oversized raspberry colored sweater. Her hair wasn't held back in a braid tonight, but rolled over her shoulders and cascaded halfway to her elbows. Falling across her face like it did, she seemed to hold an air of mystery she didn't normally possess when it was pulled away from her features.

"I hesitated to ask, because I wasn't sure you'd enjoy it," he finally said, pulling his gaze back to the road. "As usual, you're full of surprises."

"Is that a good thing or a bad thing?"

He chose not to answer, shaking his head as he turned on his blinker. "What's your favorite Christmas song?"

"Traditional or on the radio?"

His eyebrows drew together as he pulled into the parking lot. "I don't know—radio I guess."

"That version of 'Carol of the Bells' with the electric guitars and the drums."

Shifting into park, Doug let his hand rest on the steering wheel. "No kidding? I would have thought that one was a little brash for your tastes."

"Brash." She looked in his direction, the wispy strands of hair around her face highlighted in the glow from the parking lot pole light. "Some of the first songs I learned on the fiddle were what I suppose you'd call brash. AC/DC. Metallica. The people I lived with when I was given the hand-me-down fiddle were borderline metal heads."

"What happened with them? The metal heads?"

"I wasn't with them long. They didn't talk to me much, but they fed me and kept me safe, so I couldn't complain."

"And after them?"

She sobered a bit, but somehow still managed to look happy. "Like I've told you before, I bounced around. People weren't really sure what to do with me, until I found Pete and Mary." The somberness slid from her tone, replaced with a bouncy lilt. "Are we going to the movie or what?"

Celeste popped another piece of popcorn into her mouth, unable to keep the grin from her face. The seat was cushiony and creaked when she moved too much, the popcorn was nice and buttery, and Doug's shoulder was touching hers above the armrest. The announcer's voice coming through the speakers was deep and dramatic, dragging her right into the action like she was one of the passengers on the train about to derail.

Leaning close to Doug, she tapped him on the arm. "Will you tell me what's happening?" she whispered, her bottom lip accidentally touching his hair.

"The whole movie?"

She nodded, resuming her place on her seat. His arm next to her shifted, then slid behind her neck, his hand settling on her shoulder.

"Okay, but I'll have to be quiet or they'll kick us out," he whispered, his nearness almost causing her to jump.

Forcing a deep breath, she nodded again, fighting the urge to snuggle against him. He stayed close, his arm wrapped around her shoulders. Minutes crept by, giving details about movies that would release soon. She couldn't focus on them, instead mesmerized by the sensation of his arm touching her back. The faint scent of cologne clinging to his neck.

"She's watching the car pull away from the house," he whispered, his beard touching her cheek. "Something's wrong, though. She's either sad or angry, it's difficult to tell from her facial expression."

The images flashed on the screen, but rather than focus on the haze, she closed her eyes.

"He just stepped through the door, and he's checking the watch he pulled from his pocket. He's nervous about something."

Celeste let herself get pulled into the sensations around her, and time passed so quickly the movie was almost over as soon as it started. The soft tone of Doug's voice explaining the actions on the screen. The actors' lines playing against the musical scores. The gentle sniffling of someone behind them who was either overcome with emotion or had the beginnings of a cold.

"She sees him. He's walking across the street in the direction of her building, and she's staring out the window. Her breath fogged up the glass, so she wiped it with her fingers. Now she's holding her fingers against the glass, like she could reach through it and touch him. He just looked up to see her there, but she pulled away from the window. Now he stopped walking and he's staring at the ground, like he doesn't know what to do." Doug straightened in his seat. "Oh, she just threw open the door and she's running at him."

Celeste nearly let out a sigh as a contented smile slipped onto her face.

"He's kissing her," Doug said, gently clearing his throat.

"I know."

He leaned even closer. "How did you know?"

"Just a feeling," she muttered, opening her eyes and focusing on the now-dark screen. "That was beautiful."

People shuffled by, the squeaks of their seats popping back into place echoed by her own when she rose to her feet. Her fingers came to rest on the seat back in front of her while Doug picked up the bag of popcorn that he'd placed on the floor.

"You ready?" he asked, his voice no longer a whisper.

Turning to face him, she offered a smile. "Yes, I'm ready."

His fingers hooked on the crook of her elbow, gently leading her from the row of seats into the aisle. Something bumped her from behind, and she pressed closer to him, grasping his arm so she wouldn't be separated. The exit from the room was easy to detect when she stepped into the bright hallway, red carpet leading as far as her eye could see.

"I can't remember when I've had such fun," she said, clasping both her hands around his arm. "I do hope they live happily ever after."

"That's pretty much the point of those types of movies, I think."

"Well, if you ask me, you should be in movies. You did a fantastic job narrating the story."

Doug pushed the door open, a gust of cool wind hitting her in the face and blowing her hair away from her cheeks. "You think so? 'Cause I gotta tell you, it made me feel a little bit . . ." He hesitated, causing her brain to begin firing off a dozen endings to his statement.

"Self-conscious," he finally finished. "I'm not a man of few words like Clint, but even I don't like to hear myself talk that much."

"That's a shame. I could listen to you talk for hours."

He stopped walking, nearly causing her to step into him. Without the movie crowd pressing against them, it felt silly to continue to hang onto his arm with both hands. She didn't release him though, her fingers wrapping his muscle beneath the shirt he wore.

She waited for him to open the truck door, but instead she felt the gentle brush of his beard against her skin, then the sensation of his lips against her cheek. Her eyelids fluttered almost like a replica of her pulse in her wrist, but she struggled to keep her breath calm as he hovered so close to her.

"Thank you for going to the movies with me," he said, taking her hand from his arm and lifting it, his lips pressing to the back of her hand next. She found herself tilting her chin up in expectation, even though she didn't dare to dream he might kiss her.

The click of the truck door opening dashed her hopes, but the fact that her hand was still in his kept the movement from dampening her spirits. Friends didn't kiss each others' hands at the end of the night, did they? Friends didn't normally spend quite so much time together either—at least that's what she believed. Not being much of a dating expert, though, she could have been woefully wrong.

And the fact that she seemed incapable of having internal thoughts without writing them across her face left her no choice but to smile like an imbecile in hopes that he wouldn't notice. Turning, she climbed up into the truck, easing herself comfortably onto the seat.

"For the record," he added, "I can't remember when I've had this much fun, either."

The truck door closed, leaving her alone in the cab with nothing but her thoughts. Ava had warned her to be cautious with her heart, but sometimes that most willful of the organs had a tendency to rebel. Despite her best efforts, she knew she was falling in love with Doug Kirkland.

And if her face was in the habit of spilling her guts, she had no idea how she was going to keep it a secret.

Chapter Ten

"Can we go shopping?"

Doug shoved the remains of their fast food lunch off the tray into the garbage receptacle, then fixed his gaze on Emily. "Shopping? What kind of shopping?"

"I made a list." She shoved her fingers into the kangaroo pocket on the front of her sweatshirt and pulled out a sheet of notebook paper. "Just, you know . . . normal stuff."

"Normal stuff." He plucked the paper from her fingers. "Toothbrush and toothpaste. Hat and gloves." His eyes drifted to the hat on her head, with the bright pink puffy yarn ball on the top. "Socks women's size nine to eleven. Deodorant. Are you even old enough to wear deodorant?"

Her eyebrows inched up as she shot a nervous glance around the restaurant. "It's not for me."

That made more sense and less sense at the same time. Moving toward the exit, he shoved the door open and waited while she stepped outside. The sun had slipped behind the clouds and put a chill in the air that he hadn't noticed earlier when he'd been cutting wood. Although he might not have noticed anyway, given the physical exertion he'd been putting in.

"Are these things for your mom?" he tried again over the hood of the truck as Emily pulled the passenger door open. She shut herself inside the cab, so he had to climb inside before hearing her answer.

"Yes and no."

That was the kind of statement that made starting the truck a lot less appealing. Twisting in her direction, he draped his wrist over the steering wheel. "It seems like that deserves an explanation."

She made a great show of buckling her seatbelt, which he might not have noticed were he not used to harping on her about buckling up every time they got in the truck. "If I tell you, will you promise not to say anything to mom?"

"That's almost an unfair request until you tell me what it is, but I'll do my best."

She wrinkled her nose before picking at her cuticles. "Mom got one of the stars from the tree at church."

Pressing his lips together, he struggled to keep his patience. "Okay. And then what?"

"It's got someone's name and a list of things they need for Christmas."

"Well, that seems like a nice thing for your mom to do."

She nodded, peeking over at him, her eyebrows partially hidden beneath her hat. "Yeah, it's nice. But I heard Mom tell Grandma she wasn't sure how she was gonna pay for stuff this month."

A wave of understanding seemed to wash over him. "And you want me to pay some of your mom's bills."

"No, not Mom's. You're always spending money on me, so maybe you can just spend it on Star Twelve instead. I promise you I won't mind."

He took a moment to answer, studying the earnest expression on her face. Emily at nine was somehow light ages ahead of him in the compassion department. No question about it—Ruth had done an amazing job raising their daughter. For a split second he wondered if she would have been so incredible if he'd been around the entire time, but he quickly shook loose from that thought. It was no use living in the past or reimagining the present.

"We'll figure it out, kiddo." He started the truck's engine. "We'll figure it out."

"Thanks so much for having me over," Celeste stated for the third time, settling herself onto a chair at the dining room table. "I'm sure it was bothersome holding dinner on me until I got off work."

Willow placed the steaming bowl of pasta in the center of the table. "Of course not. Clint's accustomed to eating at odd times, since I get caught up in what I'm doing and forget what time it is. Besides, we've been eager to get to know you better."

A smile lit up Celeste's face even though she twisted her hands together in her lap like a picture of nervousness. "I couldn't help but notice you have a Christmas tree up already. Doug insists it's too early to decorate, even though it seems like we've already been geared up for the holidays at the park for ages."

"Don't let Doug's *bah humbug* attitude get in the way. To be honest, I'm surprised that you . . ." Willow glanced at Doug, her eyes finishing the statement she stopped. ". . . noticed the tree. What with all the decorations you normally have at the park, I mean."

Doug drew his eyes away from Willow and focused on Celeste instead, who kept her gaze drawn to the table as the smile slid to a more neutral expression. He knew from experience that she was reading volumes into Willow's moment of silence.

"It was hard to miss the blinking lights."

The inexplicable urge to rescue her surged through Doug's veins as he shifted in his seat, grabbing his napkin from the table. "Celeste can see certain things. Bright lights, vivid colors. Kind of like looking through a fogged-up window."

Celeste offered a quick nod. "Yes, sometimes I can see almost perfect, but usually in a tiny patch of my vision and only for a second or two."

"She must have never seen you, or she'd have run for the hills," Clint offered from his end of the table.

"Oh, I did see Doug once. Only for a second though." Her neck flushed pink, but instead of keeping his attention glued to her, Doug glared at Clint, who merely offered a shrug.

"Would you like some pasta?" Willow asked, digging a serving spoon into the dish as she awaited Celeste's response.

"Yes, please." Celeste paused briefly while Willow placed the food on her plate. "Doug tells me you paint fairies."

"Did he tell you that? I'm a little surprised, since he seemed so miffed that I painted him as a little tree bark-winged fairy captain."

Now it was Doug's turn to feel heat filling his veins. "I wouldn't say I was miffed, it's just a weird feeling's all. Clint told me he felt weird when you painted him into your drawings too."

"True, but Clint tends to avoid attention in general. You, on the other hand . . ." Willow offered a sweet smile, as though that would make her words less of a barb. "I wish you could see the paintings of little Cap, Celeste. He's so sweet with his gossamer wings and tiny muscles."

A laugh slipped from Celeste's lips as she picked up the fork beside her plate. "I can hardly bear the fact that I can't see him now. He sounds so darling. That seems like a life goal to me, to have oneself painted into Willow's fairy world. You should be proud, Doug."

"Should I?" He narrowed his eyes at Willow. "Would it bother you if Willow painted you into her fairy land?"

Celeste placed her fingers over her lips as she chewed a bite of her pasta. "No, not especially. But if she did paint me, I'd so desperately wish to see it."

The image of Cap sitting at the edge of the forest with the bird came flitting to Doug's mind, but he kept the information to himself as he piled some pasta on his plate. Maybe someday he'd tell Celeste that Willow had painted her, but for now, he'd keep the information in his hip pocket.

Clint headed across the yard to the detached garage, Doug one step behind. It hadn't been surprising at all to Doug when his brother announced that he was going outside. He could only handle so much idle chatter, and one extended dinner with someone he didn't know had probably set him over the edge.

"What do you have in mind?" Clint asked as he grabbed the handle for the garage door, shoving up until it sprang into action, lifting above their heads.

"I've decided to use a log and make Em a fairy house. I plan to hollow out a place near the bottom with a working door on hinges. A couple of windows on either side. Might be nice if it had a table and chairs inside. Nothing elaborate, but I know Willow's an expert at that stuff."

"She'll like that." Clint walked to the far side of the garage to the makeshift wooden table next to the wall, grabbing a lined pad of yellow paper and a carpenter's pencil.

"You think so? I've had a hard time coming up with a gift since I don't want to upset Ruth."

Clint scratched the side of his beard before sweeping the pencil across the paper. "Why would getting Emily a gift upset Ruth?"

"Just something Celeste said about not causing friction when I suggested getting Emily a dog."

"Yeah, that'd do it. Ruth can't have a dog at her apartment."

"I know." Doug shoved his hands into the pockets of his jeans as he rocked back on his heels. "Listen, speaking of Ruth . . . I was wondering if you might do me a favor."

Clint gave him a sideways glance from the crude drawing he was creating. "I don't want to be in the middle of any conflict. You know I can't stand that."

"It's not a conflict." Pulling his hands from his pockets, Doug wrapped his arms across his chest instead, leaning his backside against the table. "Emily told me this morning that Ruth's having a hard time. I guess she overheard her talking to her grandma about struggling to pay the bills. From what I could gather, it sounded like she had to replace the transmission on her car."

"Oh?" Clint dropped the pencil to the table, wrapping his fingers around the edge of the wood surface. "I'm sorry Emily's worrying about that kind of stuff."

"Yeah, well I don't want her to. I'd like to give Ruth some cash, but I know she won't take it if I offer it."

Clint leaned back far enough, he might as well have taken a step away. "She won't take it from me either, if that's what you're thinking."

"No. But I thought she might if it was a tip." He slid his hand into his back pocket and drew out the wad of bills he'd stuffed in there earlier. "Maybe someone you know would be willing to place it on the table, like an anonymous person? She'd have to take it then."

Clint made such an uncomfortable face, Doug would have sworn he'd just stepped in dog doo. "I don't know—"

"Or give it to Jess at the diner. She could slide it onto Ruth's table incognito-like. I'd do it myself, but the woman thinks I'm scum. She likes you though, doesn't she?"

Clint's brow scrunched together. "Jess?"

"Yeah, I'm sure if you asked she wouldn't breathe a word about it to Ruth." He held the money out in front of him, waiting as Clint eyed it with such wariness, it could have been a snake. "It won't bite you, I promise."

With the most exaggerated sigh imaginable, Clint reached for the money. "You owe me."

"I owe you then. You can ask me to pay up however you see fit."

With a nod, Clint went back to sketching the little furniture.

"It seemed like Celeste got on with Willow pretty well," Doug said, watching as Clint ran his pencil over the line a second time.

"I have a feeling those two could talk circles around each other all day." Clint reached up to scratch his beard again. "She's nice, though. I wouldn't have thought you had it in you to pick a nice girl."

A chuckle slipped out before Doug processed Clint's words. "Like I've told you before, we're friends."

"Yeah." Clint nodded as he pressed his lips together. "Same as when I met Willow. Friends."

Chapter Eleven

"Pa, don't be silly! If I was gone, who'd play the fiddle for you?"

"Exactly."

Doug found himself smiling in spite of the fact that he'd seen their little skit too many times to count. The truth was, he'd sat on the steps of the tiny cabin so often that it was starting to feel like a second home. And he'd grown so accustomed to having Celeste close to him, he could barely remember what life had been like before he'd spoken to her on the phone.

A wrong number. Just a mistake made by a random woman when she'd written down the ten digits. He was no stranger to dealing with mistakes in his life, most of them of his own making. But this was beginning to feel like it hadn't been a mistake. Like it had been some grand design all along, and he'd stumbled into it blindly.

As much as he liked to think he was in control of his own universe, he couldn't have concocted a plan like that one. When it came to matters of the heart, he'd always been a bit myopic. Acknowledging the problem seemed a step in the right direction, but what if his line of vision in that regard would always be as clouded as Celeste's was in day to day life? Her heart didn't have any problems seeing the big picture. It almost had better than perfect vision, pulling in all the colors of the vast universe.

If he went in headfirst, he felt sure things would sour too quickly. Like the first strains of Christmas music after Thanksgiving, bright and melodic and filled with a kind of wistful hope. What if Celeste was a Christmas song, and he was something more along the lines of January the twentieth? Past the romance of the holidays, all the way to the bleak grayness of winter and the disappointment of broken New Year's resolutions?

Yep, that would sum up the issue pretty tidily. If Celeste was Christmas music, he was the first week someone decided not to go to the gym after all.

"Hi."

He glanced up, the crowd suddenly gone and Celeste standing in front of him. "You snuck up on me."

"Did I? I guess I've developed a kind of sixth sense about when you're around." Her smile was all sweetness. "Or fifth and a half sense, more accurately. My shift ends in ten minutes. Where are we going?"

"It's a surprise, but I have a feeling you'll approve. For now, I'll wait out of the way."

She wrinkled her nose before turning to head back into the cabin. He expected that she and Roy had some sort of end-of-the-day ritual they performed, putting things away and locking things down. He'd never wanted to get in their way, preferring to stand on the periphery.

With a quick glance upward, he took in the lights spanning the length of the building. The place was definitely a winter wonderland if he'd ever seen one, minus snow. Emily was at that age where she expected it to snow for Christmas, because of course it should, since she saw snow on every holiday movie. Having lived in the area for the majority of his life, he knew Christmas snow was a tall order. It wasn't even cold, not really. Night was falling and he couldn't see his breath in the air.

At least in that one detail, lack of visual evidence was actually a lack of existence.

"Have fun, Emily!" Willow called from her doorway as Emily was stepping up into the truck.

Emily waved before reaching for her seatbelt without having to be reminded, an eager smile lighting her face. "Hey Celeste. Did Dad tell you where we're going? I'm totes excited."

Doug nearly let out a groan at that weird word Em had picked up. From school maybe? More likely from that silly kids show she was watching on TV the other night. They'd made up enough words during the course of that program he'd found himself wondering if they were actually speaking some nutty alternative form of English.

"No, he said it would be your surprise, so I'm dying to find out."

Emily's eyes were dancing in Doug's rearview mirror. "My Sunday School class is going to a care facility tonight. Mom couldn't come so Dad's taking me. He thought you might want to sing Christmas carols with us."

Celeste turned her focus to him, like she could somehow see straight through him even if he seemed a bit fuzzy. "You're singing?"

"No way. She was referring to *us* as in her classmates."

Mischievous giggling bubbled up from the passenger side of the truck. "You will most definitely be singing. I'll see to it myself."

"Then I'll wait in the truck," he said without skipping a beat before glancing back up to find Emily's eyes in the mirror. "Your mom said she had to work some kind of party or something?"

"A Christmas party where people eat finger chicken and laugh too loud," Emily stated. "She didn't care though. Yesterday she came home from work crying but she said it was good crying."

So Clint's money drop the day before had actually worked as planned. He nearly breathed a sigh of relief.

Celeste partially turned in her seat, catching Doug's attention. "Finger chicken? What's that?"

"I think she means chicken fingers. Fried strips of chicken."

"She knows what that is, Dad. She's not really from the 1800's."

"How do you know they didn't have chicken fingers in the 1800's?" he asked.

"Maybe chicken feet, but not chicken fingers," Celeste stated. "I really am excited now. I've never heard either one of you sing. I'm sure you're both wonderful carolers."

Emily sang well, her airy voice ringing through the room like only a child's could. She blended with the other kids until they all sounded like one person, with the exception being one boy who seemed to end every note by adding a crescendo.

Doug was a different story. Celeste had nudged him in the ribs at one point to ensure he started singing, but he'd only sang out for a few seconds before his voice quieted to almost nothing. He was terrible. Almost laughably terrible, if such a thing were laughable. She knew not to snicker, though, because she herself was not a capable vocalist. Since she was well aware that singing ability was not her forte, she lip-synched as they sang the familiar choruses.

"Away in a Manger."

"Joy to the World."

"We Wish You a Merry Christmas."

If Emily noticed, she didn't say a word.

It was late when they delivered Emily to her mother's apartment, and Doug insisted that Celeste walk to the door with them to meet Ruth. She hadn't considered the possibility before, but when Doug suggested it an immediate feeling of dread filled her—not because she thought Doug still had feelings for his ex, but because she was woefully aware that there could be a comparison. Standing side by side with the woman who was Emily's mom, would she measure up?

Ruth's voice had been kind, although it held a hint of weariness. Whether it was from a hard day waitressing or the annoyance of Doug bringing another woman to her door, Celeste couldn't be sure. Still, she didn't say anything ungracious or give her the impression that she wasn't welcomed in Emily's life, so she managed to hold her wobbly smile in place while she said goodbye to Emily's mother.

And in the span of the few seconds while Doug was saying goodbye to Emily, she prayed with all her might that God might let her get a glimpse of Ruth. Even more fervently than she'd prayed that she might catch a glimpse of Doug. Perhaps mercifully, she was denied the request.

If she didn't see the other woman, maybe she wouldn't continue to taste the insecurity.

"Looks like John and Ava have already turned in," Doug said as they pulled into the driveway. "The house is dark."

"I told them not to wait up." Celeste twisted her fingers together in her lap, keeping her focus tilted downward. "Thanks for taking me with you tonight. It was fun to learn something new about you."

"Something new?"

"That you can't sing." A smile tipped up the corner of her lips, but she didn't look in his direction. "It's nice to know I'm not the only one."

He sat silently for a few seconds. "I don't know, there was something musical about your singing. Kind of like a dog howling in the wind."

She let a laugh slip out. "Had I known we were so perfectly matched, I might not have worried about it so much beforehand."

The cab of the truck grew silent again.

"In the singing department," she hastily clarified. "I meant singing, of course." Bringing her hand up, she brushed a strand of hair behind her ear. "I would have loved seeing the faces at that care facility tonight. They seemed so happy to have the kids there."

"I'm sure there are days you wish you could see more than other days."

"Yes, and other times I just wish I could look around me for five minutes to see whether I was terribly out of sync. Ava assures me I look like the other women my age, but that doesn't stop me from feeling like a fish out of water."

He made a brief humming noise. "I can't say as I'm the one to ask about that, because you're different than anyone else I've ever met."

The words themselves were innocent enough, but she felt a sting all the same. "Because I can't see."

His hand wrapped around both of hers, the unexpected touch causing a jolt through her veins. "No, because you see things differently. Before I met you, I was the type of guy who never would have stopped to look at the sunset. You—you're not content to notice the things around you. If you can't see the sunset, you'll still sit there staring in its direction, wrapping yourself in the light. You notice the unseen."

Her heart pounded erratically against her chest, projecting all kinds of images onto her imagination that had no business appearing.

"I've adapted to the life I find myself in," she stated. "It's exactly the same for you. When you were on the oil rig, you were Deke, making money as a bachelor. Back here you're Doug, dad to Emily."

"Muddling along."

"All any of us do is muddle along. If you meet someone who has it all together, they're lying."

He laughed at that, and she took the opportunity to extract one of her hands.

"Would you be willing to grant me one request?" she breathed, her words barely more than a whisper.

"You make it sound like I'm a genie." He twisted his hand against the one he still touched until their fingers were intertwined. "Anything, Celeste."

His words should have emboldened her, but she still felt the emotion catch her voice as she extended her free hand between them. "Can I see you? I mean. . ." She left her hand in the air but curled her fingers back.

"Yes."

The shape next to her was nothing but fuzz and subtle hints of spicy cologne, and somehow one hundred percent flesh at the same time. Knowledge of that fact made her pause long enough that his hand wrapped around hers between them, drawing her arm across the cab of the truck until she felt the curve of his cheek beneath her fingers. Extracting her other hand from his grasp, she made it a mirror image of the palm on his face, so that both hands framed his cheeks. She traced her fingertips down his beard to his neck, then the slope of his nose, and finally smoothed her fingers over his forehead.

"You have a scar," she whispered as she brushed his eyebrow.

"Yeah. One time Clint and I had a light saber fight with sticks in the back yard."

"Who won?"

"The stick."

She smiled, but the lightness from his words left her as soon as his hand touched her cheek instead.

"Do I pass your inspection?" he asked, rubbing a thumb across her cheekbone.

She gave a slight nod. "I like your face."

His grin shifted his beard against her palm. "That's good, because I like your face. I'm quite partial to it, actually." He inched closer until his breath touched her cheek. "Is this okay?"

It was more than okay. It was all she could think about at the moment, and what she'd been imagining since the first time he'd taken her somewhere in the cab of his truck. She barely managed a nod before his lips were on hers, sending her heart barreling down to the tips of her toes. She settled her fingers against his neck, accidentally finding his pulse. The beat of his heart tapped against her fingertips while he continued to kiss her, like she'd slipped into her own magical movie moment. She'd never dared to dream that she could have a man like Doug. Was it possible even now?

He pulled back, settling his forehead against hers. Clear vision or not, even with her eyes closed, she sensed he was smiling before she heard his words.

"It feels like I've been waiting forever to kiss you."

Although she agreed, she kept the sentiment inside and offered nothing but a smile in return.

Chapter Twelve

Celeste almost felt like she was tromping up the steps in her snow boots. Ava had insisted she wear them even though they'd both heard the weatherman say there would only be a dusting. Not even enough to stick to the ground, if his predictions were proven correct.

The springs on the screen door protested as Doug pushed the wooden frame open, giving the impression that they were stretched tight and ready to burst. As soon as she'd stepped into the living room of the cabin, the wood popped closed against the door frame, trapping the warmth inside along with the hints of wood smoke and—

"Cedar!" she stated as she closed her eyes, taking the time to inhale. "Doug Kirkland, I believe you have a tree in your home."

His footsteps came to a stop on the hardwood. "Turns out a guy can only take so much nagging. And when it came down to it, I do like the scent of fresh-cut wood. It's probably the only excuse I'll have all year to bring the outdoors into the house."

A spark of warmth settled inside her heart as she shrugged out of her coat, which Doug immediately took from her hands. "You can pretend to be grinchy all you want, but I know you're practically bursting with Christmas spirit. Your heart has grown at least three sizes since I met you, and that was barely two months ago."

"Don't praise me too much. I barely got a Christmas tree by December twenty-third. Not impressive."

She held her hand out to her side, catching sight of the greenish shadow in the corner. When her fingers connected with the branches, she paused and let her hand rest in place. "You've had a busy month spending time with Emily and making her fairy house, not to mention the time we've spent together. It's amazing to me that you got a tree at all."

He stepped up behind her, placing a gentle hand against her waist. "I got it for you and Em. And I hope you don't mind that I let her put most of the decorations on it this morning."

"What kind of decorations?"

"Normal stuff, I guess. Popcorn strings and snowflakes cut out of paper."

A laugh slipped out as she ran her fingers over the greenery until she touched one of the popcorn strings. "You spent your morning making popcorn strings?"

"Yes."

"I've never been more attracted to you than I am at this moment."

"Really?" He cleared his throat as he shifted behind her and moved a little to the right. "We cut out those tiny snowflakes for hours. I still don't have all the glitter off my fingers."

"You never said anything about glitter."

"Sure, loads of it. Tons of glue. Shiny little stickers shaped like stars."

"Now you're just showing off." She pulled her hand away from the tree and turned in his direction. "So you mostly decorated the tree? What's left?"

"Emily thought you should put the angel on top. It made her think of you."

"Because I'm an angel?"

Doug placed the fabric against her palm, and she instinctively flattened her hand when she felt the fragile structure. "No, although I wouldn't argue that reasoning. I bought it at the park. Emily said that's special because that's where we met you."

The irrational sting of tears pricked her eyes. "What is it made of?"

He released one of those familiar frustrated half-sighs. "You would ask me that. Some kind of mesh that's stiff or starched maybe. Burlap. Lace. Kind of a mixture of colors and textures in muted grays and tans."

"It sounds pretty."

His hands cupped hers around the angel. "The top of the tree is about your arm's reach. I can get a chair for you to stand on, or pick you up."

She could imagine him picking her up and knocking the tree over in the process. "Maybe you could do it for me? I'm sure Emily won't mind that I asked you to help."

He went silent, and she dropped her gaze to his chest. Not because she didn't want to look at him, but because she was slightly afraid he was studying her again. He did that too often for her liking.

"Of course not. If you want me to put the angel on the tree, I will."

She gave a subtle nod as he removed his hands from hers. "Thank you. What else did you still have to put on the tree?"

Doug's grunt as he placed the angel on the tree left her with all kinds of thoughts running through her imagination. He'd had to rise to tiptoe, maybe. He'd moved a little too close to the tree and the branches tried to engulf him.

"What are you smiling at?" he asked, interrupting her musings.

"Was I smiling?"

"Was I smiling," he repeated with humor in his voice. "In answer to your question, I have one more decoration, but it's special. You might not want to put it on the tree."

This time her smile was purposeful. "I'm all aflutter with anticipation."

"Aflutter? Emily would have a heyday with that expression." His boots shuffled against the floor as she waited for him to continue. "Do you remember when we had dinner with Willow and Clint and you told me you wished you could see how Willow would draw you? The truth is, she drew you a while ago, but I didn't know how to tell you. You're the songbird Cap tries to coax out of the woods."

"Oh." She turned her gaze toward the tree, focusing on the smudges of green again. "And did it work? Was Cap successful?"

"I'm not really sure." He faced the tree beside her. "The thing is, Cap probably doesn't deserve for that to happen. He's done a lot of dumb things in his life . . . made too many mistakes. The songbird is pure goodness. Unspoiled beauty. If she went with him, it might change everything about her."

She considered his words as she closed her eyes, breathing in the fresh scent of the Christmas tree. "Probably. It's impossible to spend time with someone and not be changed in part. But I think Cap is missing one important element."

His voice quieted. "What's that?"

"It's Christmas. A season for miracles. When perfect love came to change everything and bring hope to a dark world."

"And that's it? You think the songbird will come into the light toward Cap because it's Christmas?"

"No. She might have a little more hope than normal because it's Christmas." Pausing, she opened her eyes and looked near the top of the tree toward the angel, trying to see clearly and failing. "But the reason she'll respond to Cap is because she loves him."

He didn't answer. Instead, his hand touched hers, fingertips barely grazing her palm before he placed something against her skin. She gently wrapped her fingers around it, the cool wood smooth to the touch. While she cradled it in her left hand, she used her right to trace its side, feeling every corner and crevice.

"It's a bird," she decided.

"The songbird," he added softly. "That's my best imitation of what Willow painted. I wanted you to see it."

Celeste closed her eyes once more, tracing her fingertips over the bird. "You made this?"

"Roy taught me a few things about whittling while I was at the park this past month. It took a great deal of practice and errors, and it's definitely not perfect, but—"

"It's amazing, like she's come to life right before my eyes. What color is she?"

"That one's just the color of the wood, but the one Willow painted has a yellow head and a red chest. Brown wings."

Her fingers swept the fine lines of one of the bird's wings as she opened her eyes, focusing on the hazy navy blue of Doug's shirt. "Thank you. Nobody's ever done something like this for me before. I don't know what to say."

Again he responded with an extended silence, but he brought his fingers down to rest them on the bird in her hand, almost like he was attempting to see it through touch along with her. The action was comfortably uncomfortable, mirroring almost every emotion Doug normally caused.

He drew in a deep breath before he started talking. "You deserve far better than me. I've known it from the moment we met when you gave Emily your taffy, and my opinion hasn't changed since. And I . . . Well, I'm the guy who erased all the contacts from his phone two weeks ago and wishes he could do the same with a dozen other things." He shifted his fingers from the bird to her cheek instead. "I'm not proud of my past, but I don't resent it anymore. It led me here—to Emily and to you."

An inexplicable surge of joy filled her heart. The thought that Doug might want a relationship with her had filled her daydreams vividly enough that she'd nearly burst the first time he kissed her, but she'd told herself not to read too much into it. With a tremulous grin, she turned toward the tree, extending the bird in its direction. "I think she belongs here with you. Where should I put her?"

His fingers guided hers until they'd safely settled the bird on a branch. When they finished, she placed her palms against his chest, sliding her hands up his shirt until she'd linked her fingers behind his neck. This close, she could almost make out his features, but her brain had no problems filling in the details.

"Be prepared," he said as his arms wrapped around her waist, "because I'm about to borrow one of Emily's cheesy Christmas tunes."

"'Santa Baby'?"

Her words made him laugh as he tightened his hold on her. "Not even close. All I want for Christmas is you, Celeste. I've been trying to fight it for your sake, but I'm afraid I lost the battle. How would you feel about dating a guy like me?"

"Like it was Christmas morning every day."

His lips touched hers, cutting her smile short, but she didn't mind at all as she leaned closer.

"I should have known you'd say something like that," he breathed against her cheek, his beard pressed to her skin. "Being with you feels like I'm living in the twelve days of Christmas, but this is more like day forty-five. Is there a gift for the forty-fifth day of Christmas? On the forty-fifth day of Christmas, my true love gave to me . . ."

"Her heart," she answered, her eyes closing as she focused on the feel of being in his arms. "Merry Christmas, Doug."

Epilogue

Doug maneuvered his truck through the parking lot into a space that was a hint too small, making sure to park closer on his side to give plenty of room for his passenger to exit. Within seconds he was around the back of the truck, opening the door for her. Celeste placed her hand in his, stepping down to the asphalt.

"Do you smell that?" she asked, making him pause and stand still beside her.

"Diesel fuel?"

"No, lilacs. They're in the air somewhere. I can tell it's going to be a beautiful day."

He smiled as they continued walking to the employee entrance and into the park. Every day was a beautiful day to Celeste, whether the sun was shining or the clouds threatened a downpour. She saw things the way she wanted to see them—or maybe the way everyone should see them. But he had to admit that his days seemed a lot more beautiful lately, too. Maybe because he'd gotten a job woodworking at the park, so he could pick Celeste up every morning and take her home every night. Maybe because he'd decided to buy a house the week before, and he and Clint were planning to build a treehouse in the back yard for Emily. Or maybe because the hope he'd found at Christmas had followed over into the new year, leaving him excited for the future.

The cabin where Celeste spent her day loomed in front of them, and he walked her right up to the front steps, pausing as Roy stepped into the doorway.

"Morning, Roy," he said, nodding at the older man.

"Doug. I saw that horse you're working on. Fine craftsmanship."

"Thanks." Doug watched as Roy turned and went back into the cabin, then he gave his full attention to Celeste. "I'll be back around when I have a break. Try not to get married off while I'm gone."

Her smile lit any dark places left in his heart. "I can't make any promises."

"I have first dibs," he grumbled, bending to place a kiss on her lips. "Remember I already gave him my two dollars. That, and the fact that I love you."

"I love you too. And I hope you don't regret the two dollars." She climbed up onto the first step, offering a parting wave, her copper hair spilling over her shoulder.

"Not for a second," he stated as he started down the hill to his own workspace. "Best money I've ever spent."

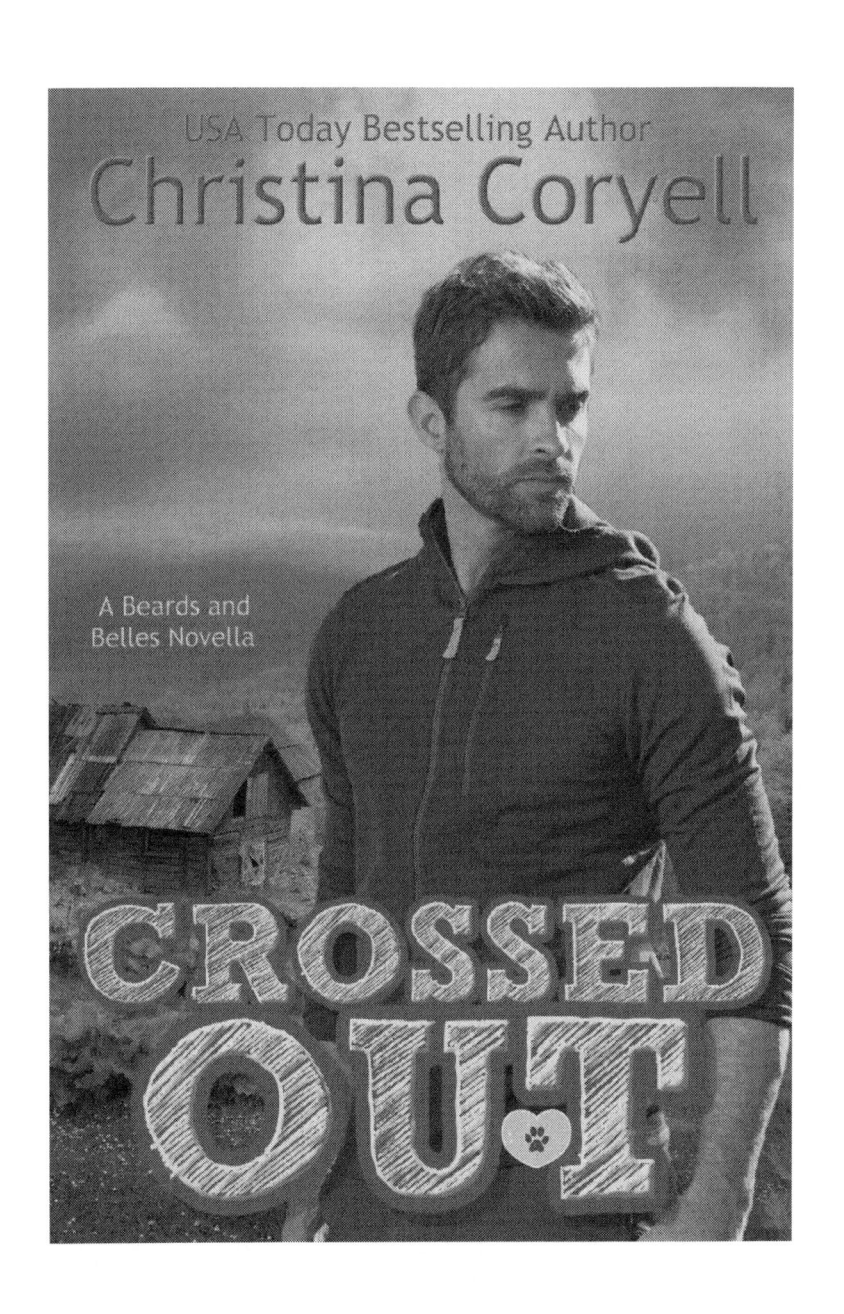

USA Today Bestselling Author
Christina Coryell

A Beards and Belles Novella

CROSSED OUT

CROSSED OUT

A ROMANTIC COMEDY

BY

CHRISTINA CORYELL

| ¹R | U | T | H |

Ruth's motto had long been *you do what you can to survive,* but some tips weren't worth earning. Even if they ended up being forty-five percent, the feeling they caused inside was worse than when she had to scrape the giant wads of used chewing gum off the bottom of the back corner booth. Glancing out the front window at the Lexus pulling away, Ruth shook her head before she peeked at the bottom of the receipt again. *Room 306, nine pm,* like she was some cheap call girl who regularly visited hotel rooms of men who sat at her tables. Guys whose names she didn't even know.

Letting out a sigh of disgust, she looked at the signature again. The first name looked like it started with a P... Pete? Perry? Presumptuous?

"Gotta love that dirty flirty money," Jess stated as she stepped past her, a steaming pile of apple crisp on her plate, vanilla ice cream melting into a pool around the crust.

Even though the moniker stung a little, Ruth couldn't help but give a wry smile. She hated the dirty flirty money as much as the next person, but Emily was going to need a new pair of shoes before long. Quick, competent service wasn't going to provide those. As much as she loathed admitting it, money she got from being a little too friendly with customers of the male persuasion was what usually tipped her finances over the column from red to black.

Besides, Jess only teased her because she was married to Pitt in the kitchen, so she couldn't earn any dirty flirty money of her own.

With the receipt and the pen between her fingers, Ruth turned and offered a sheepish smile to the man in the booth by the window. "More coffee, Pap?"

He lifted a couple of fingers as he shook his head, his hand trembling where he held it in the air. "I'll pass. You oughta tell guys like that to take a hike, Ruthie. A nice girl like you deserves better."

Stopping beside his table, she dropped a hand to the surface beside his coffee cup, leaning a little closer to her favorite customer. "I have a feeling there are no nice guys left out there. Except you, of course, but flirting with you probably won't earn me a better tip."

A low chuckle slipped out as he put his hand on his coffee mug again, a slight tremor accompanying the movement. "Maybe if I were sixty years younger. And if I ever paid my tab."

Wrapping her fingers around the elderly gentleman's shoulder, Ruth gave a little squeeze. Roger Pittman – affectionately called Pap by everyone at the diner – was Bill Pittman's father. Since Bill owned the place and ran the kitchen, Pap sat in the same booth by the window nearly every day. She'd grown to love the man over the years, but he never had a bill to pay, so her service was just that.

Service.

"Save me a seat for my break," Ruth said as she stepped across the dining room, sliding the pen behind her ear before grabbing a rag so she could clean the table Mr.

Predatory had just vacated. Pausing next to the bar stools that framed the counter, she stretched to tiptoe and leaned back, giving her muscles an easy tug. Being on her feet all day kept her in good shape, but it also caused enough tension in her back to make her feel like a tightly coiled spring most days.

"You and Em doing anything after school today?" Jess asked, reaching for a plate of eggs that just slid through the open window between the dining room and the kitchen. "Hanging out with grandma?"

"Willow's taking her for one of her jaunts in the woods. They're looking for fairies." Twisting her mouth to the side, Ruth scrunched up her nose as she thought about Emily's artistic aunt. "It's pretty hard to compete with fairies. Everything I do pales in comparison."

Jess chuckled before stepping past her with the eggs. "Moms are supposed to be uncool. It's in the handbook."

"Why didn't anyone tell me there was a handbook?" Ruth turned and stepped across the room, hastily wiping the tabletop she'd cleared. The salt and pepper shakers weren't even, so she adjusted them, twisting the pepper until the seam in the glass pattern lined up perfectly with the salt. With her pinky finger, she pushed the napkin dispenser back a centimeter or two.

"Perfect," she whispered, tossing her rag back to the counter where she'd retrieved it. Fighting the urge to whistle, she grabbed the folded newspaper from where she'd placed it behind the counter, pulling the pen from atop her ear. The crossword puzzle beckoned like a lush island in the middle of the crowded dining room. Her daily respite, allowing her to mentally escape for a few moments before giving her all to other peoples' needs again. The only *me time* she got some days, at least until she climbed into bed alone at the end of the night.

Line one across tempted her, but before she had a chance to read through its words, Jess rapped her knuckles on the countertop next to Ruth's elbow.

"Before you take a break, get that fella at the end of the bar, would you?" she whispered. "I've left him waiting too long."

Suppressing a groan, Ruth dragged her paper across the back edge of the counter until she was standing in front of the guy, who had his head bent over so far, she worried he might be sleeping. While she considered whether or not to clear her throat, the top of his stocking cap bobbed up a smidge and she caught sight of two very dark eyebrows, tilted downward. Angry scowl, or hungover and avoiding the overhead light?

Either way, just her luck.

"Hey," she said, the cheerfulness of her tone almost grating on her own nerves. "Sorry for the delay, but Jess got caught up in delivering her food, so I'll help you in the meantime. My name's Ruth. Can I get you a cup of coffee or a sweet tea?"

"Coffee, black."

The fact that he didn't even bother to look up to acknowledge her presence sent a pinprick of annoyance through her side. She could take just about any reaction from a customer as long as she didn't seem invisible. Instead of noticing her continuing to stand in front of him, though, he wrapped his hand around the black box in front of him and pulled it closer to his chest.

Dropping the paper to the counter, she shook her head as she took the few steps to the coffee pot, grabbing it along with a fresh mug from the stack. If she were feeling especially feisty, she'd give him a takeaway cup from the beginning. Maybe encourage him to skedaddle so she could take her break.

"Black coffee," she announced, carefully placing the steaming mug on the counter in front of him. "Could I interest you in some breakfast this morning? Ham and eggs, or maybe biscuits and gravy?" She inched closer, the buttons of her shirt coming into contact with the counter. "Unless you're too interested in whatever you've got there to care about food."

Angling his head up, he centered his gaze on her, two frown lines dimpling the skin between his eyes. Based on his mood alone, she imagined they were always there, along with the disinterested air that made his face seem longer than it was. Angular cheekbones led to creases on either side of his mouth that disappeared behind a short brown beard. Accentuating the gloominess, he'd topped the look off with a depressingly drab gray stocking cap.

"Toast, wheat," he said, going back to whatever interested him on the countertop.

She let her eyes linger on the coffee mug, twisting the handle until it was at a ninety-degree angle to the edge of the surface. Jess sometimes claimed Ruth had obsessive compulsive tendencies, but she just liked things to be orderly. Things she could control, anyway. The things she couldn't control were driving her nuts as they always did.

"Wheat toast," she repeated, adjusting her tone to the appropriate upbeat volume. "That's all?"

Releasing an audible groan, he leaned back and shoved a hand in his pocket, pulling out a folded bill. Placing the five on the counter in front of him, he motioned toward it with his hand. "This is going to be your tip."

Now it was her turn to get those little lines in the middle of her forehead, but she quickly tried to school her features. The last thing she needed was premature wrinkles. "Wow . . . okay then. It's usually customary to wait until after you get the bill so you can base the tip on service you receive, but—"

"Which is why I'm putting it out there now. No amount of flirting or breezy chatting is going to increase it, so don't waste your breath." He leaned back just enough that she could see the item drawing his attention was a camera. Not a cheap camera, either, but one of those high-dollar numbers with the giant zoom lens and tons of gadgets.

"No worries," she muttered as she took a step away from him, mentally swatting at the imaginary cloud of darkness she felt creeping into her space.

He definitely didn't need to fret about her flirting with him now, not with the salty attitude he was wearing. As though her silent glare had actually turned up the heat in the room, he tilted back in his chair and began to tug his sweater over his head, the flannel shirt beneath it rising until it showed a white T-shirt against his abdomen. The guy was wearing more layers than the chocolate fudge cake Pitt pulled out on special occasions.

Wheat toast. Who went into a greasy mom-and-pop diner and ordered wheat toast and black coffee? He might as well have walked in and ordered a peanut butter and jelly sandwich like Emily requested for an after-school snack.

Ignoring the usual routine of putting the ticket in the window, Ruth stepped down the long corridor and went around the side of the divider, emerging into the kitchen. Pitt gave her a cautious glance from the corner of his eye as he flipped a sausage patty on the griddle.

"Special order?" he asked, his gruff voice even scratchier than normal.

"Super special," she said with a subtle lift of her eyebrows. "Special enough that even I can take care of it."

"Oh boy." Sliding the sausage onto the edge of the plate, Pitt turned to place the food he'd just plated on the open window. "Rough morning?"

"Nothing I can't handle." Popping two slices of wheat bread into the toaster, she readied a bowl of various jellies and butter packets. "Do I have any words stamped on my forehead today?"

Spatula paused in midair, he offered a wary glance. "Words?"

"You know, like desperate. Trashy. Kick me."

Pitt offered a harrumph as he turned back to the griddle. "You lost me at trashy. Need me to come to the dining room?"

"Not unless you want to scare off the customers."

Offering a coy smile, she grabbed the freshly toasted bread and plated it, carefully positioning the edges atop one another. Having words on her forehead was one of her deepest fears. She'd had the odd smudge on her cheek or her chin from handling the newspaper print and cleaning tables at the same time, but so far she'd never actually managed to transfer an entire word. Still, every time something odd happened, she imagined the scene from *Never Been Kissed* when Drew Barrymore fell asleep with her stamped hand pressed against her face. The poor woman didn't realize until it was way too late that she'd unknowingly branded herself with the word *loser*.

"Order up." Her cheery voice sounded fake as could be, but she still smiled as she stepped past Pitt once more. It didn't feel right not to be cheerful at work. Exhaustion followed her on a daily basis, but she still managed to be upbeat for the customers. She never let any of her emotions rest on her face.

She saved that for after Em went to bed, and usually told her problems to a half-empty bag of chips and a carton of chocolate milk.

The grumpy dude at the end of the bar was still huddled over the counter, his coffee untouched, but she placed the plate against the slick surface, letting it clank against the counter. "Wheat toast," she announced, watching as he lifted his head. Her eyes caught sight of his Adam's apple and drifted down to the neck of his T-shirt before the newspaper came into view by his elbow. Grabbing the corner of it, she jerked it from beneath his arm.

The word "RUTH" was spelled there plain as day in what she had to assume was his handwriting. As were many other words scattered about the puzzle, all in the same boxy script. And underneath, where the clues should have been, there were scribbles. Line after line of scribbles.

"You did the crossword puzzle?" she asked, incredulity lining her tone.

"Some of it." He grabbed a packet of butter and began slathering it on his toast. "Didn't have time to finish."

Her jaw clenched as the black lines swam together on the newsprint. "Who said you could do that?"

A derisive laugh slipped out. The same kind she gave Emily when she asked if she could have brownies for dinner. "You set it right in front of me."

He took a bite of his toast, chewing as though he hadn't just stolen something from her. Mindlessly gnawing away at a piece of bread as though he hadn't ripped away her precious five minutes of mental solitude.

Who wore stocking caps indoors anyway? It wasn't the dead of winter, and he wasn't one of those skateboarder kids trying too hard to look unaffected.

Shrugging her shoulders, she tossed the paper to the corner of his plate. "Well, you ruined it."

This time he turned his full attention to her, using the back of his hand to brush at the corner of his mouth. "All because I filled in a few answers?"

"How do you know if they're correct? I might get to down number four and find out that you answered one across wrong, but I wouldn't know how to fix it, would I? You crossed it out."

"Crossed it out?" he repeated, dark eyes narrowing.

"The scribbling with your pen." She brushed her finger back and forth across the paper in a motion that felt manic the instant she started. "You crossed out the clues when you finished reading them. I highly doubt the answer for one across is Ruth."

Clearing his throat, he lifted his eyebrows. "The legendary Babe."

Drawing herself up a little straighter, she drilled him with a glare. "Babe?"

"Babe Ruth." Placing his finger on the paper, he pointed at his printed answer. "R-U-T-H. He was a baseball player."

"I know who Babe Ruth is." Glancing at the countertop, she grabbed the bowl she'd filled with butter and jelly, pushing it out of his reach.

"You're punishing me by taking away the butter?"

Her fingers trembled as she thought about the unreasonableness of her response, so she crossed her arms over her chest to still them. "You're finished."

"I'm finished." As though contradicting his words, he took the coffee mug in his hand, lifting it to his lips. The narrow squint of his eyes made her want to look anywhere else, but she stood her ground, arms still crossed. Jess had turned to look at her from the other end of the counter. Pap was peering in her direction, too, his eyes all but pleading with her to step back. Indignation warred for its spot, though, and as long as this guy kept staring at her, she wasn't giving an inch.

He finally glanced away, rising to his feet and reaching into his pocket again. "Guess this'll cover it." He tossed a handful of ones on the counter and grabbed his sweater from the back of the chair, pausing to grab the messenger bag he'd dropped by his feet. Then he picked up his camera, cradling it in the crook of his arm as he turned and headed toward the door.

Ruth watched as he left, ribbons of uncertainty filling her veins. It wasn't normal to have such an intense reaction to a crossword puzzle. She knew that somewhere in the recesses of her mind, but she also knew the sight of his handwriting on her paper sent her blood boiling all over again.

Refusing to stare at the puzzle, she settled her gaze on his back as he pulled the glass door open. His jeans were snug and tucked messily into his hiking boots, the laces undone and dangling as though he hadn't been concerned enough to tie them. His exit should have been welcomed, but instead an uncomfortable knot formed in the pit of her stomach.

As soon as he was safely behind the door, she let her eyes sweep down to the paper for the final time.

Picking up the pen, she traced over the letters he'd written, spelling out her name on row one across. R-U-T-H.

It should have made her feel better, but instead the sight of the two strokes of the pen mingling together left a clear sense of apprehension resting on her shoulders.

| ²T | A | T | E |

Standing on the sidewalk in front of the little diner, Tate forced a deep breath into his lungs. He had known better than to mingle among people today. Everything in his gut told him to hunker down and wait out the storm, but his mind told him he'd go crazy sitting in the cabin. So he went out in public, ate toast, and berated a waitress whose only crime was being attractive enough to draw attention from other male patrons.

The whole thing was just too . . . normal. Ordering breakfast. Listening to happy chatter. Overhearing the elderly guy by the window tell the waitress she deserved better. For Tate, the thought of her flirting with him seemed offensive on a day like today, even if she only would have been doing it for the money.

Doing things for money felt egregious today, period. Maybe something inside his psyche had snapped, and everything he'd done up until now would feel wrong. He'd never be able to return to his job. He'd have to move to the woods, live in a tent, and eat food he grew with his own hands.

Even the sun felt too bright, like the entire world was mocking him with its sameness.

Taking a step off the sidewalk, he forced one boot in front of the other. All the well-meaning people had told him that's how it would work: one day at a time. Get through one day, and then another, and then another. Eventually he would realize he'd made it through a week's worth of days, or a month's, and he would find himself moving on. It wasn't even that he'd been struggling with normal life today, though. He'd been almost numb, until he couldn't get the camera to work. The camera had pulled him off kilter, sending him into a downward spiral that ended with wheat toast and throwing one-dollar bills at an innocent person.

Squeezing his eyes closed, he paused in the parking lot. Had he really done that?

His left hand clenched and unclenched as he imagined her face in his mind, eyes blazing over the fact that he wrote on her newspaper. He should go back in and apologize. Any other time that's what he would do. But any other time he wouldn't have crossed her in the first place.

The camera shifted in the crook of his arm and he popped his eyes open, glancing down to make sure it wasn't slipping. All the action did was remind him that this wasn't any other time. It was square one, and there was no clue to help him fill in the blanks.

Insignificant plots of land had no reason to possess stately names. This wasn't a farm or a ranch, or even some public property set apart for birdwatching or botanical gardens. The place barely encompassed eleven acres, all lined with mature trees but not much else. The mountain view wasn't anything to sneeze at, but only if one positioned oneself at the sole clearing on the property. Turn away from the clearing and it was a forest. A forest nestled on the edge of the Smoky Mountains, but still a forest.

The sign hanging above the driveway welcomed him back yet again, its inscription carved into wood like he'd seen in movies about summer camps. Darrow Acres, a name that might make someone think it was a haven for weary souls. A setting for adventure or endless hours of enjoyment.

Tate stilled the engine of the Jeep, letting his eyes linger on the cabin. What he could see of the cabin, anyway. It was hidden by vegetation, the wood railing the only thing that drew the eye to the fact that there was a walkway from the driveway to the front porch. A stone chimney climbed up the wall, reaching past the logs marking the wall until it was visible against the towering green trees. The place was eighty years old, called a charming antique by his father. Of course he'd failed to mention that the inside was covered with fading wallpaper and appliances so ancient, he felt like he'd entered an episode of the Beverly Hillbillies.

But a man could see for miles on a day like this one, and that was the selling point, right? At least for someone who had an interest in that sort of thing. Normally Tate loved a good view, but not today. All he had an interest in at the moment was time travel. If he could rewind the past few days, he might not be in this situation. He'd go right back to the point where his dad told him he was sick a few weeks ago. Maybe a little earlier so he could spring himself into immediate action. He wouldn't have tried to get his affairs in order first before asking for a three-month sabbatical from work. He'd have shown up a month ago so he could spend time with his father, not giving himself only a day and a half before he was gone.

A shadow shifted on the porch, and his spine stiffened against the seat before he realized it was the dog. None of the spunk she'd exhibited upon his arrival a few days ago marked the animal now. She waited near the steps, ears hanging down past her jowls with her brown fur tangled and matted on her upper legs. The dark eyes in the chocolate-colored face only served to make her look more depressed—mournful maybe. The dog was taking the loss hard.

He didn't have much to offer there. He'd never been a dog person. Couldn't have had one in his line of work even if he wanted to. How was one supposed to comfort a dog? Have her adopted by someone else? Would it be detrimental on her to remove her from the cabin? She'd been at Darrow Acres for four or five years now. Sending her away felt cruel.

Keeping her almost felt crueler.

The dog lowered herself to the porch, her face on her paws indicating her disinterest in anything Tate had to offer. Probably best. He was in no mood to mingle with people or canines.

The face of that waitress filtered into his mind again, her brown hair swept into a ponytail and her pronounced cheekbones causing little hollows in her cheeks. "The legendary babe," he muttered, shaking his head at his own stupidity. He'd probably ruined her day, too. She'd ruin some other customer's day, and they would go home and ruin their family's day. An entire catastrophic turn of events set into motion by his being a jerk.

Starting the engine of the Jeep again, he peered over his shoulder as he backed out of the driveway. He should undo whatever he could of that situation, if possible. Especially since it might be the only thing he could control at the moment.

Tate pulled on the glass door, cautiously stepping into the diner and letting his gaze slide across the other patrons. A married couple were chatting, others were looking at their phones, and the lone man who had been sitting by the window before was gone. The familiar tan shirt of the servers caught his eye and he directed his attention to the nearest waitress, her sunflower blonde hair piled on top of her head. Same waitress who had initially directed him to the bar, roughly fifty with her eyeliner fanning away from her eyelid like a black streak against her temple.

"Back for more?" she asked when she finished delivering her plates to a table in the center of the room.

He tugged off his stocking cap, pulling it down to his chest. His scalp tingled, giving him the distinct impression that static was making his hair stand on end. "Wanted to apologize to Ruth."

"Oh yeah?" A smile quirked up the corners of her mouth, spreading wrinkles over her cheeks as her eyes gave him a once-over. "She already went home for the day."

A couple of rapid blinks of his eyes were all he could manage as he looked down at his hands, pressing the cap to the book. He hadn't thought about her not being here. Extending the peace offering, he brought his gaze up to the woman's face. "I don't suppose you could give her this for me?"

"Crossword puzzles?" Her pencil-darkened eyebrows rose against her forehead as she accepted the book. "Who should I tell her dropped them off?"

Squeezing the cap in his hand, he took a step backward. "Just tell her I'm sorry."

The door gave way behind him as he pushed through, finding himself on the sidewalk again. He'd tried—at least he could rest on that sentiment at the end of the day. Nothing could make him feel good about the encounter, but the fact that he'd tried to rectify the situation made him feel a little less bad.

EMILY

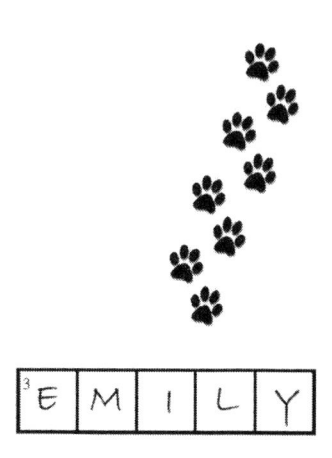

Emily could talk the ear off a tick, according to Ruth's mother. A true statement on certain occasions, but at other times she clammed up tighter than a kid trying to hide all evidence that she stole the last M&M. Both of those opposite tendencies Ruth handled with ease, but pleading always made her feel like a sucker. The bottom lip sticking out, the puppy dog eyes, even the way Em's cheeks shifted downward to make her look like a basset hound. It was all too much to take.

Somehow her daughter had succeeded in this go-round, and Ruth was currently driving her to the park. Not just any park—a dog park. Which might not have been so odd if they'd actually owned a dog.

Emily befriended dogs the way most kids befriended . . . well, other kids. Instead of talking about Billy, Tommy, or Janie, she came home talking about Danger, Pickles, and Camilla the Red. There had been some severe bouts of confusion before Ruth had figured out that Camilla the Red was one of the neighborhood canines. Emily had asked permission to play kickball in one of the neighbors' yards, not start her own doggie day care.

And forget seeing one of those dog shelter commercials on television. Emily would start sobbing and begin shaking the quarters out of the top of her piggy bank like she could save the whole lot of them with the change she'd found in the sofa cushions.

"What made you want to go to the dog park?" Ruth asked, sweeping her hair away from her eyes before hitting the signal to turn right.

"Willow took me there. She was looking for new 'spirations for her fairies. She thinks dog parks have lots of 'spirations, but I didn't see any."

A grin threatened to break out on Ruth's face, so she fought it by biting her bottom lip. "I think Willow was probably looking for inspiration," she explained. "Inspiration means things that spark ideas, like the scenery at the park could make Willow think of things she could paint."

Emily slouched in the seat, her pink skirt with the tulle overlay directly contrasting with her striped black knee socks and mid-calf black boots. Her shirt had the likeness of a fawn pug on it, so Ruth supposed that made the outfit come together.

Or not.

Emily turned her face toward Ruth, wrinkling her nose. "Dogs and fairies don't go together. They'd probably eat them."

Valid point. Emily had thought Willow Fairies were amazing long before she actually claimed Willow as her aunt, but Ruth was almost certain her daughter still didn't understand the detailed process of creating the intricate scenery.

"What do you have in your sack?" Ruth asked, pointing to the black satchel Emily had at her feet. Emily sat up a little straighter, lifting it to her lap.

"Dog toys I got at Mrs. Nelson's yard sale, 'member? She only wanted a nickel for each of them."

"How could I forget?" Pressing the brake, Ruth slowly pulled into a parking spot. If Emily had a weakness other than dogs, it was yard sales. When something cost less than a dollar it had to be priceless, no matter what type of junk it was. Used dog toys were pretty high on Ruth's list of unacceptable purchases, but if it came from Mrs. Nelson's, Emily had managed those when Ruth's mom was on duty. Kids at yard sales were nearly impossible to corral. Grandmas watching kids at yard sales were like wild mustangs, throwing caution and endless quarters to the wind.

"Well, here we are," Ruth announced as she quieted the engine. "What should we do?"

"Introduce ourselves to the dogs," Emily stated so matter-of-factly, it seemed like it should have been a foregone conclusion. But as her daughter stepped out of the car and slammed the door behind her, Ruth could do nothing but send up a little prayer for sanity in the confines of her car.

Not once in her twenty-six years had she ever introduced herself to a dog.

| ¹L | U | C | Y |

Lowering himself to one knee, Tate snapped another picture, peering down at the screen on the back of his camera. The sight almost made him smile, the way the photos were telling a story. A couple more and he'd have himself a narrative worthy of sharing with the world.

Not that he was into sharing at the moment.

He'd brought the dog to the dog park hoping that something would spark a little life into her bones. Being at the cabin alone for the last week had been bad enough, but watching that dog mope around had been like sharing a home with a ghost. Creepy and disturbing.

Tilting the camera, he angled for a better picture of the little girl, whose hair was pulled into a messy braid down one shoulder. Her outfit was perfect nonsense—mismatched and confused, like Pippy Longstocking meets Princess Peach.

Unexpected fingers covered his lens, and he leaned back, focusing his gaze upward.

"You better have a really good reason why you're taking pictures of my kid."

The sight of that familiar face sent him off balance enough that he fell backwards until his rear plopped in the leaves. She'd been pretty back at the diner, but with her hair falling around her face and the late afternoon sun streaming in to highlight her cheekbones, she looked like a model for outdoor equipment. The kind who would peek back as she was walking up the mountain just to make sure you were following, all the while giving that coy smile because she knew you'd follow her anywhere.

"Dog," he stammered, pushing himself back up on his haunches. "She's playing with my dog. I'm a photographer."

"Said every pedophile who ever lived. I've seen videos where guys use puppies for the express purpose of kidnapping children."

His palm pressed into the wet leaves, brittle and slimy at the same time, while he shoved up to his feet. Once he was standing, he thought he would feel more at ease. Looking down at her instead of up didn't make him feel like he was on solid ground, though.

"I know you," she said, narrowing her eyes. "Crossed out."

"Excuse me?"

"The guy at the diner with the crossword. I was willing to accept the apologetic gesture you left until a few seconds ago. What's your dog's name?"

The rapid questions seemed to snap out faster than gunfire. He glanced around trying to assess the damage before he could catch himself. "The dog's name? Um . . ."

"Um? You can't remember your dog's name?"

Wrapping the camera strap over his neck, he brushed at the back of his jeans to try to remove the leaf debris. "The dog's name is Lucy."

"You named your dog Lucy?"

The skepticism lacing her tone made him cringe enough that he felt his cheek rising as his left eye squinted. "My dad named her. Said she hitched a ride on Roaring Fork just like the ghost back in the day."

"Obsessed with ghosts, your dad?"

The little girl threw what looked like a dilapidated toy goose, prompting Lucy to chase it through the grass. "Ghosts? No. Must have been an old legend he heard somewhere, I guess."

"Legends? And I thought Gatlinburg was just a tourist trap." She adjusted her stance, folding her arms over her chest. "Convince me you're not a psycho, because I'm still dangerously close to calling the police."

Biting the inside of his cheek, he brought his hand up to scratch the side of his beard. He'd been asked for credentials plenty of times, but not once had anyone asked him to convince them he wasn't a psycho. How did one go about that?

"You want to look at my photos?"

She let out an exasperated sigh as she extended her hand, wiggling her fingers.

An anxious surge of adrenaline pulsed through his veins as he placed the camera in her palm, pushing the arrow so the most recent photo he had taken appeared on the screen. "Just push this button here," he said, pointing before pulling his hand back.

A pink tint swept over her cheeks as she scrolled through the photos, but then her eyes softened a little and she tilted her head to the side. "These are good. Scary good." Craning her neck, she inched closer to the screen. "I haven't had her picture taken in forever. She looks so grown up."

Shaking her head, she glanced at him before returning her attention to the camera. "Speaking of mountain legends . . ."

He reached out and stripped her of the camera before she could finish her question. "The name's Tate Darrow. I'm a photojournalist, most recently a war correspondent. Feel free to Google it so you don't think I'm a psycho."

He'd added that last bit to his statement as a barb, but she didn't look offended. Instead, she pulled her phone from her back pocket and began typing into it. Rubbing a hand across his face, he looped the camera back over his shoulder and focused again on the kid and the dog. Lucy was actually running again, doing that happy pant she'd performed the first time he'd met her.

Hard to believe it hadn't even been two weeks ago.

"Tate Darrow," Ruth repeated, letting her eyes linger on him a little too long for his tastes. "You're a bit scruffier in person, which is amazing considering the fact that these last pictures are actually of you embedded in the desert. How do you look rougher in the quiet heartland of America than you do amongst the militia?"

"That enemy was less hostile." Dragging in a deep breath, he looked toward the other end of the park. "Where's your dog?"

"I don't have a dog."

"What kind of psycho goes to a dog park without a dog?"

"The kind who's desperately trying to make her kid happy." She pressed her palm against her jeans, the sleeve of her cherry-red sweater hiding part of her hand. "Ruth Erickson. The smallish person introducing herself to your dog is Emily."

He took her proffered hand, enclosing it in his fingers. The sweater sleeve kept him from completely feeling her palm, but her fingers were cold. He immediately drew his hand back, shoving his fist into his pocket. There was something unsettling about human connection when he'd spent so much time lately sequestering himself with only the dog for company.

"I'm still unconvinced about whether you're a nut," she breathed, returning her attention to her daughter.

The man didn't appear to have a comeback for that statement, instead making his eyes sort of squinty as he nervously glanced around the park. It was impossible not to notice that he was wearing lots of layers again, his jeans bunched up at the top of his boots like he couldn't decide whether he should tuck them in or not. Those boots were untied and loose at the top just like before, as though he'd dressed in a hurry and pulled them on at the last minute.

Who was to say he hadn't.

Ruth watched Emily give the dog directions on which toy they were going to play with next, and the dog good-naturedly wagged her tail in answer. It was a nice distraction, because Ruth felt the distinct pull of her gaze trying to slip over to Tate, and she was determined to withstand the temptation. He was a little prickly with his sharp answers and standoffish demeanor, but there was something she found attractive about him. Not in the same manner as the tailored businessmen who sometimes graced the dining room of the diner, but that was a good thing. More like the old westerns her dad watched where the gun slinging cowboy would ride into town all rough and tumble, demanding attention.

She needed to get a handle on her imagination posthaste, before she decided the man was Clint Eastwood in a stocking cap.

It was probably the vague answers he provided to her questions that she found intriguing, anyway. Hostile enemies. Ghosts. Old mountain cabins. The mere suggestion of those ideas lent a little excitement into her life, and she yearned for excitement.

"Your crossword skills are top notch," she said, keeping her eyes glued to Emily.

"My what?"

"Crossword." She chanced a look at him, finding her eyes unable to turn away once they made a connection. "The answers you filled in on my crossword puzzle were right."

"Yes."

A smile slipped onto her face as she watched his profile, studying the way his cheek sunk in almost like he was trying to purse his lips. Staring at a stranger's mouth wasn't proper, though, so she forced herself to look away.

"Yes you're vaguely answering, or yes you knew they were right?"

"Why would I write them down if I didn't know they were right?" He looked at her then, his gaze sweeping over her as she pretended not to notice from the corner of her eye.

"You never venture a guess?" Ruth peered over her shoulder, spotting a park bench about fifteen yards away. Taking a step backwards, she moved in that direction. "I've never had anyone tip me at the beginning of a meal before. How was the toast, by the way?" She brushed a stray leaf off the bench, lowering herself until the coolness from the wood seemed to soak right through the back of her jeans.

"Can't say that I noticed one way or the other." He followed her lead, sitting about a foot away on the bench before leaning forward and propping his elbows on his knees.

"You seemed a little preoccupied."

Tate kept his focus laser-pinpointed on the dog, watching Emily and Lucy play tug of war with an old rope. The bobbing of his Adam's apple was enough of an answer for Ruth.

"We've never lived anywhere we could have a dog," she said, letting her gaze return to Emily as well. "In the apartment where we live now, there was an extra five-hundred-dollar deposit for pets, along with an extra fifty dollars a month rent. It might not seem like a lot, but fifty dollars is fifty dollars."

"Probably about ten tips from grumpy men at the diner."

An abrupt turn of her head caught the briefest hint of a smile, as though he was trying to be incognito about it but couldn't hold it in.

"I don't meet many grumpy men at the diner, and when I do they usually don't tip."

He clammed up again, reaching up to adjust the stocking cap on his head. It barely moved before he dropped his hand back to his lap.

"We get along fine," Ruth continued, focusing on Emily trying to remove a leaf from her tulle skirt. "Emily and me, I mean. I don't want you to think I'm complaining about money, because I'm not."

Tate cleared his throat but didn't move.

"Doug—her dad—has only recently been back in the picture. He broke things off with me before Em was born, and then he escaped Tennessee as fast as possible after high school. Now he works at a theme park here. But her Uncle Clint's always been a lifesaver, letting her get off the bus at his place ever since she started kindergarten." She took a breath and pressed her lips together to quell the urge to spout more personal information. "Sorry. Server side effect, making it easier to talk to strangers. Feel free to tell me to shut up."

He looked down at the camera sitting beside him, running a finger across its edge.

"That's not the camera you had at the diner the other day," she said, watching the movement of the unoccupied hand he held against his thigh. His fingers constantly bent and straightened, almost like he was trying to crack his knuckles.

"No."

Emily let out a tinkling giggle, and Ruth focused her attention on the dog running in circles around her daughter. The two of them looked perfectly content together, almost as though the arrangement had been preordained before Ruth even pulled into the parking lot. Instant friendship between two creatures who seemed completely unalike.

Yet she sat on the park bench with another member of the human race, wondering if she'd completely lost her touch. Usually at the diner she could make someone talk just by giving a friendly smile and leaning a little closer.

"Are you taking photos of old Smoky Mountain landmarks? The cabin I saw in there?" She peeked at his hand against his thigh, where his fingers had stretched stick straight and were now drumming against his jeans. "I'm sure those old cabins make an intriguing subject, catching them rising from the mist. With the right lens you could make them look like they were taken from another time period altogether."

"No, I prefer action shots."

Her eyebrows lifted as she looked down at the grass in front of her feet. "I only asked because I saw the picture of—"

"That was nothing."

She turned in his direction, studying his profile again while his hand came to rest on the top of his camera. "Oh, do you—"

"I should get going," he stated, rising to his feet.

Before she had time to stand, he was halfway to the dog. Ruth had barely shaken the back of her legs to remove the cold denim from her thighs by the time he had the dog on her leash, headed in the direction of the parking lot. Emily stared after the pair of them, that worn out limp goose dangling from her fist.

It was almost tempting to laugh at Em's forlorn expression, lifting one eyebrow while a sheer look of disbelief passed over her face. She didn't seem like the halfway grown girl Ruth had seen on the camera. She seemed small and insecure and confused.

Ruth knew the look, because she'd perfected it herself over the years.

"Everything okay?" she asked, placing a hand on Emily's shoulder.

Emily gave a disgusted little shrug. "I don't think that guy's a dog person."

Ruth let her arm drop until it was draped around her daughter. "That's a pity. He's not a people person either."

⁵CROSS

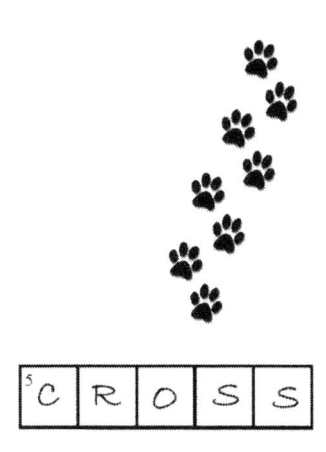

Ruth had just stooped to pick up a discarded napkin that had fallen to the floor when Jess placed a hand on her shoulder, leaning close enough that Ruth could smell the remnants of cigarette smoke clinging to her breath. "Your friend is back."

The stack of plates balanced against the crook of her arm rattled a little as Ruth glanced over her shoulder to the booths by the window. Eastwood, as she'd taken to thinking of him, was sitting at the booth directly behind Pap . . . the one with the little slash in the seat. It had been almost two weeks since she'd seen him at the dog park, and she hadn't expected to run into him again in the diner.

Hadn't expected to run into him again, period.

"I'll get him in a sec," she muttered to Jess, hauling her armful of dirty plates back to the kitchen. If the guy was showing up to rattle her, he was doing a swell job. She'd handled an entire room full of five-year-old soccer players Saturday without once losing her breezy attitude, but seeing his familiar gray stocking cap sent a little hiccup of panic into her chest.

Drawing in a deep breath, she brushed at the front of her shirt to smooth out any wrinkles and grasped the notepad in the palm of her hand, pulling her pen from behind her ear. If he was cross, Pap would surely say something in her defense. Not that she wanted to rely on someone to come to her defense. She wasn't a blathering princess sitting on a balcony waiting to be rescued. She was a strong, modern, working single mother who took care of her own problems.

She stepped around the corner, slamming her shoulder into the wall in the process and jarring the notepad onto the floor. No matter, she thought as she bent to retrieve it. Strong and poised weren't exactly synonymous.

Neither were grouchy and unattractive, she realized as she caught sight of him gazing out the window. Of course her heart was in full betrayal mode, lurching into an erratic beat when he came into view just like it had every time she thought about him after their last meeting. She hadn't experienced an illogical emotion-based crush like this since she fell into pre-teen Hollywood love with Aaron Carter, blushing every time she saw his face on one of those heartthrob magazines. And maybe Doug back in high school, but that realization should have been enough to kick those stupid butterfly flutters to the curb.

"Black coffee?" she asked as she stepped up to his table, staring at the notepad in her hand rather than waiting for his reaction. He didn't readily answer, so she glanced down at his fingers drumming out a rhythm on the tabletop.

"Working hard," he said, giving a brief shake of his head. "Four letters. Starts with A. Ends with T."

Narrowing her eyes, she leaned down enough to peek over his shoulder, catching the distinct firewood smoke scent clinging to his sweater. Clearing her throat, she stared at the newspaper in front of him and the point of the pen he had poised above the first block.

"At it." Straightening, she forced a calming breath. "Now, do you want the coffee or not?"

He leaned back against the booth seat, one leg outstretched under the table as he turned his chin up until he was looking at her face. His eyes were golden brown, the color of cognac, and she held his gaze while he lifted his eyebrows. "Why don't you surprise me?"

Disbelief settled over her like a rain-heavy cloud. "Surprise you?"

"Yeah." He returned to the crossword, rolling his shoulders a little as he leaned his elbows on the table. Same exact clothes he'd been wearing every time she'd seen him. It was almost enough to make her wonder if he slept in his Jeep, but the man was a highly acclaimed photographer. He'd received awards and even been at some high-society functions in Washington, D.C., wearing a suit and the whole nine yards.

She had admittedly Googled him a few too many times.

Turning on her heel, she headed for the kitchen. If it was a surprise he wanted, it was a surprise he would get.

Ruth had been gone for an inordinately long span of time. Long enough that he could have driven to another coffee shop, ordered a to-go cup, and come back and sat down without her noticing. But her absence might have been a good thing, because when he'd leaned back and looked up at her, he'd felt that same familiar jolt he'd experienced at the dog park. The inane feeling that he already knew the woman somewhere soul-deep.

He'd also gained the knowledge that her eyes were a misty gray blue, and she had one noticeable freckle on the right side of her nose. Knowledge that wasn't going to assist with anything but filling her out in those mental pictures he was conjuring up lately.

The whole thing was understandable, wasn't it? She was the only person to converse with him in any material way since he'd been in Tennessee. Granted, he had been hiding away in that cabin with nothing for company but the dog, but still . . .

"Surprise," she said, settling a mug in front of him on the table.

Pulling his arm away from the crossword puzzle, he leaned back and stared at the drink. Some sort of frothy whipped topping rose into a peak above the rim, leaving the contents of the cup a mystery. He tossed her a glance, which he immediately knew was a mistake. Her face was a little flushed, a strand of hair sweeping down over her forehead where it had escaped her ponytail.

"It's hot chocolate," she continued.

His gaze ricocheted back to the mug, staring at that foam again. "Like a kids drink?"

"Yeah. You seem like you need a little reminder about the pleasant things in life, but don't worry. It's bittersweet dark chocolate and kind of salty, so it fits you."

That statement sent a cough sputtering out of his throat and almost made him want to smile, but he pushed his spoon into the whipped topping instead, raising a scoopful above the mug.

"Don't suppose you want to finish my crossword?" he asked right before shoving the giant spoonful of airy, sugary cream into his mouth.

"Why? Did you give up?"

"Met a little resistance, so I'm thinking them through."

She settled into the booth across from him, pulling her bottom lip between her teeth as she studied the paper. Her knee touched his, so he sat a little straighter and pulled his legs back. The woman had beautiful cheekbones. The kind some women tried to create with makeup when they were preparing for photos. She also had fresh, dewy skin, reminiscent of girls he remembered from his college years. Sitting together with her, he could almost convince himself they were on a date.

He dug the spoon deeper into the cup and pulled out a mixture of fluff and cocoa, dripping thick off the spoon like melted chocolate chips. Leaning forward, he placed it in his mouth and waited for the ensuing sugar high to commence.

"This one's belt," she stated, placing her daintier letters in the middle of his boxy answers.

He didn't comment as he pondered the taste of the chocolate, finally swallowing the concoction. It was strangely intriguing, the sweet and salty. And he hadn't tasted hot chocolate in years.

"How old is your daughter?" he asked, thinking that might get to the bottom of the age question swirling in his mind without having to ask outright.

"Em's nine, and I fully expect copies of those pictures you took so I know you don't have any nefarious purposes."

He felt his brow furrowing as he took another spoonful of the chocolate. "I assure you, I have no nefarious purposes."

"Which of course you would say if you had nefarious purposes." She paused only long enough to fill in a few more letters. "Nice catch with Capra."

The letters FRANK automatically came into his line of vision on the crossword puzzle, but he scooped up a little more whipped cream so he could pick up the mug and drink like a grown man instead of sampling it like a bowl of soup. "I don't know many twenty-year-olds who do crossword puzzles."

She groaned but didn't meet his gaze. "If you had been listening when I told you my daughter was nine, you would know it's mathematically improbable for me to be twenty. It's fortunate that you told me to Google you and I already know you're thirty-four, so I won't ask you any insulting questions of my own. Besides, I think it's perfectly normal to do crossword puzzles all the time."

"Except it isn't." He lifted the mug, taking a sip of the rich chocolate.

"Done," she announced, pushing the paper in his direction. "Would you care for some breakfast? Wheat toast maybe?"

His brow wrinkled in consternation as he pulled the paper closer, surprised she'd finished so quickly. "I think I'll have the veggie omelet." Glancing up to meet her gaze, he tilted his head to the side. "With wheat toast."

Sliding the veggie omelet onto the table, Ruth settled herself across the booth from Tate Darrow, unable to stop the flitting sense of unease from swooping over her. The man had been in a room with the highest government officials in the land. He'd seen things she'd only imagined. What could she possibly say to interest someone like him?

He ignored the food and instead stared at her across the table, like he was waiting for something. An explanation for why she sat down, probably. Especially when he hadn't invited her to do so. She wasn't ready to offer a reason, though, because she didn't have a good one.

She found him intriguing as a fellow human, that was all. It had nothing to do with his Eastwood-esque appeal.

Picking up his fork, he turned his attention to his meal.

"I think you owe me something for the photos you took of Emily," she blurted. "You didn't request permission, after all."

His head instantly shot up, and he pinned her with his gaze while he brought his napkin to the side of his mouth. "You want me to pay you for taking photos?"

"No. Not monetarily, at least. I was just hoping you'd answer some questions. Appease my curiosity."

He settled the fork on the side of his plate, linking his hands together atop the table. "Shoot."

Jess offered a quizzical look as she walked by, plates in hand, but Ruth kept her focus on Tate. "The pictures of the cabins on your camera . . . what are you working on?"

Quickly clearing his throat, Tate seemed to shift a little in his seat. "I'm not really working on . . ." He took a deep breath. "That's my dad's place."

His answer was unexpected enough that she couldn't readily think of a reply. He leaned closer, hunching forward over the table and shoving his plate to the side. "I just lost my dad. Took a long sabbatical so I could spend time with him, and he passed two days later. Buried him the day before I met you, actually."

The heaviness that settled on her heart didn't feel like empathy for a stranger. "I'm sorry."

"And that morning the camera he gave me as a graduation gift decided to stop working." He lifted one hand to his beard, sliding his palm against his face. "Granted, the thing's a decade old, but of all the days to decide to quit . . ." He settled back in the booth, pulling the plate in front of him and grabbing his fork. "Anyway, I'm sorry for being a jerk that day."

She felt all the edges she wanted to keep as armor soften a little as she watched him eat his omelet. "Apology accepted. And I'm sorry I freaked out about the crossword puzzle."

He nodded but continued eating his eggs.

"I'd love to see the cabin sometime. It looks incredible."

His gaze lifted only about halfway, focusing somewhere on the table in front of her. "Yeah, okay."

"Emily and I are free Saturday."

Pulling the newspaper to his side of the table, he scrawled out a word at the top, shoving it back across so she could see it.

PUSHY.

Unable to fight the smile attempting to plant itself on her face, she took the pen and wrote her own word beneath it.

SELFISH.

He looked up at her, squinting his eyes beneath the stocking cap.

"Because you have a gorgeous mountain cabin and you don't want to share it with anyone," she offered, her cheeks heating a little at his intense scrutiny. "Just a pity, that's all."

With a resigned half-smile, he offered a slight nod of his head before writing only two letters at the top of the paper.

OK.

⁶WORDS

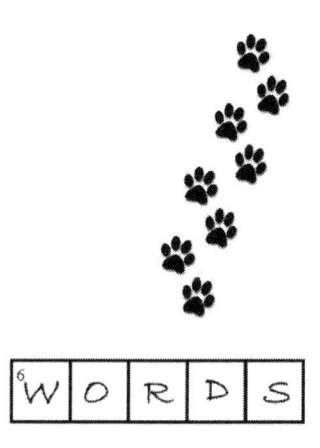

Lucy lifted her head from the multi-colored rag rug, her nose pointing in the direction of the door. Tate heard the engine noise mere seconds later, but it didn't fill him with the same sense of anticipation exhibited by the dog. His was more a lump of discomfort in the pit of his stomach.

There was no logical reason for the amount of disquiet he felt at the mere thought of Ruth. While he couldn't deny her natural sort of beauty, there was no rational argument for the two of them to be friends—on paper, anyway.

Narrowing his eyes, he nearly growled at himself as he rose from the chair in the corner. If staying in this drafty old cabin had made his dad lose his mind, he might need to keep a closer watch on his own mental faculties.

The dog began pawing at the door, letting out a high-pitched whine that caused him to furrow his brow. When they were alone the dog seemed older than the hills, content to mope around and sit in front of the fireplace like she was waiting for the grim reaper. One glimpse of that kid, though—Emily—and she'd reverted back to a frantic puppy state, running and playing in the park. It was a bit disconcerting to see her so full of life at the mere sound of a new car driving onto the scene. Was he horrible enough that the dog would rather die than live with him?

Releasing a lengthy sigh, he twisted the doorknob with gratefulness that the dog couldn't talk. Speculation about her feelings was bad enough. Hearing the canine say she hated him would be salt in an already painful wound.

"Lucy!" Emily shouted as she slammed the passenger door of the old Toyota, bounding halfway across the yard before the dog reached her and tapped its paws against her abdomen. The two of them fell to the ground, Lucy planting sloppy kisses on Emily's cheek as she rolled on the grass.

"Mind that you don't leave the yard," Ruth said, closing her own door more gently than Emily had.

He expected her to head toward the porch, but instead she drew her gaze skyward across the towering tree branches overhead. The corners of her lips inched up as she studied her surroundings, her arms folding themselves over her chest. Sunshine filtered through a patch of leaves to cast a pattern of light across her hair, tinting it with red and golden lines. She nearly melted into the scenery like she was part and parcel of the package as a whole.

A pang of longing flickered across his mind at the knowledge that he'd rarely ever seen unabashed wonder on the face of a stateside human before. With the exception of a few children and rural folks he'd encountered overseas while he was working, he'd only seen it on one person: his dad. He'd fit with the scenery here too, although Tate hadn't liked the image then.

He took the first step, staring down at the ground beneath his feet. The wood railing at his side beckoned for him to touch it, but he refused as he stuffed his hand in his pocket. The less interaction he had with the place, the better. Besides, he'd probably get a splinter.

"Mr. Tate, can I give Lucy a bone?" Emily propped herself up on one elbow, holding a plastic bag aloft. "Mom let me buy some and they're made of bacon."

He nodded his agreement as he watched Emily rise to her feet. Lucy patiently waited while the girl rifled through the bag, the only sign of the dog's discomfort the rapid thumping of her tail against the dirt.

With a shake of his head, he stepped further down the walkway, heading to Ruth's side. She had moved a few feet away from her car now, her arms still over her chest and only her profile visible as she continued to study their surroundings.

"Guess you found the place okay," he said, peering into the brush to try to see what she found so fascinating. Nothing caught his attention.

"Yeah, you gave top-notch directions." A bright smile lit her face as she turned it his way. "Darrow Acres, like something straight out of a novel."

"Guess I always thought it sounded like a ridiculous dude ranch. But my father believed it needed a name, thus the crude sign."

Her smile faltered a bit. "You're using crude to disparage the homemade nature of the sign, I take it?"

"No, I'm using crude because it's a little distasteful to see my name up there. And because the sign is tacky with the hand-lettered R's that don't have curved edges. It has all the warmth of a Halloween pumpkin carved with an ordinary butter knife by a harried and careless parent."

A giggle slipped from her lips as her eyes widened. "Wow. That's the most words I've heard you string together at once, and it only solidified the fact that you're a grumpy old booger."

That description took him aback. Not necessarily because she'd wounded or offended him, but more because the words almost stuck. He was beginning to feel like a grumpy old . . . booger.

"You don't like that I said that," she continued, dragging her attention back to the scenery.

"I doubt most people would enjoy being called grumpy, old, or a booger."

"True, but who could possess such a view and still be in a bad mood?"

He glanced around, his gaze naturally drifting to the canopy of leaves encompassing the space. "I take it you're a tree lover."

"I have a soft spot for nature. It makes me feel small enough to forget my problems for a moment. And you can't look at that tree in front of you and not feel a little awestruck. It has to be the largest yellow birch I've seen in quite some time."

"I can't say as I'm acquainted with many yellow birch varieties." He shifted his gaze to the line of trees to the left. "That tree there—"

"Mountain maple."

He paused with his mouth ajar, words sticking to his lips like they'd been affixed with glue. "The mountain maple, yes. It seems to be Lucy's particular favorite. I have a sneaking suspicion that a squirrel lives in its branches."

The grin on Ruth's face was so bright and warm, he found himself wondering how he'd put it there, just in case he wanted to replicate the effect later. "I suspect there are a great many unknown critters on Darrow Acres." She stepped away from her vehicle, wandering toward the tree line. "Do you mind if I ask you a personal question?"

"Most likely, but social etiquette would require me to say no. Besides, I doubt you would listen."

She turned toward him, the directness of her gaze causing his sweater to feel too warm. "You've been wearing the exact same clothes every time I've seen you. Are they your favorites, or are you especially eccentric and own several copies in those exact colors?"

His nose twitched like he'd suddenly developed a nervous tic. "I have plenty of other clothes, but I haven't bothered to get them out of the Jeep."

"Because?"

Another twitch, but this time he held the back of his hand against his nose to hide the telltale movement. "In case I have to hurriedly leave when the meddling townsfolk get too nosy."

"You sound like a villain from *Scooby Doo*. Are you going to tell me the truth or leave it at that?"

Somehow he'd earned her undivided attention, which hadn't been his intention. Since he had no desire to be studied the way she'd been studying the trees, he moved in the direction of Emily and the dog. "I took one bag inside when I got here because I figured the rest could wait. But it couldn't. Or didn't. In either case, I haven't been able to make myself take the other bags inside."

"Why not?"

"Because I don't want to." Glancing in the direction of the cabin, he gestured to it by extending his fingers. "I don't want *that*. I don't want a crumbling cabin or a cantankerous dog or a father who won't tell me he's sick until it's too late to do anything about it." Cringing, he closed his eyes and pressed his fingertips to his forehead. "This is a colossally bad idea. The talking to people thing. I shouldn't be doing it."

"That's debatable."

Tate opened his eyes in time to witness Ruth stuffing her fingers into the pockets of her jeans. "Debatable?"

"That you shouldn't be talking to people. It seems like you need someone to talk to, or at least to shine a light around you so you can see clearly. Your cabin's not crumbling, and Lucy certainly doesn't seem cantankerous to me."

A sharp bark clipped the end of her words as Lucy darted past them, chasing Emily toward the trees.

"About your father," she continued, a hint of tenderness slipping into her voice, "would you like to tell me about him?"

"No." He stared down at his boots before moving in the direction of the porch. The sweater was too warm for the afternoon sun, but he couldn't take it off without drawing attention to her previous comment about his clothes. Maybe if he moved into the shade he'd be more comfortable.

Turning as he reached the steps, he expected to see Ruth standing next to Emily but was surprised when she was right in front of him. Close enough that he grabbed the railing before he realized what he was doing, catching the hem of his sleeve on a wood sliver. "I never could understand why Dad moved here. When I was in Syria, he retired from the University of Virginia and disappeared. The mountains took him from me."

"How so?"

He met her eyes with his gaze, not bothering to answer her question. None of the women he'd ever dated had worn their hair like hers. They'd been more pulled together, smoothed out. Her dark hair was parted down the middle and windblown like she'd been hiking the mountains all day.

"Have you ever seen what happens to a hot dog in the microwave when you don't poke holes in it?" she asked.

With a quick blink, he found his eyes zeroed in on her lips as they moved. "A hot dog?"

"Yes. If you don't give it an avenue to release steam, it explodes."

"The hot dog explodes." He directed his attention back to his sleeve, gently tugging against the wood sliver that held him tight. "Sorry, I'm not sure what you're getting at."

"My point, hot dog, is that I'm a fork ready and willing to stab you. A fork you can walk away from at the end of the day without having to worry about whatever you said coming back to haunt you. And maybe, if you're lucky, I'll save you from exploding when you're here alone and there's no one to pick up the pieces."

Tate pulled on his sleeve again, achieving nothing. "That was horribly morbid."

"Fine, I'm not good at metaphors." Her fingertips touched the back of his hand while her other hand wrapped around his wrist. With one tug, she had him free of the railing. "This place seems to have quite the hold on you."

Running a finger across the stretched-out thread on his sweater, he shook his head. "Very funny."

"Take it off, I'll fix it for you."

"What, the sweater?"

"No dummy, your boot. Of course the sweater."

Tate stretched his arms above his head, tugging the sweater up until it shielded his face. For a second, Ruth squeezed her eyes shut and contemplated running back to the car. Stick a fork in him like a hot dog? Was she a complete and total idiot? His button-down shirt rose underneath the sweater, exposing the tail of his white T-shirt against his abdomen. Shirt untucked. Jeans tucked into his boots. Everything about him was odd and new and—

Exciting.

She shook herself a little as a reminder to knock it off. He wasn't exciting. He was goofy and grouchy and almost unhinged. And his hair was a little longer on top, she realized when his stocking cap came off with the sweater. He held both in his hands, but the sweater was the only one he extended. Sans cap, he seemed a little more unsure of himself.

Ruth took the sweater from his hand, turning it inside out while he watched. "Do you take a vow of silence while you're embedded in these war zones? Because I have to tell you—you're completely terrible at conversation."

"Normally I'm a brilliant conversationalist."

"I can picture you now, sitting at a party with your D.C. friends, rambling on about ghosts with your jeans tucked into your boots. Was your father a professor?"

"What?" He quickly scratched the side of his head before stretching the cap taut between his fists. "Is this that fork thing you were talking about? Or are you normally this abrupt?"

She tugged the errant thread through to the underside of the sleeve, then made a little knot to tie it off. "You look good without the sweater. I mean, red is a nice color on you."

He looked down, like he'd forgotten what color his shirt was. "Thanks."

"And your hair too. That unruly look fits you."

"I'm fairly certain that was an insult."

"Except it wasn't." With a flourish, she extended his sweater. "Good as new, so long as you don't look underneath."

"Another metaphor?"

One side of his mouth tilted up, instantly making him seem more approachable. And a lot more attractive, which her stomach seemed to notice before she did. Clearing her throat, she took a step back.

"To answer your question, no," he said as he carefully inspected the sweater sleeve. "My dad wasn't a professor. He worked maintenance at the university for thirty years."

"I see. What made him move here, to the cabin?"

He carefully draped the sweater over the railing before turning his attention to her with a lift of his eyebrows. "I know exactly what you're doing, and I'm not a hot dog."

"Touché." Ruth studied the railing, gently placing her hands atop it so she wouldn't catch on a wood splinter like Tate's sweater had. "I've never lived anywhere but Gatlinburg. It's been my long-held belief that certain choices I made in high school limited my options." She glanced at his profile, then down at the cap still in his fist. "And don't ask whether I still believe it—I'm slowly adapting to a different mindset. It's a process."

"Hmm, I can see your reluctance. Flirty waitressing is a lucrative career."

"Was that a joke? Are we making jokes now?"

"Merely an observation. I heard you talking about it at the diner, remember?"

She couldn't remember, actually, but she crossed her arms over her chest and kept her arguments locked inside, just in case he was right.

"Sort of," he muttered, quietly enough that she turned to stare at the side of his cheek.

"Sort of?"

"Joking. I gave it a shot. Didn't care for it."

"Of course you didn't." Unable to keep the smile from her face, she turned just in time to see Emily throw the worn goose toy across the yard. Lucy darted after it as though it were the real thing. A timely reminder to keep herself guarded. Tate might have inched out of his shell a little, but darting after him after the first hint of his humanity appearing would be a huge mistake.

⁷| G | O | A | T | S |

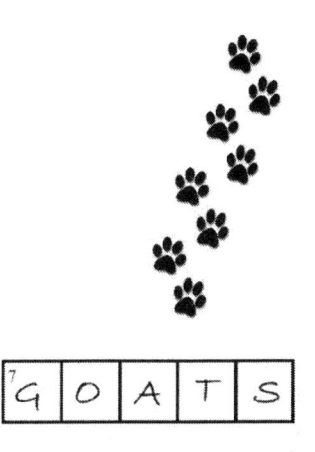

With two mug handles held firm in the crook of her finger, Ruth pulled the coffee pot from its warmer. A break couldn't come fast enough. The customers had been nonstop this morning and included a woman whose eyes had been so glued to her phone that she allowed her little guy to spread jelly all over the salt shaker. To make matters worse, Ruth had found it impossible to flirt with the familiar man at table two an hour earlier, and as a result she got no tip at all. One stupid comment from Tate about flirty waitressing being a lucrative career and her normal perky personality had shriveled up like a decade-old prune.

"Casanova's back," Jess whispered, the distinct mingled scents of peppermint and smoke filtering over Ruth's senses like a fog.

Half expecting the guy who'd stiffed her for a tip earlier, Ruth glanced over her shoulder. Tate Darrow sat at number four, folded up newspaper on the table in front of him.

"I'm pretty sure Casanova actually wanted people to like him," Ruth whispered back, settling the mugs on the counter.

"He's kind of cute," Jess added, following her words with an over-the-top wink.

"Like a pet skunk."

Jess turned her back to the counter and stared at Tate, causing Ruth to do the same. He sat with his elbow on the table, one hand atop the stocking cap on his head. At least today he was wearing a navy hooded sweatshirt instead of his standard sweater.

"I've heard skunks can make great pets," Jess continued.

"Maybe after they've been disarmed. That one still attacks when you get near him." She pinched the tip of her nose and widened her eyes before grinning at Jess, who rounded the corner and disappeared into the kitchen.

"Two fully caffeinated cups of joe," Ruth stated as she set the mugs on table six. "Missed you boys at breakfast this morning. Getting a late start?"

"Really early start, more like," the guy on the left said. "Earlier than Pitt would have started cooking breakfast. Is it too soon to get lunch?"

"Yes, but I'm sure he'd make an exception for the two of you. You both want the special?"

"Yes, ma'am."

She couldn't resist a quick peek at the back of Tate's neck as she returned the coffee pot to the counter. One hand had moved to rest there just below his hairline, while the other was perched with a pen above the paper.

After a trip into the kitchen to ask Pitt about the lunch special, she returned to the counter and grabbed her own copy of the paper, along with a pencil. Without saying a word, she slid herself onto the vinyl seat across from Tate, placing her newspaper on the table in front of her. He'd already completed several of the answers, which she'd have known even if she couldn't see his boxy handwriting in the little spaces. The harsh slash marks through the clues were more than enough to let her know he'd finished them.

"You do know this isn't a public library," she stated, filling in the boxes on one across. "Normally people who take a table here order something."

"Sure. And normally waitresses take orders instead of seating themselves at customers' tables."

"A true statement. I knew you'd need help with your crossword, though. There's an air of confusion about you."

"Are you sure it's not skunk scented?"

Ruth drew her gaze up from the paper, settling it firmly on his dark eyebrows. They were drawn in concentration, not giving her any attention.

"You weren't supposed to hear that."

"Probably not. Just for the record, it wouldn't bother me if you liked me, but I'm not sure I'm ready to disarm just yet."

A smile began to form on her face, so she looked back down at her newspaper. "No, I think you enjoy being a stinker too much to allow that."

He laughed. Barely and very quietly, but he still laughed. She counted it a triumph.

God help him, Gatlinburg was making him lose his mind.

First the dog—the two of them had actually gone to the dog park on their own the afternoon before, and she'd followed up on their hasty jog around the premises by licking him on the hand. A dog kiss from the ghost hound who had previously hated him.

Second, he'd pulled the kitchen appliances into the middle of the room and started re-staining the cabinets. He wasn't supposed to make the cabin homier. Wasn't even supposed to want to be there.

And third . . .

Ruth. No matter how he tried, he couldn't get the woman out of his head.

"What brings you out of hiding this morning?" she asked, followed by her lips moving as she silently read the clue for the crossword puzzle.

"Believe it or not, I enjoy doing the crossword with you."

"I don't believe it." She made a tidy checkmark next to clue twelve down instead of crossing it out like he had.

"You don't believe I would actively seek out your company?"

"No, I don't believe there's something in life that you actually enjoy. Ooh, twenty-three across will stump you for sure."

He dropped his gaze to the paper in front of him and checked his own answers. "Mohair."

"Seriously? You got that out of *goat product*? I'm impressed."

"Sudan is one of the top exporters of sheep and goats." He paused while the writing on the paper seemed to fuzz together at his lack of interest. "That tidbit of useless information had nothing to do with me knowing the answer."

He looked up from his paper and focused on Ruth instead, who exhibited a hint of a smile at his words. Her hair was swept up into a messy bun at the back of her neck, one piece falling down over the side of her cheek. He had the sudden thought that it would be fun to photograph her.

Maybe at the cabin, with the sun filtering through the trees and a wistful smile on her face.

"Don't tell me you're finished already."

Her words shook him out of his trance. "I was just thinking about photos."

"Of goats in Sudan?"

"No, no goats." He leaned back, letting his wrist rest on the edge of the table. "Have you had your photo taken recently?"

"Sure. My mom took a picture of me with Emily in front of the church on Easter."

His mind immediately filled in the blanks of that mental picture, dressing Emily in a pink number with lace falling to her knees, next to Ruth in a pastel blue cardigan with pearls around her neck. "Wow. Classic standing on the church steps? Not . . . hunting for eggs or eating giant chocolate rabbits?"

"Heavens no. Mom doesn't rabbit on Easter. No bunny loves you like Jesus." Ruth's eyes settled on his, twinkling with a hint of mischief. "It was a sweet picture though. Somehow she caught Emily mid-sneer and captured the precise moment the wind swept my hair across my lip gloss so it plastered to my cheek. Good times. Have you ever taken pictures of goats? Now I'm curious."

Tate couldn't help but grin at her rapid change of subject. "Um, yes, come to think of it. In Scotland."

The smile slid from her face. "I detest you. Is there anywhere you haven't been?"

He placed the pen on the paper, giving up on the crossword for the moment. "A lot of places. I haven't been to New Zealand. It's on my bucket list."

"New Zealand's on my bucket list," she mimicked, wrinkling her nose. "You know what's on my bucket list? Virginia."

He almost laughed, but something in her demeanor instead had him furrowing his brow. "You're telling me you've never been to Virginia?"

"Never."

"How is that possible? It's only a couple hours' drive."

"Thank you for the geography lesson, but I've seen my share of maps." Ruth returned her attention to the newspaper in front of her. "My parents were never the traveling sort, and I've not had the opportunity to get out much as an adult. More important things to worry about."

He waited for her to look up at him again, but she didn't. Her lips moved as she read the next clue, then lifted the pencil eraser to place it on her cheek while she thought.

"You really should get out more," he stated, picking up his pen.

"Now you sound like my mother."

"I suppose that makes sense. I'm not crazy about rabbits, either."

That remark elicited a slight giggle. "Emily is with Doug this weekend. Maybe I'll live wild and go to Walmart or something."

She placed her tiny little checkmark next to the crossword clue, glancing up to catch him staring at her. He brought a fist to his mouth to clear his throat, then tried to focus on the crossword puzzle in front of him. "If your choice is Walmart or something, I'd choose something."

| ⁸S | P | U | R |

The knock sounded on her door just as Ruth had a very full spoon of chocolate-covered cherry ice cream pressed to the roof of her mouth. She paused with the spoon hanging from her lips, indecision flooding her veins. Interruptions weren't welcome tonight. Not when her situation called for *Steel Magnolias* and sleep that carried her safely through to the sunlit hours.

To answer the door or not to answer, that was the prickly question. It was probably Mrs. Oliver from next door asking Ruth to water her plants or collect her mail while she went to visit her daughter. She could pretend not to be home. Could even hide in the bathroom to make her absence more convincing if need be.

But if she didn't help Mrs. Oliver, she'd feel guilty about it all weekend.

With her full bowl in one hand, she pulled open the door with the other, spoon still in her mouth. Instead of Mrs. Oliver, her eyes landed on Tate Darrow.

"This is not a good look on you," he said, letting his eyes sweep downward as he took in her attire.

She stood up a little straighter, releasing the doorknob so she could pull the spoon from her mouth. The ice cream stuck to the roof of her mouth, giving her an instant lisp. "Thweat pants ah pewfectly acceptable for an evening alone, thank you vewy much."

"I was talking about the spoon. Not a great choice for mouth gear." Sucking in the sides of his cheeks, he narrowed his eyes. "Am I interrupting the beginning of one of those stereotypical chick flick things? Woman shooting whipped cream straight into her mouth while she watches sappy romances and feels sorry for herself?"

With the bowl held close to her abdomen, she leaned against the door frame. "You couldn't be more wrong. I'm enjoying a dessert and watching *Steel Magnolias* and . . ." *Feeling sorry for myself,* she nearly added.

He gave an almost imperceptible nod, stuffing a hand into the pocket of his jeans. "Quite possibly the biggest bowl of ice cream I've ever seen. Chick flick protocol would lead me to presume you're eating your feelings. Do you want to talk about it?"

"No." Taking a step back, she crossed to the kitchen and placed her bowl on the counter. "You do realize it's weird to show up at my doorstep, right? Especially since I haven't given you my address."

"No weirder than people without dogs going to the dog park."

She let a laugh slip out before resting her palms against the island counter to face him. "Apples and oranges. The dog park is a public place. I won't ask how you knew my address if you tell me why you're here."

A hint of a smile tipped up the corner of his lips as he stepped into the room and closed the door behind him. "Jess gave me your address."

For a split second she pondered being upset at Jess for playing matchmaker, but seeing him remove his jacket and drape it over the back of her couch erased all her protests. It was impossible to miss the fact that he didn't add why he was at her apartment. Not that she minded him being at her apartment, really, but having a handsome man in her living room was a new sensation. She never invited men over. Had only been on a handful of dates since Emily had been born, and none of them had turned into anything serious enough to warrant an invitation to her home.

Looking away, she focused instead on the creamy-hued door of her freezer. "Do you like chocolate-covered cherry?"

"What?"

"Ice cream," she added, opening an overhead cabinet door to grab an empty bowl.

"Sounds good, thanks."

Best not to overthink things, she reminded herself as she tugged open the freezer door and grabbed the tub of ice cream. She wasn't dating this guy. They happened to run into each other a few times, and she let Emily play with his dog at the cabin once. He definitely hadn't asked her out. That she would have remembered.

Did he think they were . . . friends? The thought almost made her mood wilt as if it were a living, breathing thing.

Shaking her head, she grabbed the oversized spoon she'd used to scoop her ice cream and gave it a quick rinse in the sink. She was perfectly capable of having a normal, friendly conversation.

With handsome seasoned international photojournalist Tate Darrow.

In her apartment.

A sudden panic forced a quick intake of breath, and she couldn't resist the urge to glance at him. He stood with his hand on the back of the couch, casually giving the room a once-over. Ruth noticed every single element of the scene at once. Tate's red T-shirt. The Tinkerbell blanket thrown over the arm of the couch. The pile of Emily's dirty clothes she'd taken out of her duffel bag so she could pack for the weekend. She definitely should have emptied that a couple of weeks ago.

If Tate thought the cabin was horrible, what must he think of her apartment with the decades-old green and brown patterned couch, the miniscule television, and the odd stain in the corner of the carpet that she couldn't remove no matter how she tried?

He caught her eye, straightening as he drummed his fingers on the couch back. "Am I interrupting your plans?"

"Plans?"

"Walmart or something."

Ruth practiced a slow breathing exercise as she scooped a spoonful of ice cream into the bowl. Relief surged through her as her lungs opened up, letting her drag in a full tug of air. "I've already been, as evidenced by the ice cream. How much do you need? A normal amount, or a chick flick sappy romance serving?"

"Let's try a normal amount."

She tossed the spoon in the sink before putting the ice cream away. "I'm very curious to know more about your experiences with chick flicks."

"I bet."

His eyes continued to rove over every inch of her apartment, taking in the old-fashioned flowered pattern of the wallpaper and Emily's hand-painted artwork from school. Unable to help herself, Ruth glanced down at her ratty T-shirt, complete with the little bleach spot near the hem, like a tiny white sunburst against the grape colored fabric. He had to be judging her. She was judging herself.

Standing a little straighter, she took Tate's bowl in hand and raised her chin. "I'd like to hear the details now, actually. How do you know so much about chick flicks?"

Tate stopped investigating the room and instead focused on her, raising one eyebrow as he extended his hand. Shaking her head, she pulled the bowl closer.

"The ice cream is being held hostage until I get information."

"That's hostile abuse of a dessert."

Turning to grab her own bowl of ice cream, Ruth ordered herself to relax before she casually moved to the living room. Sitting at the end of the couch, she placed Tate's bowl on the coffee table and her own firmly in her lap. Instead of taking a seat at the other end, he rounded the opposite side of the sofa and parked himself directly in the center, only inches from her. From that close proximity, it was impossible to miss his subtle lean closer to the ice cream.

"Nope," she said, pushing it farther from his grasp. Scooping up a heaping spoonful from her own bowl, she eyed it with a comical amount of delight. "This is so, so good."

He sighed as he plopped back against the couch cushions. "Fine, but I get to ask a question of you afterwards. Turnabout's fair play."

"Fine."

This close, his eyes almost had a green tint mixed in the brown hue. Between that and his almost-curling at the ends hair she rarely saw thanks to his usually-present cap, she was having a hard time keeping her gaze averted.

"I've always had a roommate to share expenses. Kenny was my roommate the longest. His girlfriend did nothing but watch Lifetime movies while he was at work. If I happened to come home while she was there watching that stuff, it's not my fault."

Ruth swallowed her ice cream and tried not to smile. "I'm sure you never actually watched them."

Tate offered a tiny shrug as she slid the bowl in his direction. "Never on purpose. My turn now? What's all this about?"

She hesitated to answer as he twirled the spoon around in his bowl, turning the vanilla and chocolate into a light brown mess. "All this?"

"You seem to be in a mood."

"A mood? Because of the ice cream?"

"In spite of the ice cream."

All the chocolate covered cherries in the world couldn't sweeten a question like that. Placing her bowl on the coffee table, she settled back on the couch, twisting her fingers together in her lap.

"I only ask because your light seems to have gone out since I saw you earlier," he continued.

"My light?"

"You know. 'See you around, Tate.' The light. That thing that makes you a memorable waitress and keeps those guys coming back every day. It can't be the food."

The bright inflection he'd used to mock her tone almost made her want to wince, but instead she shook her head. "Just tired, I suppose. Can I get you anything to drink? I have water, apple juice, coffee." She rose to her feet, not bothering to wait for his answer. Her tone sounded too airy now, like she was trying to force something that didn't exist.

The bowl and spoon she'd been using rattled in the sink as she set them down, the remains of ice cream pooling into a puddle of mud at the bottom. The image seared into her brain, drawing her attention like a crime scene. If something that looked so delicious only moments ago could look like dirt now, what hope was there?

And Tate hadn't answered about wanting a drink. He probably didn't want anything but to conjure up an escape route.

"He's proposing tonight," she blurted, her fingers wrapping around the edge of the sink for support. "My ex wanted Emily to come over for the weekend because he's using her in an elaborate proposal for his girlfriend. It doesn't bother me, really. He's turned his life around and I want him to be happy for Emily's sake." She paused and glanced up at the ceiling. "It's not like I want him to be alone just because I'm alone. That would be ridiculous. And there's no way I could ever dislike his girlfriend, because she's a really nice woman. Sweet and innocent and . . . blind. She's not even drawn to him because he's attractive. She likes his personality. You sure you don't want some water?"

The deafening silence in the room left only the ticking of the clock on the wall and the sound of her heartbeat pounding in her ears. Maybe she'd imagined all that in her head and hadn't announced it to the room. If she had, he'd have commented, right?

Jingling sounded behind her, the unmistakable noise of keys clanking together, and in that moment she knew. She'd said every word. Every. Humiliating. Word.

Turning to face the living room, she drew in a deep breath. Tate would leave now, and she would smile bravely and pretend she didn't care. Except he wasn't moving toward the door. Instead, he stood in front of her, his eyebrows slanting down the way they always did when he studied her.

"I'll rinse the bowls out," he said, motioning with his head for her to move out of the way.

Stepping to the side, she watched his hands as he turned the knob for the faucet. "Well, then what am I supposed to do?"

"Pack a bag, and be quick about it. We'll have to leave soon if we're going to get to Virginia before nightfall."

9. RIDE

Tate propped himself up on his elbows, glancing around the dim room while his mind adjusted to the change of scenery. It wasn't the cabin he was waking up in this morning, but a queen size bed at a historic Virginia hotel. He blinked to clear the fog while his gaze landed on the nightstand, the magazine resting there clearly stating that Virginia was for lovers.

Could have been why the front desk clerk looked at him strangely the night before when he'd paid for two rooms and given Ruth her own key.

This shouldn't have made him feel uncomfortable, though. This was exactly the kind of thing he normally did. Come up with a plan and execute immediately. Find a potential story, buy a plane ticket, and disappear for months. It was squatting in the cabin that felt all wrong, not spur of the moment decisions.

"You know what's on my bucket list? Virginia," she'd said. Those few words, and he'd gone straight into research mode. *Find the closest town, book a hotel, plan out the day's activities.* He and Ruth would be heading out on the shuttle in a couple of hours to the top of the mountain.

The trail promised seventeen miles of easy biking back to the bottom. Maybe when they got back they could relax and enjoy a leisurely dinner before he drove her to Gatlinburg.

He'd planned their trip well before he arrived at her apartment the night before, but watching her begin to self-destruct in front of him had made something snap. She was easily the most enigmatic, naturally charming person he'd ever met. The fact that she felt second best to anyone made him want to shake her a little bit. Or shake that ex of hers, maybe.

And on top of it all, in any other situation he'd want to date her. Whatever his internal wrangling, it all hinged on that fact in the end. She wouldn't, or maybe shouldn't, be receptive to the idea. There was Emily to consider, and he wasn't going to become a full-time Tennessee resident. Any talk of a future seemed like a non-starter, and a relationship would be doomed from the beginning.

A hollow knock rang through the door, interrupting his thoughts and leading him to stretch his arms above his bed before rising. The air conditioner kicked on in the corner, emitting a buzz so all-consuming he could almost imagine the floor vibrating as his bare feet hit the carpet.

With a swift twist, he popped open the lock and pulled the door open a couple of inches. "Ruth?"

"Am I too early? My body is accustomed to being awake before the crack of dawn, but I gave you two extra hours while I worked on the crossword book you gave me."

He reached up to scratch the back of his head, accidentally releasing the door so it snapped back into place. Fixing an apologetic look on his face, he pulled it back open. "Sorry about that. I just rolled out of bed, but if you give me five minutes—"

"You sleep in your clothes?"

That was all the impetus he needed to make him look down at his rumpled jeans and Army-green T-shirt. "Doesn't everybody?" Her eyes opened wide enough that he almost regretted joking about the subject.

"No, but I can see why you would, embedded in your military war zones halfway across the world." That familiar indecisiveness popped into her expression, like she was comparing herself to some imaginary standard and not measuring up. "I'll pop back over to my room and give you some time."

She backed away from the door and took a step away before he could get himself into the door frame and peek out at her.

"Truthfully, I'm just low maintenance. And maybe a little lazy."

"What every girl wants to hear," she said with a hint of humor in her voice, throwing him one token smile before she scanned her key card and disappeared.

He stood there for a moment, staring at the empty space she'd occupied only seconds before. Something debilitating had happened since he'd set foot in Tennessee, because there was a time he'd been able to talk to other human beings and carry on normal conversations. A very recent time.

A pre-Ruth time.

Ruth centered herself over the bike, one sneaker on the ground and one perched on the opposite pedal. She couldn't even remember the last time she'd attempted to ride. Third grade? Fourth? As long as it had been, she sincerely hoped the mantra *it's just like riding a bike* actually held true.

Tate was next to her looking a great deal more cool and aloof than she felt as he fastened the strap of his blue helmet beneath his chin. Her mind wanted to wander back to a few hours before when she'd knocked on his door, but she forced her attention to the trees in her periphery. There was no sense thinking about his messy hair and the way he'd rolled out of bed . . .

Well, like she imagined Clint Eastwood would roll out of bed in one of those old westerns. If he'd had a six shooter on his hip and told her to make his day, she might have swooned.

Which was stupid. Stupid! Single mothers trying to make better lives for their daughters were not allowed to swoon when cowboy sorts rode into town shooting . . . photos and stuff.

"You going to be okay?" he asked, staring at the helmet she gripped with both hands.

"Time will tell," she murmured, lifting the helmet to her head. "When was the last time you rode a bike? Don't tell me—coasting around the streets of Italy or something similar."

"I actually have a bike that I ride sometimes so I don't have to deal with traffic. The answer to your question is . . ."

Ruth snapped the buckle underneath her chin, accidentally catching her skin in the process. A finger forced between the strap and her neck let her know she wasn't still attached to the plastic, but didn't make it hurt any less.

"To tell the truth," he continued, "I'm not sure. Within the last year."

The timing of his last bike ride wasn't really the point, but she had managed to learn he wasn't a novice. A previously random fact that now held the potential to make her present situation more embarrassing.

"How about you? When was your last ride?"

"I'm pretty sure it might have followed an episode of *Rugrats*."

"*Rugrats*. Were you watching this episode, or was it Em?"

"Definitely me."

"So very recent."

"Very." She pulled her stationary leg off the ground while she pushed the pedal, the bike wobbling a few feet before she planted her foot back on the dirt. "Very, very recent."

He pulled up next to her, hands wrapped firmly around his handlebars. "I've heard it's easy to get back into the swing of things. Just like riding a bike."

"That's very helpful, Captain Obvious."

Tate's lips broke into a smile. An actual smile. Not one of those half-hearted smiles she'd seen him give at the diner. It was downright disarming.

"Would you like assistance?" he asked. "I could hold onto your bike while you get it going."

"Walk behind me like I'm a four-year-old? No thank you."

"I meant hold your bike from here."

The wind kicked up behind her just as heat crept up her neck. She made a show of pulling her jacket's zipper an inch higher, careful not to shift on the bike.

"Hey, you're mountain biking in Virginia," he said, turning his head to take in the panoramic view. "A perfect thing to cross off your bucket list. Can't think of anything I'd rather be doing."

"I'd only make a check mark instead of crossing it off, and you don't have to patronize me."

"I'm not patronizing you." He paused and reached up to scratch his cheek in front of the helmet strap. "Maybe a little. I'd rather be zip lining in Peru. Kayaking in Belize. Only if you could come along, of course."

She narrowed her eyes as he turned to face her once again. "I'll let you know if I have any trips to Belize coming up in the future. For now, I'm ready to give this a try. Are you going to hold the bike?"

His palm clasped her handlebar. "Got it."

With a deep breath, she pressed her foot against the pedal and sent the bike crawling forward at a snail's pace.

"The trick to staying balanced is having a little speed," he said, shuffling along beside her.

She forced her feet to move faster, keeping her gaze focused on the path in front of her. With each wobble, she gripped the bar tighter to keep it straight. Tate's hand never left her bike, pacing her like he was accustomed to moving like a tortoise.

"You're getting it," he added, shooting a little surge of pride through her veins. With a hasty nod, she cast a glance at him. Huge mistake.

Her front wheel veered to the left, careening into his before her pedal met his bike chain. The bikes intertwined and bobbed back and forth before violently separating, sending them in opposite directions. Ruth shoved her foot in the dirt and held her bike upright as she glanced at Tate, who tipped over in a perfect imitation of a slow-motion people falling highlight reel.

Her mouth dropped open as he fought to lift the bike from his thigh from his new place on the ground. The apology was on the tip of her tongue, but instead she found herself gaping at him. Grease from the chain marked a line up the leg of his jeans, made more visible when he rolled onto his back and propped himself up on one elbow.

"I can't ride a bike," he stated, squinting one eye as the sunlight cascaded over him like a halo.

"Seriously? You told me you currently have a bike."

"You're misunderstanding. I was letting you know what you should have said earlier. When I said, 'Hey, I arranged for us to bike down the mountain,' that was your cue."

"I can't ride a bike," she repeated quietly.

"See? That wasn't so difficult."

"No. Do you need some assistance?"

"Absolutely not, don't move a muscle." Shrugging one shoulder, he slid his backpack strap away from his arm. Before she had time to wonder what he was doing, he'd managed to unzip his pack and pulled his camera to his lap. The instant it tilted up in her direction, her eyes widened.

"Are you kidding me? I'm wearing a helmet."

"Somehow makes you more stunning. It would be a shame to waste this light."

He focused on his camera instead of her, but she couldn't keep her eyes pointed in his direction. Peering to her right, she took in the backs of two seasoned bike professionals as they headed down the trail at a swift pace. Insecurity gnawed at her, urging her to turn her back or at least pop a hand in front of her eyes. Ignoring its promptings, she finally returned her attention to Tate.

"Give it up," she said, wiggling her fingers in front of her.

He held the camera between his palms, cradling it near his chest. "Why?"

"Turnabout's fair play, and it would be a shame to waste this light."

"Are you kidding me? I'm wearing a helmet."

She didn't relent, and with the biggest sigh imaginable, he leaned forward to hand her the camera.

"Is this for the blackmail?" he asked. "I can't think of any other reason you'd want to photograph me in this embarrassing predicament."

"Totally for the blackmail." With the bike leaning against her inner thigh, she brought the camera up to her face. Forget the fact that she had no idea how to use it. Tate Darrow flat on his rear beneath that bike with a self-effacing grin was a mental picture it would take a long time to erase.

10. BURNED

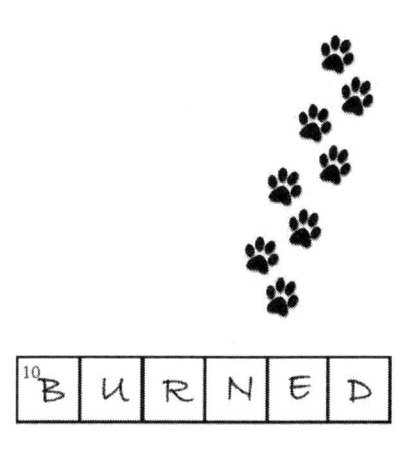

The pizza sitting between them on the table sent up a ribbon of steam, the cheese still bubbling where it touched the outside crust. Too dangerous to bite into just yet. Ruth had to be content to wait it out, knowing she would be burned if she rushed.

Tate leaned back against the booth's vinyl seat, his wrist on the table while his fingers tapped out a rhythm. She couldn't remember if she'd ever met anyone quite so fidgety.

"What did you think of it?"

His words were surprising enough that she could only blink as she pondered a response. "Think of what?"

"Virginia."

It was cute the way he really thought Virginia was on her bucket list, like some exotic place she'd only dreamed of visiting someday. As world wise as he should have been, he obviously had trouble detecting the sarcasm in her answer the day before. The only reason Virginia was on her metaphorical bucket list was because she'd never been anywhere, so she didn't dare allow herself to picture a faraway locale.

She couldn't even imagine anything exotic when he'd asked what she wanted for dinner, squeaking out pizza like Emily might have done.

"It's fantastic," she answered, fiddling with the cloth napkin on her lap.

Where would she have wanted to go, if she had the choice? She wouldn't dream of popping off an answer like Tate did—Peru or Belize or the far side of China. Maybe Virginia really should have been the extent of her traveling bucket list. Pennsylvania if she dared to push her boundaries.

"I'm ninety-nine percent certain I'll be sore tomorrow," he continued. "It's been years since I've had a bike wreck. Decades maybe."

She cringed as she grabbed the parmesan cheese shaker, twisting it between her hands. "I know it doesn't change anything, but I'm sorry about causing the accident."

"You're not sore, I hope."

"Only my pride."

"I'd say. My pride might never be the same." Grabbing the spatula from the pan between them, he lifted a slice of pizza, its cheese playing tug of war with the pieces left in the circle. Leaning forward, he slipped the slice onto her plate. "Was that Emily you were talking to while I was in the men's room?"

Ruth slid the cheese shaker back toward the wall. "Yeah, the proposal went off without a hitch. Doug is officially engaged to be married."

Saying the words aloud caused an ache so deep in her chest, she couldn't begin to understand its source. As far as she had deciphered, the needling discomfort had nothing at all to do with Celeste. It was impossible to be jealous of a legally blind woman who managed to naively see the world as a beautifully enrapturing place when life was usually so mundane.

The beginning swells of panic rocketed around her lungs, threatening to cut off her air supply if she didn't get things under control. Yet another way she succeeded in feeling like the most ridiculous woman in the world. Having a panic attack over something important felt almost normal. Mounting bills, threatening creditors, job worries, fears about her daughter's well-being—those seemed like legitimate reasons for panic. She always managed like a trooper during those situations, though. It was the commonplace days—the ones that melted into one another with nothing of significance—that made her want to burrow into a hole. She couldn't imagine Celeste doubling over and gasping at the thought of nothing changing. Who had panic attacks over nothing?

"Ruth?"

A gasp of breath escaped her lips as she looked across the table at Tate, one eyebrow lowered as his curious gaze fixed on her.

Pizza. Soda. Diversions usually calmed her brain enough to thaw the freeze. Going for the slice Tate had placed in front of her, she lifted it and took a bite, her thoughts immediately transferring into another realm when the cheese and sauce affixed to the roof of her mouth like a spoonful of molten lava. If she were at home, she would have spit it back onto the plate, but never in a million years would she do that in front of Tate. Sucking in a breath, she tried to push the bite aside with her tongue to relieve the sting. As a last-ditch effort, she grabbed her drink, pulling as much soda through the straw as she could manage.

Before she could come up with a plan, Tate was by her side, his hand tracing circles on her back. Her emotions ricocheted from humiliation to admiration and back again before she managed to compose herself.

"I'm fine," she mumbled, finally having cooled the bite enough to swallow it. "I may need some kind of graft on the roof of my mouth, but I'll survive."

"You sure? You seemed far away for a minute."

Far away.

She was a measly one hundred-thirty miles from home, but he was right. Everything important seemed as far away as could be.

"That seems like a big job, refinishing the hardwood."

Tate closed the Jeep's passenger door behind Ruth and followed her away from the parking lot. "Maybe, but I need something to keep me busy so I don't spend all my time staring at my dad's notebooks."

She lowered herself to the park bench outside her apartment building and sank her sneakers into grass the landlord probably should have trimmed last week. "Full of lofty ideas, those notebooks?"

He only hesitated for a few seconds before he seated himself beside her. "No, they appear to be the random rantings of a man gone insane."

That was the kind of statement she didn't know how to answer, so instead she made a game of linking her fingers together in her lap, twisting them one way and then the other. "You don't like to talk about your dad, do you?"

She glanced at him in time to see one corner of his lips inch up, but he kept his gaze on the parking lot. "It was never a problem before, but now I have no idea what to say.

Not once in all my conversations with him did he tell me about why he moved here or what he was doing in that cabin, so to find those notebooks after he passed away felt like stumbling onto this secret life."

Staring out into the inky twilight, Ruth forced herself to ponder an appropriate response. Acting rashly earlier had left her with a burn, and she wasn't about to go there again.

"What was he like, your dad? Before he came here, I mean?"

"Reliable. Steady. No-nonsense."

"Sounds like you're describing my old Toyota."

That comment made him smile. If she could figure out the secret to coaxing out his grin, she'd replicate the action over and over.

"Maybe those weren't the best adjectives to use. He was a hard worker, and there was never a question about whether he'd be there for me if I asked. He would always show up, without fail."

"He had to have been a hard worker, being in maintenance all his life."

"He went to college for a year, but never figured out what he wanted to do. Then his future kind of got decided for him." Tate stretched his arms out in front of him, inspecting the back of his hands against his knees. "He met my mom at the beginning of the year, and by the end of the year, it was apparent that I'd be joining them."

"What happened after you came along?"

"He took the job at the college and raised me the best he knew how."

"What about your mom?"

Tate paused while he leaned back and lifted one leg, propping his ankle against the other knee. His posture almost seemed to relax. Had the shoe been on the other foot and

Ruth been on the receiving end of the questions, she'd have been folding herself into a ball of nervousness.

"She was a scared kid, too afraid of what her family would think to take me home. My dad stepped up and took responsibility."

The matter-of-fact way he stated those words settled deep in Ruth's heart and stirred a wave of empathy. Would Emily have ended up telling a similar story some day? But Doug had returned, changing everything.

"Have you ever—"

"Tried to find her?" Tate turned his gaze to the sky, making Ruth follow his line of vision to stare up at the dark expanse. "I know who she is, and I almost worked up the nerve once. Went so far as searching her information on one of those Internet people finders, but what I saw there stopped me in my tracks. Two kids, thirteen and eleven. Every time I thought about standing at her doorstep, the what-ifs rolled through my head. What if she'd never told her husband about me? What if it caused a rift in their marriage? What if I ended up splitting the family apart? I couldn't risk impacting those kids."

Tate's hand rested on his thigh, and with her heart in her throat, Ruth reached over and placed her fingers over his. Not once had she bad-mouthed Doug to her daughter, but compassion in her heart? Would she have cared if his life got disrupted? Did she even care now?

Tate turned his hand over and laced his fingers through hers, gently rubbing his thumb across her knuckles. "Sometimes I remind myself that it's a miracle I'm alive. She could have easily chosen another route, and it goes without saying that I'm glad she didn't. So far this life's been a pretty good ride."

Ruth contented herself to stare at the sky, relishing the feel of Tate's hand in hers. The importance of bucket list vacation destinations faded into the periphery, replaced by gratitude for simply experiencing the warm night sky with this man. And of all the things she had in her life to be thankful for, in that moment she said a prayer of thanks for Tate's presence beside her.

[11] BOOK

Emily sprang from the vehicle the minute Ruth put it in park, not even bothering to close the passenger door behind her. With a groan, Ruth stalled the engine. She remembered some of the other girls back in junior high being boy crazy to the point that they could barely converse about anything else, but with Emily she was certain the obsession was going to be dogs. Always.

Probably way better than obsessing about boys in the long run.

"Emily, you should be polite and ask before you—"

Tate opened the door of his Jeep, sending Lucy barreling after Emily. So much for the impending valuable tip on polite behavior, as if Emily would have heard it anyway. Her brain was probably hitting on only one cylinder: *Must pet dog. Must pet dog.*

Stepping out of the vehicle, Ruth pushed her own door closed before rounding the front of the car to close Emily's. "Your dog's out of control," she said, loud enough that Tate could hear her where he was exiting his Jeep two parking spots away. He speared her with a look that spoke volumes, but she shrugged as she closed the passenger door. Emily wasn't out of control. Overly rambunctious maybe.

He stepped closer until he was only a couple of feet away, his messenger bag draped over his shoulder and the camera he normally carried glaringly absent.

"No photos today?" she teased, stepping away from the asphalt until her sandals padded through the grass.

"No, a friend recently told me that I'm too focused on the lens. I should look at the view outside it now and then."

How was she supposed to respond to that? She'd been the one who gave him that mini lecture a morning ago at the café over the crossword puzzle, but the word *friend* poked her in the heart nonetheless. For the first time in a long time—maybe ever where men were concerned—she felt like Tate saw her. Really saw her.

And had decided he wasn't interested.

They'd held hands when they returned from Virginia, but that was the extent of it. Her imagination wanted to build on that action, but her brain told her it was only a moment of solace after he'd related his history. A bonding moment between two *buddies*. He'd visited the café every day she worked that week to do the crossword, but he hadn't touched her again. Hadn't asked her out either, although he'd suggested this dog park visit, almost like he was using Emily and Lucy as buffers for their time away from the café.

That realization stung.

He shoved his hands into his jeans pockets as he walked beside her, still wearing his stocking cap although it was a warm spring afternoon. Emily would be out of school soon. Tourist season would ramp up. Her tips would get better but her hours would be harder. Same as every year since she could remember.

"I brought you something," Tate said, burrowing into her hectic thoughts.

"Oh? Is it ice cream?"

The two of them reached the park bench they'd sat on the last time Emily and Lucy played at the park, and he sat down and pulled his bag up beside him.

"Do I look like I have ice cream?"

"A girl can dream." A quick look in Emily's direction revealed Lucy had found a stick, and girl and dog were each holding one end as they danced in a circle. "What did you bring me then?"

As soon as she settled herself next to him, he pulled a leather-bound book from his bag.

"A puzzle."

"Is this what I think it is?"

Tate found himself leaning closer as Ruth pulled back the cover, staring at the first page. "It's one of my dad's books."

Her blue eyes seemed to brighten a little in the sun as her bottom lip dropped just enough that he could see her teeth. He'd gotten too close. Knew it with every breath in his lungs, but he still kept going to the café every day, sitting across from her while she did her puzzles. Even now his fingers almost ached with his need to touch her, but Emily's happy squeals from nearby reminded him why he couldn't.

"Tate, why are you giving me your dad's book?"

Peering down at the page she had open, he reached over and tapped his finger on the paper. "Read that."

One dubious glance was all she gave him before she focused on the words before her, clearing her throat. "You can't help a bird from flying over your head, but you can keep it from building a nest in your hair."

He could see confusion mixed with sympathy writing itself over her features, but he turned the page and pointed again, ignoring her nonverbal protest.

"Enchanted lake," Ruth read, staring at the words underlined several times. "Find it after days of fasting and continuous prayer."

With a sigh, he leaned back while he waited for her response. Her eyes swept over the pages again before she turned her gaze up to him.

"I'm not sure what you want me to say," she whispered.

"Say you'll help me." Turning his entire body in her direction, he scooted closer on the bench. "You can't deny that you love a good puzzle, and I have a gut-deep feeling you're the person who can siphon the meaning out of this one."

When she didn't answer, he lifted his arm to place it behind her on the bench, allowing his fingers to settle against her shoulder. She withdrew her gaze from the book and stared at her daughter playing with his dad's dog. An unlikely duo. Had he imagined a friend for Lucy during those first few days, he would have pictured her with an aging individual who never ventured farther than the front porch. But then she'd been morose and lifeless like those old coon dogs in cartoons with their jowls hanging almost as low as their bellies. Nothing like the lively pup she resembled now.

"Life is kind of like a crossword puzzle, if you think about it," he said as Ruth tilted her head slightly until it rested on his arm. "We're inhabiting a tiny spot in the universe, organizing hints and clues in order to form answers for our most important questions. Sometimes it's only after you have the answer that you can look back and see the clues clearly."

Her fingers swept across the page of the book in her lap, lighting on the bit about the enchanted lake with a tap of her finger.

"Take Emily and Lucy, for example," he continued. "I never would have seen that one coming, but now that I see them together, I think the dog was looking for someone to bring her back to life. My presence couldn't have done that."

Emily let out a high-pitched squeal as she plopped to the ground, letting Lucy plant a slobbery kiss to her cheek. If he watched the two of them hard enough, he might be able to ignore the way Ruth seemed to be settling against his side. If he were really focused, maybe he could resist the urge to pull her against him.

The wind picked up, grabbing her hair and pushing it across his cheek. With a sharp breath, he rose to his feet.

"Give it some thought," he tossed at her as casually as possible as he moved in the direction of those squeals.

The entire world being a set of clues. Of all the ridiculous, idiotic notions. If this were a set of clues, Ruth would have to surmise that she was being sent on a relentless goose chase in an effort to drain her sanity.

Every day he visited her at the café, and for what? Her expertise on crossword puzzles? Did he really think she could somehow unlock the story that had emerged from his dad's scribblings? Had it all been for nothing—the weekend away? The sharing of so many hours? The way he had his arm draped over her shoulder a moment before, daring her to melt against him? As soon as she'd start to think they were having a moment, he'd exit stage left as fast as his legs could carry him.

It was enough to leave her muddled up in a state of consternation as he joined Emily and Lucy, grabbing the stick the dog had just dropped and tossing it in the direction of the trees. She'd spent a great deal of time in bed the night before trying to decipher why she liked Tate so much, but she'd come up empty. Maybe it was possible to like someone for no specific reason at all.

Or maybe they were like two random pieces of a jigsaw puzzle who seemed to have nothing in common but the fact that they connected.

She nearly let out a groan as she closed the book in her lap. Now he had *her* thinking life was a puzzle, which wasn't helpful.

"Tate's a cat!" Emily yelled, crouching down beside the dog. "Get him, Lucy. Get that cat."

Lucy lunged forward, playfully growling at Tate while he jumped away, making a move behind Emily for cover. The sight of him peeking around her daughter at the dog caused Ruth's heart to ache. Before she had time to give it any further thought, he whisked the cap from his head and tossed it in her direction. It landed on the edge of his messenger bag, precariously close to sliding off into the grass.

His stocking cap would have been fine sitting right there without her intervention, even had it landed in the grass. Perfectly fine.

And had she left it alone, her daughter wouldn't have caught her smelling it like a lovesick teenaged girl.

"It's not like I'm going to say anything."

Ruth's cheeks heated afresh as she tightened her fingers on the steering wheel, not removing her eyes from the road in front of her. "I told you, Em, it's a mom thing. Second nature from having to pick up your laundry and check to see whether things are clean or not. Is it embarrassing that I did it to Tate? Yes, but that's the end of it."

"Okay. Except I've seen you do that laundry thing to towels in the kitchen at Grandma's house, and your face didn't get red."

"That's not even *close* to the same thing."

Emily started humming while Ruth focused on her blinker, pushing it up so she could turn right. The subtle ticking noise that accompanied it almost fell in rhythm with Emily's song. Which was . . .

Some Day My Prince Will Come

"Ugh, Em. You have to stop. Life isn't a fairy tale."

"I don't know what you're so worried about. If you want to be in love with Tate, it's totally fine with me. I know I didn't like him at first, but only 'cause I could tell Lucy didn't like him and he wasn't a dog person. Now she thinks he's okay so they must have made friends. Besides, his house is cool and I like to play there."

"You think that's how I should go about choosing a man? Just find someone whose house is cool?"

"And someone who has a dog, of course." Emily stretched her arms in front of her, giving an exaggerated yawn. "Playing with Lucy sure wears me out. I bet I'd be a hundred percent better behaved if we saw each other more. I might even take naps."

Ruth pushed her discomfort down enough to shake her head at her daughter. "You would never take naps."

"For Lucy I would. Think about it, Mom. Spending more time with the man you like, me taking naps. It's a win-win for everyone."

A smile slipped onto Ruth's face at her daughter's silly words, but it didn't remain long. It couldn't be a win-win when she was certain everyone was going to lose-lose.

12. RAFT

Ruth wobbled a little as she sliced the oar through the water, but somehow managed to stay upright on her paddle board. She'd been leery of wearing the life jacket, but the instant Tate's camera emerged from the bag he always carried, she'd said a little prayer of thanks for the extra layer of covering.

Lucy swam by with a stick between her teeth, heading in the direction of the shore. For the sake of her play time with the dog, Emily had kept her promise about Ruth's cap sniffing incident. Tate was still none the wiser, but he'd stopped wearing the head covering after that. Her gaze naturally floated to the man where he crouched on the shore in his board shorts and a T-shirt, the lens pointed in her direction.

"If I didn't know better, I'd swear you were trying to get footage for *America's Funniest Home Videos.*"

"Are you open to that?" His easy smile seemed as new as the board shorts he wore, and he hadn't ripped the tag off those until they left the cabin an hour before.

"Highly doubtful."

Emily threw the stick again, and Lucy launched herself away from the bank as she paddled in Ruth's direction.

"How many times have you done this?" Ruth asked, trying to avoid direct eye contact with Tate's camera. No matter how many meetings she had with that side of the lens, she feared she would never grow comfortable.

"Taken photos?"

"Yes, taken photos. I'm asking how many times you've taken photos."

Again with that smile. Forget her legs going all jelly-fied on her. Soon she'd have problems with coordination all together if he kept that up.

"No, I've not paddle boarded before. Believe it or not, most of my travels have kept me busy with work-related things. Floating around definitely falls into the leisure category."

The front edge of her board tipped, and she leaned back with a jerk to keep herself from upending. "Let me know how that leisure works out for you when you get your board on the water."

He turned to say something to Emily, and Ruth carefully lowered herself to her knees before sitting on the paddleboard. Despite his initial gruffness, Tate had ended up being really good with her daughter. Just the right level of quick wit to keep up with Em without overpowering her. Able to relate to her without talking down to her. He might have been everything Emily needed, although she couldn't claim that without qualifying the statement with the fact that it could have been selfish on her part. She'd let him grow on her like the creeping vine hanging over the corner of his cabin, and she had no desire to do any pruning.

From her standpoint on the water, the only thing keeping him from fitting into the picture was the fact that he didn't want to be in the frame.

And unfortunately, that was kind of a huge component.

Forcing his eyes closed, Tate tilted his face toward the sun and attempted to regroup. He was standing by a river in the middle of nowhere, Ruth was on a paddle board waiting for him, and Emily was happily playing with Lucy on the shore. That combination would have made him more uncomfortable than sniper fire in the desert two months ago, but instead it was starting to feel normal. Better than normal on days like today.

He couldn't see the photos on the camera he held in his hand due to the sun's glare, but he knew what they held. Capturing Ruth mid-wobble on that board was accidental, but he'd also caught her mid-laugh. The excitement that laced her beauty was contagious. Palpable. Part of him wanted to share the photos he'd captured of her with some of his colleagues back home, but the selfish side of him won out. For now, she was only his.

Even thinking that statement felt bizarre, because he'd determined from his very first memories not to need what this experience offered. Attachment. Stability. He'd longed for the freedom that came with not knowing what tomorrow held, with the camera being the only constant in his life. The only constant beside his dad, that is, until he'd escaped to his hideaway in the mountains.

"Want to know what I think?" Ruth said. "You're too chicken to try this and you're using your camera as a shield."

A warm wind kicked up, blowing the hem of his board shorts against his thigh and bringing with it the faint scent of wildflowers. Something purple dotted the grass in the distance, but he fought the urge to point his camera in that direction to get a better glimpse. His eyes were fine, and he didn't need a shield.

Not that Ruth had meant to offer a metaphor for his life. She was talking about the paddle board, and only the paddle board.

"I wanted to let you get comfortable first so I didn't outshine you with my balancing skills," he stated as he lowered his camera to set it on their stack of towels.

Emily stepped into his line of vision and momentarily blocked his view of Ruth, winding her scrawny arm to launch the stick into the water. Lucy lunged after it, doggy paddling past Ruth's board. Instead of staring after the dog, Emily turned and gazed up at him, one eye squinting against the sun and her crooked smile exhibiting one tooth missing on the bottom left.

"Thanks for letting me play with Lucy while you and mom raft, Mr. Tate. She makes me happier than a pig in mud."

It was impossible not to smile in response, but what was he supposed to say to that? The kid liked to spout off weird sayings that she probably heard at one point or another from her granddad, but instead of making her seem like an odd duck, it made her seem more relatable. Combined with the sight of her stick-thin arms, it also made his protective instinct rise another notch.

"When did you lose that tooth, kiddo?"

One of her two braids dripped water over her shoulder as she plopped a fist on her hip. "Last night, finally.

The tooth fairy gave me two whole dollars. Grandma says it's almost yard sale season, so it happened just in time."

Lucy stepped out of the water, shaking her wet fur and sending droplets spraying everywhere. Emily squealed and launched herself into the river, settling along the shallow edge where Lucy paused beside her and waited patiently.

They were probably soul mates, Em and that dog.

Turning to grab his board, he peeked at Ruth. She stared at the shoreline just past where he stood, her posture relaxed and countenance serene. More than serene, really. Tilting toward awestruck. The woman was captivated by her tiny little corner of the universe, and she'd never even trekked beyond its confines. What would she think of the rest of the world?

"How long are you going to stand on the shore, Tate?"

Ruth turned her face to watch him, her hair hanging over her shoulder just like Emily's had been a moment before. He wished he had an answer.

The towel she'd been using to dry her hair smelled of fabric softener and cedar, and she didn't feel a bit guilty about holding it to her face and breathing in the scent. It wasn't like it was a signature fragrance on an article of clothing, just a random item that smelled good. The fact that it was in Tate's cabin was a moot point.

"Everything okay in there?" Tate asked, his knuckles rapping against the door.

Not really.

"Almost done," she said, gazing at her reflection in the bathroom mirror. Almost done wasn't a lie, but she couldn't say everything was okay. Not when her appearance announced that she'd been on the water for hours. And not when the knowledge that Tate saw her as nothing but a friend was starting to cause fractures in her heart.

A responsible woman would put a stop to it. She wasn't going to be the only one hurt when this thing fell apart. Emily was beginning to be attached to Lucy like the two were long lost friends. She knew Emily and her dog fascination. The sudden loss of Lucy was going to be like watching an endless rerun of that sad commercial with the dogs in cages as Sarah McLachlan serenaded their every movement.

None of it was okay, and she had to tell him.

Now.

Taking a deep breath, she pulled open the door and stepped into the hall, nearly smacking into Tate. Before she had a chance to say anything, her palm was flat against his chest and she was close enough to smell the hints of medicinal coconut left over from his sunscreen.

"Tate, I need to—"

"—think we should—"

She bit her lip as his words trailed off and he reached a hand up to his hair, glancing at her fingers against his chest. She should move them, but even though her brain ordered her arm into motion, it didn't comply.

"Sorry, you go first," he said, folding his fingers over hers against his chest.

It was really tempting to lean into his arms, but what if he didn't reciprocate? Was it worth the risk?

"About Emily," she finally breathed, keeping her focus on their hands so she wouldn't have to make eye contact. "With Emily, I—um—it's the relationship with your dog. I'm worried about the relationship."

"With the dog," he repeated, his fingers tightening over hers. "You're worried about my dog's relationship."

"Yes, because I think she might be getting too attached." She dared to look up, her gaze instantly catching on his. "Emily might be falling in love with the dog."

"I assure you, the feeling's mutual."

Ruth inhaled, fighting the anxiety trying to strangle her breath. She'd managed to muddle everything, making him talk about the dog because she'd been too chicken to lay it all on the table. Was this the punishment—that they were really talking about the dog now?

"See, that's the thing. Situations being what they are, I'm worried about how she'll feel when inevitably . . ."

Despite their close proximity, Tate managed to move a step toward her, bringing his free hand up to cradle her cheek. The warmth of his palm against her skin erased a bit of the tension, easing the pressure from her chest.

"I don't live here," he muttered, giving a gentle shake of his head. "It feels like I do at the moment, but a week from now I'll be back home getting ready for my next assignment. Putting that kind of expectation on . . . the dog . . ." His breath brushed against her neck with his heavy sigh. "Our lives are different. Me and . . . the dog."

"I can see your point, but shouldn't what she thinks factor into your decision?"

"What she thinks?"

"Everything you're saying makes sense. It sounds like the very definition of playing it safe, but aren't you usually encouraging people to be risk takers? You're supposed to be a risk taker, aren't you?"

His eyes got squinty, like they did when he was studying a particularly difficult crossword clue. "I don't know what else to do here."

All she could do was look up at the man who had turned her world upside down, thinking about how the whole thing had started with a crossed out crossword puzzle. Crossing things out took guts. Confidence. The man normally had it in spades.

"Are we still talking about the dog?" she whispered.

Instead of answering, he leaned toward her, his lips unexpectedly meeting hers. It was a soft kiss, but he didn't pull away, so she weaved her arms around his neck. If this was going to end up being her one-and-only shot at kissing Tate, she was going to make it memorable.

After a moment, she realized that memorable was an understatement. Kissing Tate was a lot like she imagined it would be to leap from the top of a waterfall in Hawaii. The fall was exhilarating, and she couldn't have felt more breathless if she were actually flying.

So she tried not to think about how much it would hurt when she finally landed.

13. FOLKLORE

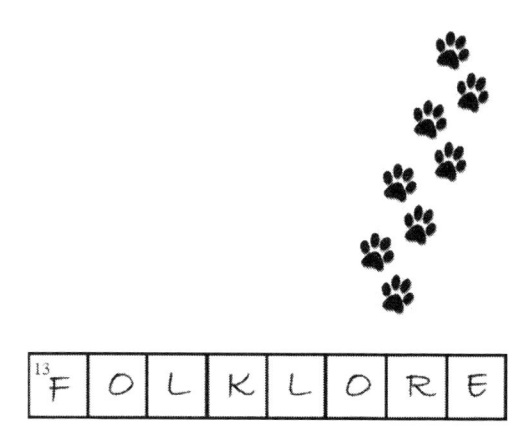

Resettling the coffee pot on the burner, Ruth turned and gazed at the booth by the window, almost wishing it were empty. The woman who sat there seemed too interested in her phone to pay attention to her son across from her, and he was too engrossed in his handheld game to order his drink a moment before. Life was too short to spend it ignoring one another's company. The memory of the lively conversations she'd shared with Tate there made their silence feel like a personal affront.

"Ruthie, I wouldn't mind a bit of that apple cobbler Pitt's hoarding in the kitchen."

With a smile, she turned and grabbed the plate Pitt had set on the open window. "Somehow he knew you'd ask." Crossing the open walkway, she slid the dish in front of Pap and settled in across from him. "It's a beautiful day. Have any big plans?"

"Just cobbler. Pitt and Jess are having a barbecue tonight and they're forcing me out of hibernation. A fella goes to visit his brother for one week, and they think that deserves a homecoming."

"They missed you," she said, gently moving the salt shaker over half an inch. "We all did. Emily and I will be there tonight, so at least you'll be able to keep us company."

He cut his fork into the cobbler. "Your friend's not coming with you?"

Instead of hurting less with each telling, the sting of Tate's departure ached more after every reminder. Shouldn't it be getting easier?

"He had to go back to work. South Africa, actually. Halfway around the world." Forcing a deep breath, she pasted on a smile. "But it all worked out like a dream. He gave the dog to Emily, so she's on cloud nine, and he's renting the cabin to us so we can stay there and keep her. A win-win for everyone involved."

Her brain stuttered over the word renting like it did every single time. Staying there for free felt wrong, but he'd insisted. When he finally came to his senses, she hoped the amount of rent he requested would be within her means. And that she'd be emotionally ready to handle that decision.

"Where's Emily this morning?"

"Enjoying a morning of yard sales with my mom. She had two dollars and fifty cents burning a hole in her pocket." Shifting forward until her elbows rested on the table, Ruth watched as Pap scooped more cobbler onto his fork. "This afternoon she'll be playing at the park with Clint and Willow, so I guess it's a good thing we have the dog now. Otherwise she'd never want to come home."

"Hogwash." Pap continued eating in silence, leaving her to stare out the window.

It wasn't logical at all, and she knew that. Guys like Tate didn't stay in one place long enough to visit the same diner every day like Pap did. The diner *was* Pap's excitement. For Tate, it was nothing but an ill-timed distraction.

If only the fact that it was illogical could negate the ache sprouting from the loss of his company.

"He'll be back," Pap announced, lips pressed together as he nodded his head.

Ruth's heart flipped into a somersault as she focused on the remains of Pap's cobbler. "What makes you think that?"

"I heard enough of that boy talking to know his life is like a giant check list, and his goal is to cross off every last thing. But he didn't cross off anything here. Left it kind of open ended. That means he isn't done."

Ruth shoved a cardboard box into the corner of the bedroom, ignoring the way Lucy whined from the doorway. It was the first time she'd been alone in the cabin to process things since Tate left. She and Emily had spent their time packing and finally moving yesterday afternoon, and she hadn't had a moment to think.

She was doing the right thing, wasn't she? It would be really weird living here, but she was doing it for Emily. And for Lucy.

Mostly for Emily.

In the darkest recesses of her mind, she hoped she wasn't doing it as a last resort to hang onto a man who wasn't really available. That would be kind of pathetic.

Yesterday she'd run into Doug and Celeste at the grocery store, and she'd been able to talk to them without feeling even a pang of jealousy. And she'd breathed easily the rest of the evening, not once going into a panic over her nonexistent love life. Maybe the cabin and the dog had given her just enough excitement to ward off those feelings of monotony.

The journal Tate had given her to puzzle over rested on the center of her bed, its pages propped open to the last section she'd read. She'd tried to convince him to take it with him when he left, but he wouldn't agree. Instead, he insisted that she'd figure it out eventually.

No matter how many times she looked at it, she felt no closer to solving the mystery than she had the day before.

With a sigh, she crossed to the bed and picked up the book, turning the page to one she hadn't read. The scribbles looked a lot like the others, so she sat down and stared at the words, reaching up to tighten her ponytail atop her head.

I watched the frog swallow the sun.

Pressing her lips together, Ruth fought a surge of sadness. Tate had shown her a few pictures of his father. The man had been forty-nine when he retired, probably planning to spend a couple of decades at this cabin in the woods. Instead he'd been gone at fifty-three, leaving behind one inherited stray dog and notebooks full of odd phrases. The idea that something that so consumed a person's time could be so woefully misunderstood left her with an odd sense of melancholy.

Turning the next page, she let her eyes rove across the words.

Roaring Fork. Came across her in the dark forest on a cold winter's night. Offered her a ride on his horse. Name was Lucy.

"Lucy," she breathed, chest tightening as a flicker of recognition began forming in her brain. "Lucy hitched a ride on Roaring Fork."

Dropping the book, she grabbed her phone and began punching in words as fast as she could type. Within seconds she had the information she was searching for: the legend of a ghost named Lucy on the Roaring Fork. Wasn't that what Tate had told her that day at the park? The dog was named Lucy, just like the ghost?

As if the dog's name had been the magic clue that let the entire crossword fall into place, she saw hints of other stories lining up in her mind. One after one she searched them on her phone, each one leaving her a little more excited than the one before.

With trembling fingers, she tapped Tate's contact on her phone. It wasn't the grand mystery he'd probably expected, but she was eager to get his reaction. At the news, or at the fact that she figured it out. Or maybe only to hear his voice.

Voice mail picked up, and she squeezed her eyes shut at the computerized words. It would have made sense to think about that before calling. Most likely it was one o'clock in the morning over there, and he'd be sound asleep.

The beep sounded, almost startling her. "Um, Tate. Hey, it's Ruth. Everything's fine here, I just wanted to tell you that I figured it out. Your dad's books, I mean. It's all folklore and stories about the area. Sayings from locals, old Cherokee traditions, even ghost stories and tales about curses."

Rubbing her palm over her face, she focused her gaze at the opposite wall. "At the risk of rambling, I think maybe that was the mystery, which wasn't really a mystery at all. He must have loved it here—the stories and traditions—enough to record them for himself. But you already knew all that, didn't you? This is just proof that he wasn't crazy, only happy. Sometimes other peoples' happiness seems weird to us if we don't understand it." She paused to take a breath. "Anyway, that's it. Hope you're taking some great photos. Emily and Lucy are getting along perfectly. They miss you. And I . . . I miss you."

Hitting the end button, she dropped her head to her hands. This was it—the great tug of war she'd feared that had always convinced her dating wasn't worth the risk. Unless she knew with one hundred percent clarity that the guy was going to stick around, she couldn't open up her heart. She'd screwed up this time, leaving it wide open. Piece by piece, she could feel it breaking.

While *Ratatouille* played in the background, Emily squeezed beside Ruth on the couch and leaned against her mother's shoulder. Sweet, big-hearted Emily. Fresh from the shower, she smelled like watermelon shampoo and the strawberries she'd just eaten. Since Emily had inherited Lucy, her life had been made complete.

Or so it seemed.

"He'll be back, Mom."

Tilting her head, Ruth looked down at her daughter. "What was that?"

"Tate. He won't stay gone forever."

Pulling her gaze away from Emily, Ruth concentrated on the screen across the room, watching the rat use the human as his cooking puppet. "Eventually he'll have to figure out what to do with the cabin, and renting to us won't be his permanent solution. But I don't expect him back here for a long, long time."

Emily shifted so Lucy could squeeze in next to her. "I'm talking about real soon. Aunt Willow didn't draw him leaving Willowdale. He's on a trip, that's all."

Why did everything always come back around to fairies in the end? It was easy to appreciate Willow and her relationship with Emily, but the obsession with the fairies as though they were real, living people was a little too much sometimes. The fascination had subsided when Tate and Lucy entered into the picture, but here they were again.

"The fairies are stories created from Willow's imagination. You know she can't actually predict the future, right?"

"No, but she's a good watcher of people. Sometimes she can see things other people can't."

A sigh slipped out before Ruth had enough forethought to stop it. "Who told you that?"

"She did."

Ruth declined to give a response, instead concentrating on the sneering cartoon restaurant critic. Emily scooted Lucy away enough to turn her body in Ruth's direction. Such a typical Emily-saves-the-world move. If she couldn't make her point in one take, she would double down and try to be more convincing.

"Aunt Willow drew Dad and Celeste into her fairy world, and now they're getting married."

"Yes, but that scenario doesn't take any deductive reasoning. Who wouldn't marry Celeste? She's pretty and practically a saint."

"Well, what about Uncle Clint? Willow drew him into her fairy world too, remember? Now they're gonna have a baby."

Ruth let out a little gasp as she turned to study her daughter. "Willow's pregnant?"

"Yeah, only don't say anything 'cause she wasn't supposed to tell me yet."

Ruth drew in a deep pull of air, feeling that familiar heaviness settle in. Why couldn't she be happy for Willow and Clint without feeling like their good fortune doubled up her bad? Without the endless tedium of her day to day life flashing before her eyes?

Emily's fingers wrapped around Ruth's arm. "All's I'm saying is, I think Tate's your Uncle Clint."

"Tate's my Uncle Clint?"

"You know what I mean. Any dummy could tell he likes you a lot. That's not telling the future. It's just seeing the *what's in front of you*."

14. PHOTOS

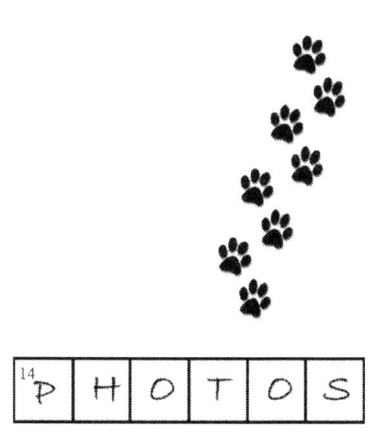

"Buddy, your post from yesterday is flat blowin' up."

Tate opened one eye enough to peer across the room at his roommate Damian, who sat at his undersized computer desk staring at his miniscule laptop. Unable to see anything substantial from his viewpoint, Tate closed his eyes again, sinking further into the fold of the couch. He wasn't jetlagged, but he figured he could get away with pretending he was for a couple more hours at least.

"Odd. Guess the colors in that one popped." But made it special? That one felt meaningless. Photos like that were a dime a dozen.

"No man, not the one of the mountains, although I'm sure it's cool and what have you. I'm talking about your Tennessee beauty."

Ruth.

He'd tried not to think about her every moment since he left that cabin, but it had proven impossible. He'd stared at her photograph more than half of his flight overseas before finally falling asleep, had replayed her message about his dad's books something like a thousand times, and fought the urge to get in the Jeep the minute he hit U.S. soil again.

"What do you mean, blowing up?"

He sat himself up on the couch, fixing his gaze on Damian's back. The picture of Ruth came into his vision from the laptop, caught mid-smile as the sun streamed around her hair. Every emotion he felt at sharing the photo rushed back. The memory of the joy he experienced at the top of that mountain. A selfish instinct to keep the experience for himself, and then the pride that eventually convinced him to share it. He'd even felt a twinge of excitement as he wrote the caption: *First time mountain biking.*

"I mean that you've got four times as many hits on this photo than any other you've ever posted."

"It's been one day. That's not possible."

"I'm looking at it with my own eyes. You've got two thousand comments."

"What . . ." Reaching up to scratch his head, Tate cleared his throat. "What sort of comments?"

"Mostly women tagging each other so they'll see it, but a few others. 'Look how happy this makes her.' 'BAE, this is what my face should look like on a date.' 'This is relationship goals.'"

Rising to his feet, Tate took a step toward Damian, studying the photo over his shoulder. "They got all that from riding a bike?"

"Probably that and the second photo of you with your bike crash."

The photo Ruth had taken. It wasn't very good quality-wise, but he'd tweaked it as best he could so he could share the experience in all its glory. Her triumph, his near-disaster. It wasn't the highest mountain he'd ever been on, not by a long shot. But it was the closest he'd ever come to actually touching the heavens.

"You've got to follow up on this. What else do you have?"

"A hundred photos of nothing."

"What do you mean, nothing? Ruth is in the pictures, correct?"

Letting out an exaggerated yawn, Tate resettled himself on the couch, grabbing his phone to pull up the account for himself. "Of course she's in the pictures. My camera had a thing for her."

"Your camera," Damian muttered, continuing to scroll through the comments. "I don't think it has anything to do with your actions in the picture. It's all about people wanting what this woman has."

Ruth's face appeared on Tate's screen, instantly calming his soul. "She's naturally photogenic."

"I'm not talking about her cheekbones," Damien said, turning his chair around to face him. "They want her joy."

Rubbing his thumb across the screen, he switched to the next photo. Ruth standing in his yard back at the cabin. Ruth with her arms lifted high at the dog park, playing some game with Emily and Lucy. Ruth on the paddleboard, eyes open wide and arms flailing. Ruth, Ruth, Ruth.

The truth was, he wanted her joy too. Desperately. For a moment, he'd had it. And then he'd left it in Tennessee.

15 YES

Offering her best smile to the little boy at table two, Ruth slid a waffle heaped high with whipped cream into his line of vision. "No way will you ever be able to finish that."

"Can too," he said, lifting his chin enough that she could see a little white scar across his cheek. Emily had plenty of those tiny white scars. Scratches, cuts, even minor burns. Signs of a life well lived.

"It's a challenge, then. I'll be back in just a bit to see if you were successful." With one tap of her fingers on the table, she turned her focus to his mother instead. "Can I get you anything else?"

"No, this is perfect. Thank you."

The morning rush finally beginning to die down, she tilted her head from side to side to try to relieve some of the tension in her shoulders. Things were going remarkably well. Emily was enjoying her summer flitting back and forth from her parents' place to Willow and Clint's. Lucy was always waiting when they came back to the cabin, eager to wear Emily out before bed time. Even her tips had started to swell with the influx of tourists. To top it off, at night, she was finally free to sit on her own porch with a glass of iced tea, listening to the crickets say goodnight. It was almost bliss.

Pressing her lips together, she vowed not to think about Tate this morning. It was bad enough that she felt his presence with every step she took at the cabin. She didn't need to eye the booth by the window during her entire shift. Knowing him had been a good experience, maybe even a gift from God, and she needed to be okay with the outcome. Because there were a lot of good outcomes.

Too many to let one little disappointment ruin everything.

While she'd been telling herself to move on, though, he'd been sharing her pictures. She didn't feel guilty about perusing his online presence, because they were friends. Friends could look at friends' photos. She also didn't feel used when she saw her face pop up, because he hadn't been sneaky about his intentions. *He might use her photos someday,* he'd said. Had her sign a release and everything.

And she wasn't going to think about it anymore.

Snatching up her newspaper from the counter, she scooted around to the other side and leaned against the bar, spreading it open. Five minutes. She needed five minutes to focus on the crossword instead of her pathetic love life.

But instead of her normal crossword puzzle, a more succinct version appeared in front of her.

"Jess?"

"What, honey?" Jess stopped short in front of her, balancing two plates brimming with eggs and hash browns.

Twisting her mouth to the side, Ruth shook her head and urged Jess forward with a flick of her wrist. The woman didn't care about her puzzle, and she wouldn't have messed with it if she did. Letting her brows slant together, she stared at clue one across.

The legendary babe.

An unladylike sputter slipped from her lips. The same clue she'd berated Tate for the day she'd met him. Thinking back on it now, the whole scene felt ridiculous, even though she could still picture his boxy letters written on the paper.

RUTH

With the first clue filled in, she moved on to number two down.

A grumpy old booger

Her eyes instantly filled with tears as she pressed her left hand to her heart, smiling at the description. It hadn't fit in the end, but she knew exactly when she'd said the words. They'd been in front of his cabin and he'd been spewing something about hating the sign.

TATE

Writing their names with the T's interconnecting was enough to make her pause and glance around the café. She half expected him to be sitting there again in his familiar spot, but instead three teenagers sat in that space. Even so, sweet anticipation filled her veins.

With her heart pounding, she read through the other clues. *Coolest kid on the planet. Cool kid's new best friend. The best kind of puzzle. These complete the puzzle.*

EMILY, LUCY, CROSS, WORDS

The answers came to her so easily, she found herself trying to skip to the bottom to see how it would end. Instead, she forced her eyes back to clue seven down and started there. *Exported by Sudan. The kind of trip we took to Virginia. Bucket list down a mountain. What happens when you eat hot pizza.*

Her fingers almost trembled as she attempted to fill in the spaces, remembering their conversation about goats and their spur of the moment trip out of state. Thinking about riding bikes and burning her mouth at the restaurant.

His dad's puzzles were in a book, *Em's word for paddle boards* was raft, and *what you found in Dad's book* could only be folklore, which left only two clues remaining.

Fourteen down: *The only thing I took with me when I left.*

"Photos."

Time seemed to stop at the sound of Tate's voice, and she glanced up to her right where he'd emerged from the direction of the kitchen. His camera clicked, catching her unaware and making her self-conscious enough to brush an escaped strand of hair behind her ear.

"The camera doesn't work as well when you're not around," he said, stepping closer.

"So you're giving it to me for safe keeping?" she guessed, turning to face him.

Unwrapping the camera from his neck, he placed it on the counter next to her newspaper. "You and this camera, you're a smashing success."

She turned toward the black piece of equipment so slowly, she felt sure he could feel her reluctance. "I'm no good with cameras."

"Behind them, no." He shook his head, taking another step toward her. "That's why I'm offering my services. I don't know if you've been keeping up with my photography, but the pictures of you are really popular."

She looked up at him, her gaze catching on his golden-brown eyes. "You're a good photographer."

His hand brushed against her waist, settling on her back as he pressed closer. "No, it's all you, Ruth. First time biking down a mountain, first time paddle boarding, none of that would matter if you weren't in that frame. It's your happiness that's contagious. I've done a lot of thinking since I left, and one of the things I want is to be the guy capturing your smile."

Lifting her fingers to his arm, she tried to keep her unanswered questions from appearing on her face. "One of the things?"

"I'd also like to be the one making you smile."

At that, she couldn't resist. Leaning forward, she tilted her head in anticipation.

"First you need to finish the puzzle," he said, offering an expectant lift of his eyebrows.

Swallowing down the desire to wrap herself in his arms, she turned and looked at the paper. "What about the fact that you don't live here?"

"I'm a freelance photojournalist. It's dawned on me that I could live anywhere."

She nodded, the letters on the paper swimming together as tears gathered in her eyes. "I should probably ask whether—"

"I love you? Very much. Emily too. Do I need to ask if you—"

"Oh, that ship sailed a long time ago. I'm almost embarrassed to admit how long ago. But I do. A whole lot." Sniffing to regain control of her emotions, she glanced up at him again. "But I was going to ask if Em and I should move out of the cabin."

He leaned down and pressed his lips to hers, inciting a chorus of applause from the other patrons in the café. A laugh slipped from Ruth as he turned his head, seemingly noticing the presence of a roomful of people for the first time.

"This would be a really good photo op," he said, tugging her close to his side.

"If you were still hiding behind your camera." Peering up at him, she touched his cheek to bring his attention back to her. "Should we? Move, I mean."

Giving a squint of his eyes, he shook his head. "No way. I have no problem staying in a hotel until you decide to make me permanent."

A statically charged calm settled over Ruth's heart, buzzing with the excitement of change even as a warm blanket of peace held her steady. "You sound very sure of yourself."

"You did say the ship had sailed." Dropping one more kiss to her lips, he inclined his head toward the paper. "Are you going to finish this thing or what?"

Sheer happiness. He'd claimed she offered it, but she was definitely on the receiving end this time. Focusing her attention on the puzzle, she read the last line.

You and me together?

Without a moment's hesitation, she filled in the three-letter answer.

YES

And for the first time in her life, she crossed out the clue.

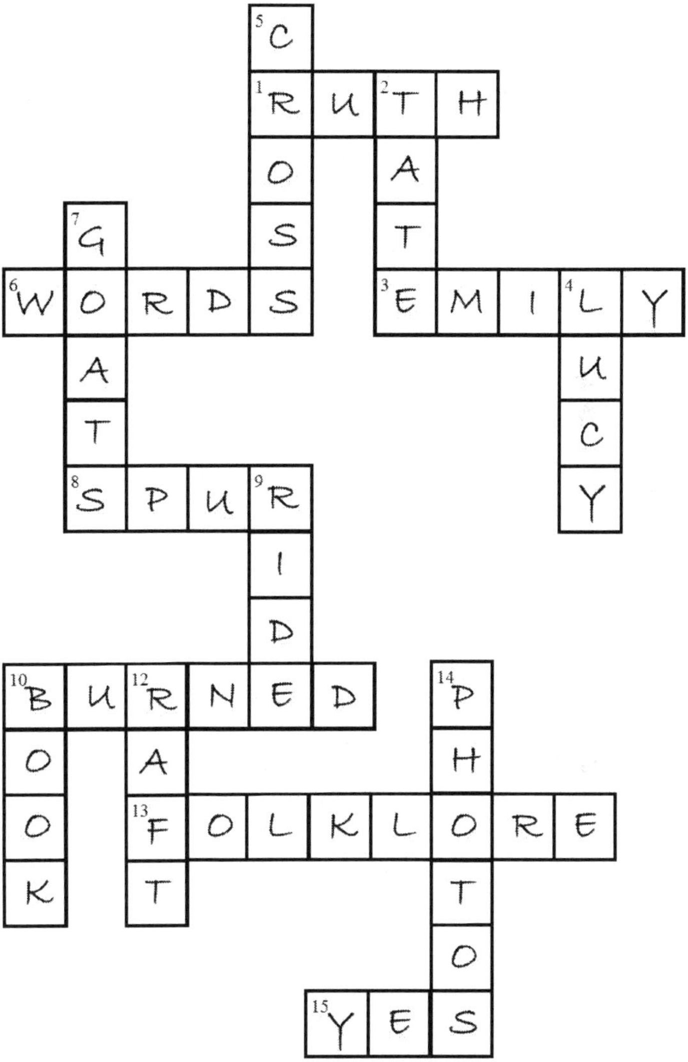

1 RUTH
2 TATT
3 EMILY
4 LUCY
5 CROSS
6 WORDS
7 GOATS
8 SPUR
9 RIDE
10 BURNED
10 BOOK
12 RAFT
13 FOLKLORE
14 PHOTOS
15 YES

Author's Note

Thanks for taking the time to hang out with me in Tennessee. It was a pleasure sharing these stories, and I hope they brought some light and laughter to your heart.

Not so long ago, I went through a difficult stretch that left me questioning whether I should continue writing inspirational romantic comedy at all. Then I met Willow Sharpe. She was quirky, fun-loving, creative, and felt like an outcast. Together, we not only crafted a sweet story about opposites attracting, but we molded a fairy universe that would set the stage for the people around her to tell their stories as well.

Was it a gamble to begin everything with a character's obsession with fairies? Maybe. But you know what I've decided? Cookie cutters have their place in kitchen drawers, but I don't want them anywhere near my fiction. If we're not going to break the mold, what's the point of creating?

So here's to the outcast. The unique. The one who seems destined to be different. The one not satisfied with generating a copy, because you want to form something entirely new.

The world would be a lot less colorful without you.

Christina

Made in the USA
Columbia, SC
25 August 2018